DAYFALL

MICHAEL DAVID ARES

DAYFALL

TOR

A TOM DOHERTY ASSOCIATES BOOK
NEW YORK

DAYFALL

Copyright © 2018 by Tor Books

A Tor Book
Published by Tom Doherty Associates
175 Fifth Avenue
New York, NY 10010

www.tor-forge.com

Tor® is a registered trademark of Macmillan Publishing Group, LLC.

The Library of Congress Cataloging-in-Publication Data

Names: Ares, Michael David, author.
Title: Dayfall / Michael David Ares.
Description: First edition. | New York : Tom Doherty Associates, 2018. |
    Identifiers: LCCN 2017039422 (print) | LCCN 2017049775 (ebook) |
    ISBN 9781250064806 (hardcover) | ISBN 9781466871144 (ebook)
Subjects: LCSH: Police—New York (State)—New York—Fiction. |
    Serial murder investigation—Fiction. | GSAFD: Suspense fiction. |
    Mystery fiction. | Dystopias.
Classification: LCC PS3601.R4655 (ebook) | LCC PS3601.R4655 D39
    2018 (print) | DDC 813/.6—dc23
LC record available at https://lccn.loc.gov/2017039422

Our books may be purchased in bulk for promotional, educational, or business use.
Please contact your local bookseller or the Macmillan Corporate and Premium Sales
Department at 1-800-221-7945, extension 5442, or by email at
MacmillanSpecialMarkets@macmillan.com.

First Edition: March 2018

Printed in the United States of America

0 9 8 7 6 5 4 3 2 1

To my friends

DAYFALL

1

Laurel Hill Cemetery was a hell of torture and death for the victims of the serial killer, but it was like heaven for him. He couldn't have imagined a better place to practice his dark art.

Founded in 1836 on eighty acres of steep hills and plateaus on the western edge of Philadelphia, overlooking the Schuylkill River, the massive old graveyard was filled with a menagerie of some of the world's most impressive architecture of death. There were hundreds of large elaborate crypts, some standing alone, some built in a line next to others, and several dozen gathered together into a section called Millionaire's Row that looked like a small town growing in the middle of the grounds. The thousands of other residents of the cemetery didn't have their own buildings to rest in, but their graves were marked with an awe-inspiring array of symbolic Victorian sculptures: obelisks, columns, towers topped by angels and other mythical creatures, arches, draped urns, and small-scale Gothic cathedrals. The stone sarcophagi were adorned with lions, winged faces, broken urns, cherubim, anchors, ivy, and ornate books too large for any human to hold.

The light from the full moon, in the early hours before dawn, created an odd grayscale twilight in the cemetery when it hit the stone and the snow. Neither was completely white anymore, the stone because of its age and the snow because of the atmospheric anomalies that were affecting the whole East Coast. But there was nothing gray about the van that pulled down the access path in the northwest corner of the grounds, stopping between a long row of crypts overlooking the river and the steep hill descending to it. The van was jet black on the outside and hell black on the inside, accommodating an evil man and his foul work.

He was known to the police and the terrified citizens of Philadelphia as the Full Moon Kidnapper—or Full Moon Killer, for those who were less hopeful—because in each of the last six months women had disappeared from the streets on this night, their bodies never to be found. But the man's name was Carl Roonan, and he was actually an employee of the cemetery, a member of the maintenance staff. He had applied for the job initially because of an unhealthy preoccupation with death—which he'd hid during the hiring process, of course—and that obsession had only grown during the year he had worked there. So had the plans that began to form in his sick mind when his boss introduced him to the wall of old brass crypt keys in a room behind the cemetery office, and the logbook that recorded the names of the tombs' owners and the last time they had been used for family burials. He was able to tell which ones would never be used again, especially in the northwest corner, which was over a hill from the office and was the most quiet and private part of the cemetery. With the river below and only a wooded mountain on the other side of it, no one could see what he was doing, especially at the early hour of the morning when he got to work.

On this particular gray morning, even though he was already confident that he was alone, Roonan looked around carefully when he exited the van to make sure there were no witnesses— except for the already dead, and the woman who would be soon. He opened the back door and lifted her out, sensing the body bag move slightly and hearing a drugged moan from inside it.

He became fully aroused, now that he was feeling safe and anticipating what he would do to the woman, and carried her to the crypt he had chosen for her final resting place.

Damn, he's big, Detective Jon Phillips thought to himself as he watched from his hiding place about fifty yards away, up on the crest of the hill. Jon realized that Roonan might be too big for him to take by himself, but he couldn't call for backup even if he wanted to. He had left his cell and radio at home, for several reasons: he didn't want his superiors to have any possible way of tracking him down and putting a stop to this un-condoned investigation, and he worried that the killer might be sophisticated enough to be using some kind of an electronics detector. He also had to admit that he wanted to take this scumbag down all by himself, because of his competitive nature and the fact that no one on the force had taken his theories seriously. Even his partner had been unwilling to join him on this out-of-jurisdiction stakeout, saying "I'm not getting fired or freezing my balls off for one of your fucking hunches." Which was probably good in the end, because this would have been harder with two people.

Jon had walked into the cemetery a day earlier during a time when there were other visitors, and lay down at this spot to test his hunch by seeing if the Full Moon Goon happened to bring his victims here.

His investigation had started with the disappearance of a woman from his rural hometown who had been partying in the city, and some rather thin clues had led him to this cemetery employee and a macabre notion of what he might be doing with the bodies. Jon wanted to check it out during the full moon night, but knew that the perp might have a way to make sure no one entered the cemetery in the hours prior, so to be safe he had to find a good hiding spot and stay there as long as needed. And this spot was ideal for several reasons: One was that it was a square family plot set apart from the other graves by a wrought iron fence that sat on a low brick wall, so no one would be walking through it and no one on the outside could see Jon when he lay prone next to the interior of the brick wall. But when he poked his head over it, he could see the entire northwest section of the cemetery, because the plot was on the top of the hill above it. He could also see two terraced rows of crypts almost as high as him to the right, in case Roonan might use one of them, and he could see a long row of crypts to the left that were built into the bottom of the hillside, next to where the black van was now parked.

Jon had guessed this particular part of the huge cemetery because the hill and river made it very private, and the guess had paid off. The only problem with his plan was that it was very cold lying in the snow, and Roonan hadn't come during the middle of the night as he'd suspected but in the early morning, when his shift started. So Jon was already suffering symptoms of hypothermia by the time he pushed himself up and out of his hiding place to head down the hill. His body shivered, his heart and lungs raced, and the hand that gripped his gun was numb enough that he dropped it once during his descent. He also felt light-headed by the time he reached the van and pulled the keys out of the ignition, throwing them into the snow far away from the vehicle. Then he turned to gaze at the long row of crypts nearby, and was no longer entirely sure which one he had seen Roonan enter. But when he trusted his first instinct and pulled on one of the big iron doors, it was indeed unlocked and swung open. It took so much effort for Jon to move it, in his weakened state, that he briefly questioned whether or not he should enter and confront the big psycho. It also didn't help that opening the door made a lot of noise, so Roonan probably knew he was coming.

Jon started down the steps with his gun and small flashlight extended. But when he reached the burial chamber at the bottom of the stairs, all he could see was the bound victim lying on her back in the middle of the cement floor. Half her clothes had been cut off, several small wounds had been inflicted on her exposed skin, and beside her lay a set of sinister-looking knives. As Jon knelt down beside the woman to check her pulse, he pointed the weak beam from the little flashlight toward the walls on every side of him, wishing he had brought a bigger one because he couldn't see into some of the crevices and alcoves of the chamber.

Finally he swung the light back to the steps he had come down, and wondered if Roonan could have snuck out that way or some other. The woman still had a pulse, however, which meant he had to be concerned with her, so he put the flashlight in his mouth and the gun in its holster, and started to untie her feet.

As he did this the killer leapt toward him from one of the dark recesses, slamming into him and slashing at him with a knife. The flashlight flew out of Jon's mouth as he sprawled onto the floor in the darkness and felt the skin on the lower back of his neck being sliced open, and then a similar sensation on his upper right arm after another thrust of Roonan's blade. But before he could be cut again, Jon somehow liberated his gun and fired two shots into the darkness in front of him. He could see in the momentary light from the muzzle flash that he probably hadn't hit anything except the walls of the crypt, but the roar of the weapon was so deafening in the enclosed space that afterward he could hear the killer scramble to find the steps and then run up them to get away. By the time Jon managed to grab the flashlight, Roonan was gone.

Jon stuck the flashlight into the limp hand of the victim, forced himself to his feet, and rode a surge of adrenaline up the steps and out of the tomb. Roonan had obviously discovered the keys were missing from the van, judging by its open door, and now was running up the hill behind the crypts—because the one on the other side, which led down to the river, was much too steep to navigate. He was also probably thinking that he could lose his pursuer in the maze of tight city streets on the other side of the cemetery. And he was right about that, because Jon was highly unfamiliar with Philadelphia, having been to the city only a few times in his life.

Jon yelled, "Stop!" but didn't wait long to begin firing at the man. And it didn't take long to realize how bad his aim was going to be. In addition to the numbness from the cold night, the recoil of the gun caused sharp pain from the wounds in his neck and arm. He looked back at the van and briefly thought about trying to find the keys for it in the snow, but remembered that the driving paths in the cemetery were very circuitous, and the man would probably be out of it and into the city before Jon could catch him in a vehicle. So he switched the gun to his left hand and took off after Roonan on foot.

The big man disappeared briefly over the crest of the hill when Jon was about halfway up, but fortunately there was a wide plateau at the top, and when Jon reached it he could see Roonan again. He was halfway across an especially ornate and crowded section of graves containing many obelisks and large markers. Fearing that his quarry would disappear again soon on the downward slope on the other side of the plateau, Jon stopped momentarily and fired several shots with his left hand. He gave up after just a few attempts, because he could immediately tell the difference from the way he would normally be shooting, and vowed that if he got out of this alive he would spend a hundred hours at the range working on his left-handed aim. He also cursed himself for ignoring the standard spiels of his captain, who repeatedly advised him and the other detectives to "prepare for anything" in such ways.

The other reason Jon only fired a few shots was that, just as he did, Roonan bounded through a cluster of large sarcophagi and was then hard to see on the other side of it. Jon forced himself forward, noticing that the shivering and racing of his internal organs had returned with a vengeance since the recent surge of adrenaline had worn off.

By the time he reached the group of tall graves that Roonan had passed through, the big man had crested the hill on the other side and was almost to the much larger cluster of crypts and tombs they called Millionaire's Row. Knowing that he definitely wouldn't be able to see the killer once he disappeared inside that small town of cement and marble, and that Roonan would be able to exit it in several directions, Jon braced his left arm on a sarcophagus next to him—not able to use his wounded right one for support—and fired a few more shots. They sailed closer to the target than they had when he'd been freestanding, but they failed to connect again, except with a wall or two in the collection of big cubic tombs that the man now disappeared into.

Jon dropped his head, sucked in a big breath of the freezing air, and leaned back on the cement structure next to him. As time slowed for a few surreal seconds, he noticed that he was resting between two sarcophagi that both seemed to be telling him that he was about to end up in a cemetery like this. One was topped by a stone casket whose lid was partially open, allowing a small cherub to escape, and the other one had an angel that was missing half of its right arm. This caused Jon to also notice that the right arm of his own coat—and his entire back—were now wet with blood, and there was a small trail of it that marked the path he had taken to get here.

He pushed himself off the cement coffin, leaving a big smudge of red on it, and headed toward Millionaire's Row.

He faced a choice when he reached the little City of the Dead— he could dart as quickly as possible through the dozen or more structures and hope to see which direction Roonan had fled out of the other side, or he could move slowly through them in case the big man was catching his breath somewhere inside of them. He chose the latter, mostly because he was tired himself by now, but also because he could always find a phone and call for a dragnet of the nearby parts of the city if the perp got out of the cemetery.

Jon also thought he might have heard some heavy breathing from within the crypts, but that could simply have been the wind whistling through them.

He moved slowly through the narrow openings between the ten- to fifteen-foot whitish buildings, holding the gun in front of him with his shaking left hand, trying unsuccessfully to clench the empty fist of his other one in case he needed it.

He was musing on the ironic prospect of dying in a cemetery when Roonan threw himself out from behind a crypt and smashed Jon into the side of an adjacent one. The impact on the front of his weakened body and the back of his wounded arm caused the gun to fly out of his hand, and the killer began stabbing at his left side with the knife. Jon was thankful now that his left arm was the one working, because he managed to block the first two blows with his left forearm against the man's right, keeping the blade from penetrating too far into his coat or skin. He then thrust his right knee—one weapon he still possessed—into the man's groin, causing him to buckle slightly. But when he did, Roonan thrashed wildly toward him again and slashed across the underside of his chin with the knife, slicing open the skin there.

An involuntary scream escaped and Jon's head jerked back against the stone wall behind him, but he also instinctively rolled away from his opponent. He staggered away from Roonan into a small open area between the crypts to get some space, but there were a few short gravestones on the ground and he stumbled over one of them. As he fell he twisted himself around so he could still see his attacker, and landed on his back in the snow between the graves. The big killer, having recovered quickly and now angrier than ever, launched himself toward Jon in another attempt to pin him, this time on the ground. But he rolled to one side, and Roonan hit only the bloody snow he had left below him.

Jon couldn't get far from him, however, because his roll was stopped by a gravestone, which he hit with his back and slopped with more of his blood. But fortunately he saw the other man making a critical mistake by pulling himself up on his knees to stand up, the process of which would leave him unstable for a few crucial seconds. So Jon fired his wounded body off the gravestone and barreled into the big man, driving him hard for a few feet before they hit the ground again and slammed into another marker in the little plot.

Jon chopped hard at Roonan's wrist with a clenched fist and freed the blade from his hand, then grabbed it himself and rolled off his body to the side, staining the snow with more blood but using the newfound adrenaline enough to stand up with the knife ready in his hand.

The killer stood up, too, shaking his head from the concussion of hitting the stone, but with enough presence of mind to see Jon's gun lying in the snow about ten feet to his left. He looked back at Jon and the knife, quickly contemplating, and Jon muttered, "No, no" through lips that were even more numb now with the loss of blood from below his chin. But Roonan chose his fate and dove for the gun, barely reaching it before Jon's own dive toward him resulted in a knife thrust into the big man's throat. This was the only way to be sure that Roonan couldn't use the gun on him, and though he didn't take pleasure in the near decapitation, Jon did think it was well deserved.

He pushed himself away from the spreading pool of blood around the killer's body, noticing the various other spots of dark red staining the off-white of the snow and cement, and leaned his ever-more-dampening back against the nearest gravestone. He felt a mixture of satisfaction at his success in the investigation, and dread that he probably wouldn't live to celebrate it.

Unable to move anymore, with no cell phone or radio, and the cemetery not opening for hours yet, his only hope of survival would be if the victim back in the crypt woke up in time to go for help, and if the Philly police happened to come to the scene and follow the blood trail before he died. But he couldn't even remember if he had untied the woman's legs well enough for her to get free, and he didn't think he had. Someone would eventually find her and she would probably survive the ordeal, but it was very unlikely that he would.

Still, this is a good way to go, was his last conscious thought.

2

When he eventually woke up in the nearby Temple University Hospital, Jon had a stretch of time alone before anyone visited him. He had no family anymore, very few people that he would call friends and no real ones. He had dated a girl a year earlier, but that didn't end well, and since then he'd been too married to his job to make another relationship work. As his dying thoughts in the cemetery had implied, stopping crime was all that really mattered to him. He suspected that would probably change someday, but he wasn't in a hurry. So during the early hours of his recovery, he mostly worried about losing his job, and subsequently his life dream, although he also spent some time staring at and taking some comfort from the hospital's official motto, posted on the wall near his bed: *Perseverantia Vincit*, which was Latin for "Perseverance Conquers."

All he'd ever wanted to be when growing up was a private

detective like in Raymond Chandler's books. He had been raised in a rural area by strict parents who would only let him read old books and watch old movies, because "they were made back when things were cleaner, before they started putting all that trash in." His parents seemed to miss the fact that, back in the 1940s, Chandler was actually quite risqué himself, for the time. But he didn't tell them that because he loved books like *The Big Sleep* and the old black-and-white movie made from it, and ate them up over and over again. He was especially drawn to Chandler because the fictional protagonist Philip Marlowe shared a name with him, and in the fertile mind of an only child he imagined himself as "Philip" and dreamed of being a private eye someday.

So after his parents basically disowned him as a teenager, he worked various jobs to pay for college classes and killed himself to get the best grades possible. Then he entered the local police academy upon graduation, because he knew by then that he probably couldn't make a living as a private detective unless he first had successful experience in law enforcement. Then he killed himself again to succeed once he was on the force, setting the tone for his current obsessive lifestyle, because it was really the only one he'd ever known. But it did manage to make him a detective by the ripe young age of twenty-five, a significant accomplishment even for a small-town cop.

Jon's first and only visitor in the hospital was the most important person he'd ever met in his life.

"My name is Anton Versa," the casually dressed older man said, without extending a hand to Jon. "I'm the Police Commissioner of Philadelphia."

"I know who you are, sir," Jon responded, sitting up higher in his bed. "I follow the force here because I'd like to be on it some-day." He thought that big city experience might fast-track his real goal of becoming a successful PI.

"Well, that's definitely not gonna happen, with the problems you've caused us here by muscling in the way you did."

Jon tensed, but felt himself relax when the gray-haired man looked around for a chair and pulled one up near the bed.

"Don't get me wrong," Versa said softly. "You did this city a great service by ending that sick bastard's reign of terror. But we can't give you all the credit in the press, or even most of it, because our own people put in a lot of work on this."

He paused and stared at Jon.

"I . . . uh," Jon said after an awkward silence, "I understand, sir."

The Commissioner shifted in the chair, then said, "You've put your own Chief in a tight spot, too, out there in Epherter, or what-ever it's called, because you weren't supposed to be here."

"Ephrata," Jon said, nodding.

"But he told me you were very good out there . . . and you really outdid yourself by catching this guy."

"Just doing my job, sir. Hopefully better than the criminals do theirs."

"This psycho had a good thing going," Versa continued. "And he could have kept going for a long time with that cemetery setup. . . . We found the other five bodies in crypts nearby."

"Just wish I could've stopped him earlier," Jon said.

"Maybe if someone had listened to you," Versa responded, in what would be as close to an apology as Jon ever expected to get from a higher ranking officer. So he let it ride, and there were a few more moments of silence. Then Versa cleared his throat and continued.

"You know how sports stars—when they do really good, but maybe they have some problems . . . ?" He paused and cleared his throat again. "They get traded, you know. Sometimes. When they're really good, and they have problems."

"Yeah . . ."

"Well, you've done really good. Damn good. But you have some problems."

"Okay . . . so?" Jon asked, shifting his bandaged body in the bed.

"Rialle King is an old friend of mine. . . . She's the Mayor of Manhattan, you know."

"I've heard of her."

"Well, she's an old friend and I owe her a few favors. And she recently reached out to other cities for a detective. Someone like you."

"What?" Jon started, and then instinctively put his hand up to the bandage below his chin as pain shot through the wound there. "You want me to go there? That place is a hellhole, isn't it? Dark all the time . . ."

"Oh, it's not that bad. Still the party capital of the world, they say."

"Yeah, they all party a lot because they're so miserable. Isn't cancer through the roof up there, and mental problems? Didn't they make it legal to sell antidepressants in all the stores there?"

"Yeah," Versa said. "But the sun's coming back."

"And then it's gonna get even worse, from what I hear," Jon said. "It could become one of the most dangerous places in the world."

"That's why Mayor King needs help," Versa said. "To keep it

from goin' there. Did you know that she's the first female mayor in New York history? And she's related to Martin Luther King."

"With all due respect, sir, I only care about solving crimes. Why do I fit the bill so well? I've never even been to New York."

"Precisely because you've never been there, and don't care about anything other than solving crimes. Mayor King can't fully trust anyone in the PD up there right now, she wants some new blood. There are forces vying, a lot of temptations for the cops. . . . She can explain it to you. She asked for someone good who's also 'incorruptible,' I think was the word she used."

"I appreciate the vote of confidence, sir," Jon said. "But I don't think I'm the right man for the job."

Versa smiled slightly and leaned forward in his seat.

"Here's why you're gonna go, and why you're gonna like it: The only serial killer that's been worse and gotten more press than our own Full Mooner is the Dayfall Killer in Manhattan. That's who Mayor King wants you to stop, that's your only job, and when you do it you can punch your ticket anywhere. Or live off the consulting and book royalties . . ."

Or open a PI office wherever I want, Jon thought.

"Plus it plays into the whole Dayfall situation," Versa continued. "Everyone is watching to see what happens in New York when it hits there first, to find out what other big cities up north, and in Europe, need to be ready for." He sat back in the chair. "You not only get to go mano a mano with a very bad criminal, but you get to be a part of something bigger."

Jon sat still and silent in the hospital bed—no more shifting around or protesting now. He didn't care much about the "bigger picture," but he did care about catching the criminal, and he sensed that Commissioner Versa had a subtle wisdom. The old cop was dangling the carrot of competition, which he knew Jon couldn't resist, and at the same time challenging him to do something more with his life.

"By the time they let me out of here," Jon said, "won't there be only a day or two before the Dayfall thing happens up there? And isn't the Mayor about to get voted out or something?"

"She has a good plan for all that, like she always does. As I said, I'll let her tell you about it.

"Besides," Versa continued, the slight smile returning, "you can't stay on a police force around here anymore. You pissed yourself twice that night in the cemetery, you know—'cold diureses' they call it. Comes with hypothermia."

"Didn't notice, actually," Jon said. "But why would that keep me off a force?"

"Well, that's gonna get out, and you know how the guys are always giving out nicknames, which tend to stick. You'd be PeeWee or Mr. Dependsable, or some other moniker you wouldn't want to live with."

"Good point," Jon said, and chuckled enough that his chin hurt again. "Like they call you Nurse Versa?"

"They do?" the man said, feigning surprise, then knitted his brow. "Now you *definitely* have to leave the area."

3

DAYFALL MINUS 30 HOURS

It was dark on the Saturday night that Jon flew into Manhattan for the first time, but not just because it was around midnight. He knew it would be dark during the morning and afternoon hours as well. The island had been perpetually shrouded in night for more than ten years, until just recently. During the last two weeks, some daylight had broken through for a few brief stretches of time that were growing successively longer and would soon culminate in an event dubbed "Dayfall," which was expected to take place after the storm system currently above the city erupted on Sunday night, clearing the sky of the last of the black clouds that had caused the constant darkness. This would allow the sun to return on Monday morning for a full twelve hours, according to the scientists, but until then the mixture of the storm clouds and the remaining sun-blockers would keep the inhabitants in one more day of night.

Jon stared in awe at the city from the passenger seat to the left of the helicopter pilot, as they approached it over the water to the south. The heart of New York had always been an impressive sight, but the recent changes to its famous skyline added a surreal quality to the view and made it even more astonishing to the young detective.

Floodwaters on the edges of the island had decreased its size by almost 20 percent, and a wall had been built to protect the remaining parts from the threat of the rising water level. This had all happened because Pakistan and India had a nuclear conflagration (commonly called "the flagger"), which changed parts of the global environment to an extreme degree. Catastrophic ice-melting in subarctic areas and Greenland caused the rising water levels, and the effect on the atmosphere caused both "nuclear night" and "nuclear winter" to fall on some of the Northern Hemisphere. Much of the northeastern seaboard of the United States, including Jon's home area near Philadelphia, had to adjust to colder temperatures, shorter days, and the gray color of the snow that had been stained with his blood at the cemetery. But the perpetual darkness, like the flooding, had only reached the coastline of the US.

New York City was at the very outside fringes of the effect, and therefore would soon be the first major city to experience full daylight, as Commissioner Versa had mentioned. Boston and Portland (Maine) would be liberated from the darkness within a few weeks, and then the northern European cities like London, Berlin, and Moscow after a few months.

Jon found himself shaking his head with incredulity that the world's most famous skyline could have changed so dramatically from the pictures and videos that he'd seen in his childhood. But then he remembered that at the turn of the century a similar transformation had occurred when the World Trade Center towers were destroyed. He knew that people had been just as astounded then that such a thing could actually happen, but he still felt stunned that it could happen twice in such a relatively short time.

In addition to the smaller size of the island and the dark ring of the Water Wall along its outer edges, he noticed that much more light emanated from the buildings in the center of the oval than the ones farther out near the wall. Those buildings had survived the not-so-sudden apocalypse of the "River Rise," as it was called, unlike their adjacent counterparts that had flooded and been torn down to use as raw material for the wall. But obviously many residents and businesses hadn't trusted the assurances that the water level had reached its peak, and had moved farther inland or left the city altogether.

Even in this semi-apocalyptic state, however, Manhattan was still far more imposing and important than any place Jon had ever lived or worked. And he had a nagging, recurring feeling somewhere inside of him that he wouldn't be able to succeed here like he had back home. But he desperately wanted to impress Mayor King, so he suppressed those negative thoughts by constantly reviewing in his mind the conversation he'd had with her before he left, on a secure cell phone that Versa had given to him on her behalf.

"You're gonna hit the ground running," she said, after she had outlined her basic plan and purpose for hiring him. "The storm's supposed to happen tomorrow night and Dayfall the next morning, so you've only got about a day to do this. We'll fly you in to a crime scene in an office building at One Hundred Park Avenue, where you'll meet Officer Halladay in the lobby."

"Yes ma'am," he answered, then wondered aloud, "Will the pilot know where to land?"

"He'll know where the nearest helipad is."

Jon asked that because he had spent the last three days in his hospital bed researching everything he could about the island (including transportation), and had read online that normally no one was allowed to fly helicopters close to the big buildings in the city. The police and EMTs could only do it in emergencies . . . so this spoke of the importance Mayor King had placed on him and his investigation.

"I hope I can help you with this," Jon told her.

"I hope you can, too," she responded. "I really think the only way we can keep the Nazis from gaining power in the city is if we find and stop this killer before Dayfall. The vote is scheduled for the day after that, and there's no way we'll win if people 'Fear the Day,' like they're being told to."

"The Nazis" was the Mayor's way of referring to a man named Gareth Render and his henchmen at Gotham Security—a private company that was poised to become the primary law enforcement authority in Manhattan, if the upcoming referendum passed in their boss's favor. For various reasons, many of the cops in the MPD sympathized with the goals and philosophy of GS, and some were even on its payroll. Rialle King saw herself and her remaining supporters as the last bastion of light for the city, fighting an uphill battle against a conspiracy so broad that she was required to bring in someone new and unadulterated like Jon.

"I also hope you have a strong stomach," the Mayor continued, "when you see what that sicko did at the office building. And I hope you're as good as Versa said, 'cause this killer seems to be some kind of ghost who can walk through walls."

"I might not be better than some of the people you have there," Jon said, trying to keep her from expecting too much from him.

"Maybe not, but unlike them I actually do have you—at least you're working for me. I don't know about any of them anymore, except maybe for your new partner. Maybe. I don't know exactly what to think about him."

That had been the end of the conversation, the Mayor having been interrupted by another call.

Jon leaned forward in the helicopter to study the city more, now that they had reached its south end. The cluster of skyscrapers that had formerly filled the tip, including the tallest one that had replaced the Twin Towers, were now gone, victims of the River Rise. In an eerie twist of fate, the 9/11 Memorial had been prophetic as well as commemorative, because its inverse fountains conjured images of the buildings descending into a watery grave.

The not-quite-as-tall buildings that still stood just inside the Water Wall were mostly dark and silent, but the lights and activity increased considerably as they flew farther into the center of the city, where everyone was presumably safer from any encroaching flooding, and where most of the businesses and citizens had moved. In a few minutes, Jon could see Madison Square Park, heavily lit with the otherworldly light of the UV lamps that kept its trees and grass green and surrounded by buildings that had taken an exponential leap in value and importance because of their location in the very center of this new New York. He especially noticed the historic Flatiron Building, which gave this now-central district its name and was also where he would be working, because it was the new MPD headquarters, and for security's sake, the Mayor's office as well. Jon remembered reading about how the Flatiron District used to be a downscale satellite to the more prestigious offices and apartments of Lower Manhattan, but now as a result of the flagger it had become the core of the Big Apple.

As the helicopter passed farther north, Jon saw that regardless of how many buildings and businesses the city had lost from its edges, much of its interior was still thriving. The towering buildings of Midtown still shone with lights fueled by commercial interests like advertising and entertainment, and even though the tourist industry had definitely taken a big hit, the brightest blast of white still emanated from Times Square. Jon wondered how many people below him were working and how many were playing, because he had read that the uninterrupted darkness had upended the normal cycle of jobs during the day and parties at night. The New York night now lasted all twenty-four hours, so the "night life" did as well, giving new meaning to the label "the city that never sleeps."

He also wondered what it was like in the almost total darkness beyond the North Wall of the city, which he had also read about and could just barely see on the other side of Midtown. The North Wall had been built across the south end of Central Park, and unlike the other stretches in the southern, eastern, and western parts of the city, it was not designed to keep the water out. There had indeed been flooding on the northern half of the island—the expensive real estate on the Upper East and West Sides had been almost entirely lost to it—but the wall there was primarily built to keep people out. There was great fear among the denizens of the southern half that vagrants from the north would invade their more protected and coveted neighborhoods, especially when many of the displaced started squatting in Central Park. And the city of New Manhattan didn't really mind losing that big landmark, because it quickly lost its appeal when it became a veritable cemetery of dead grass and trees. There was no way anyone could supply enough UV lamps or artificial heat to keep a park that size alive.

4

The nearest helipad turned out to be a rather notorious one on the top of the MetLife Building above Grand Central Station. Jon had found out in his research about the city that it had been used for public transportation in the 1970s until a horrible accident closed it down. One of the rotor blades from a helicopter had broken off when the landing gear malfunctioned, causing the aircraft to turn sideways. Whirling out of control, the blade struck four people waiting on the rooftop, killing three of them instantly, then plunged over the skyscraper's west parapet. After striking a window and breaking in two about halfway down the eight-hundred-foot gray tower, one piece continued down to Madison Avenue and killed another unsuspecting pedestrian.

This was one of the reasons, John had learned, why commercial helicopters hadn't been allowed to land on any of the big buildings for many years now. It was also a reminder to him of how anything could happen in New York.

After a long elevator ride down and a walk of a couple blocks, Jon arrived at One Hundred Park Avenue, an older International Style office building with a facade of white brick piers separated by vertical stripes of glass and aluminum spandrels. It sat on an L-shaped plot, thirty-six stories facing Park Avenue and a smaller wing extending back on the Fortieth Street side. Above the base the main tower rose to a set-back top with an illuminated "100" shining just below the roof.

Jon met Frank Halladay in the lobby after milling with a growing crowd of reporters for about five minutes, because his new partner wasn't considerate enough to come down ahead of time and wait for him to arrive. Halladay also wasn't much for introductions; as soon as he found Jon and led him through the turnstiles, he dove right into details of the case.

"This is Exhibit A," said the sandy-haired man, gesturing at the security measures. He was in his fifties and slightly out of shape, but tall enough at six foot two to still present an imposing figure, especially compared to Jon's five-foot ten-inch frame. "State-of-the-art security and surveillance here and at the two freight entrances. Not so airtight inside the building, as you'll see, but we can't for the life of us figure out how he got in."

This was obviously the reason for Mayor King's reference to the killer as someone who could "walk through walls."

"I'm wondering about the roof," Halladay continued as they headed for the elevators. "Because it'd be so hard to sneak in from the ground, and there are no cameras up there. But there's nowhere to land up there, either, as you found out. You had to walk from the MetLife Building, right?"

Jon said, "Yes" as an elevator arrived and they got in. The older man hit the button for the fourth floor and asked, "So how do you like the Big Apple? Is it true that you've never been here before?"

"Less crowded than I expected," Jon answered, ignoring the second question.

"Did you walk through Grand Central on the way?" Jon nodded, and Halladay continued, "Yeah, the thinning out is definitely noticeable in there. . . . It's still busy, but it's not Grand Central Station, if you know what I mean."

Jon nodded again, and smiled slightly to acknowledge the joke. It wasn't all that funny, but he didn't want to alienate his new partner at the beginning.

"About a third of us have left the city," Halladay explained. "And a lot of the subways have been shut down because of the flooding."

"Why did so many people leave?" Jon asked. "Constant darkness get to them after a while?"

"Yeah, and other things. Only a few ways to get on and off the island now, and just the general quality of life is lower, 'cause the city is hurting for money."

"And a lot of people are wearing those masks," Jon added. "Some interesting fashions."

"They don't know whether the air here can really kill you, or even hurt your health. But you heard about that, huh?"

"Yeah."

"So why aren't you wearing one?"

"I don't expect to be in this city for very long," Jon answered. "Why aren't you?"

"I guess I don't expect to be on this planet for very long," he said with a crooked smile. "Or really want to."

The elevator stopped and they stepped out into a utilitarian hallway, leading Jon to presume that this wasn't a typical floor of rented offices, which would likely be more stylish.

"I'm taking you to the places we know that he went, in order," Halladay said. "His first stop was the security camera room, which puts a kink in my roof theory, because there's pretty good coverage of the path from the roof entrance to the elevators—probably 'cause they're worried about jumpers or the quarter-mile-high club. But maybe the perp knew how to wriggle around the cameras, or took the chance that the guy watching them wouldn't notice."

Halladay nodded to a police guard standing outside the room, pulled aside the yellow tape on the door, and opened it. "Whatever happened, the camera guy was surprised. As you can see."

A uniformed rent-a-cop sat in a chair in front of the banks of video screens, having swiveled around to see who had entered the room. The man's hand was on his gun but the weapon was still in its holster, and a seeping bullet wound stained his forehead.

"Smart," Halladay said as he waved his hand at the screens. "Uses a silencer to be safe, takes out this guy, can see a lot of things from here. Where the cameras are and aren't. Who in the building is vulnerable. This was during the latest stretch of daylight, of course, so a lot of people stayed home from work out of fear, while others wanted to be outside out of fascination. So when the killer was here, there were a lot of people working alone in various parts of the building. He picked out a couple, and you're about to see what he did to them."

"But he couldn't tamper with the recordings?" Jon asked.

"No, not without some kind of very high clearance. Which he definitely didn't have, because . . . look."

Halladay punched a button in front of one of the bigger screens in the middle, and un-paused a loop that he and the security personnel had found earlier. It was a shot from a hallway ceiling outside an elevator entrance, and it showed a middle-aged female in office attire waiting at the door and then walking through it when the elevator arrived. Then another figure flashed in from outside the camera's view and blocked the door before it could close. He was wearing something that covered most of his face—either a piece of ski apparel or one of those health masks. The killer was short but muscular, built like a bowling ball. He pulled open his jacket as he blocked the door and liberated some duct tape that seemed to be attached to the inside of the coat, next to some other objects that sparkled with light briefly before he passed out of view and into the elevator.

Jon wondered what he'd just seen, but fortunately Halladay or some technician had appended to the brief recording a slow motion version of those few seconds.

"Those are knives," Jon said after watching it.

"A whole collection of 'em," Halladay agreed. "That's how he's done most of his victims, and that's one of the reasons you're here, I'm thinking. Didn't the Full Moon guy in Philly like knives, too?"

"Yeah," Jon said, pointing to the bandage that still graced the bottom of his chin. "I'm not much of a fan."

"This is the only video memento we have of our perp's little trip to One Hundred Park Avenue," Halladay said, returning to the task at hand. "There are only cameras on the elevator doors on some floors, at the discretion of the tenants. And we don't get much from this clip, except to give the research staff some work trying to find out who might make custom leather jackets for serial killers . . . or chefs or cutlery salesmen or whoever might buy something like that."

"Too bad there wasn't a camera inside the elevator," Jon said.

"No. . . . It's actually *good* there wasn't a camera in there."

The big detective led Jon out of the room and reattached the police tape, and soon they were back in an elevator heading up to the fourteenth floor.

"Did I hear the rumor correctly?" Halladay asked, studying the ceiling of the car. "That you've been given a private number for the King?" When Jon didn't answer, he added, "Must be nice."

Jon didn't answer again, and the elevator reached its destination.

"He got on with the woman the floor above this," Halladay said as they exited. "Stopped it in between the two floors to do his dirty work, then pried a door open and crawled out. We brought it down to this level."

Jon didn't hear the end of what his new partner was saying, because they were standing in front of another elevator that was diagonally across the hallway from the one they had ridden. And inside was the body of the unlucky woman who had found out what the knives were for. Her face was unmolested except for the swath of duct tape covering her mouth, but her lower midsection was a bloody mess from what was apparently a series of stabs and slashes directed at her genitals, or womb, or both. The Full Moon

Killer in Philadelphia had defiled that part of women's bodies for his own twisted pleasure, but for some reason this Dayfall Killer was destroying them.

"It's like Jack the Ripper," Halladay said.

"How many of the previous vics have been this same M.O.?" Jon asked.

"All of them. But one out of the first seven was a male, and number eight, who's upstairs, is also a male. And he's only done that three times."

Halladay pointed to the back wall of the elevator, above the body, where some letters were scrawled in blood. They spelled, TIME DIEM.

"What does that mean," Jon said, "'time of day'?"

"No, I guess you say it 'timay' and it's an imper . . . er . . . or whatever it's called. A command. It means, 'Fear the Day.'"

"Oh," Jon said.

"Don't worry, someone had to tell me, too." The older cop started to move away to the next scene, but Jon put his hand on an arm to stop him.

"He exited on this floor, right?" Jon said. "Because the camera above didn't get him leaving."

"That's right."

"Where's the blood?" Jon asked, looking around at the floor. "There's so much in the elevator. . . . How did he not get some on his shoes and leave a trail?"

"Good question. Maybe he was really careful. Maybe he wore plastic bags on 'em and put those bags in another plastic bag."

"And the knives," Jon added. "He's not gonna put them back in his jacket all wet, is he?"

"Maybe he wiped them with something and put that in the bag. And maybe he took that bag and its contents to the perfect place for his next kill, where he could flush it all down the cludgie."

"The what?" Jon said, as they started moving again and ended up back in an elevator.

"It's a Scottish word for the toilet," Halladay said.

"I thought I heard a bit of an accent."

"Yep. I come from a long line of distinguished Scotsmen, who served the motherland and then this country for centuries. If anyone rates a private number for the King—"

"Your father was a New York detective, right?" Jon interrupted. "And your grandfather was a beat cop."

"How the hell did you know that?" Halladay's nonchalant exterior had cracked a little for the first time.

"I did some checking on you."

By now the elevator had arrived at the eighteenth floor, and they were walking the hallways toward a bathroom that would be a janitor's hell for the next day or two.

"This asshole is good at what he does," Halladay said on the way, his slight annoyance seeming to have vanished. "He not only knew where to end up so he could flush his cleaning supplies, he knew how much time he'd likely have to commit another murder and leave the building before someone figured out one of the elevators wasn't working."

When they reached the men's bathroom, there were two men with a fold-up gurney hanging around just inside the door, in a more spacious part with sinks and lockers on each side, before it narrowed into urinals and stalls in the back.

"It's about time," the older man said with a grimace. "Can we finally get the bodies out of this building, before they paint over them?"

"Very funny," Halladay said. "I told you I wanted my new partner to see them as they lay, and he's gonna see them as they lay. And you're gonna leave the room now so we can talk. You can wait outside or go clear the other two—we're done with them."

The older man frowned again, and gestured to the younger one to exit with him. As he left he also gestured to Halladay, with his middle finger. But Halladay just watched him go.

"These 'reverse surgery' guys—like I call 'em—don't like to be jerked around," he said. "Pretty depressing job as it is."

Jon remembered from his research that New York was unusual in that it didn't have a coroner's office, just the Office of Chief Medical Examiner, or OCME. But he didn't have time to consider what that might mean practically, because his partner pulled him toward the back of the bathroom to see the corpse propped up in a sitting position on one of the toilets. The lower abdomen was mutilated on this one, too, and the last small remnants of blood in the body were still dripping into the white-and-red bowl below it.

"He chose a small male, and a weak one at that," Halladay explained. "Maybe even a jobbie jabber." Jon could only guess what that expression meant, and didn't want to know. "Not chancing too much resistance, I'd say, like accidentally picking someone who's taken karate classes. But this was definitely a male, 'cause he cut some things off him and threw 'em across the room."

Halladay nodded toward the floor on the other side, where

before he looked away Jon glimpsed a small pile of bloody body parts. Despite some prior experience with violent murder, the young detective still gagged a little at the sight.

"Why shoot the camera guy but cut up the others?" he asked, keeping his mind occupied.

"Been thinking about that," the older cop said. "Maybe the risk angle. . . . A security guy could give him trouble unless he takes care of him quick. Or the blood issue . . . not wanting to have too much to clean up that early in the game. Or maybe he just had to take care of the camera guy to get to the people he wanted to cut up. . . . Could be some personal or passion motive we haven't been able to figure out."

"Seems unlikely, with seven other vics cut up just as bad. You haven't found any connections between them, right? Only that they happened when the sun was out?"

"Yeah, otherwise they appear random, as far as we can tell. Hell, a lot of crime has no real point to it, but I just can't buy the idea that the Dayfall is causing all this."

"Which theory?" Jon asked. "The psychological stuff or the scientific idea of it being in the air?"

"Neither," Halladay sneered. "'Yer arse and parsley,' as my grandpa used to say. But people are starting to panic enough that it might end up being—what do you call it?—a self-fulfilling prophecy. You got people injured and dying in the 'chaos crimes' that have been happening in public places at the same time, and you got this guy"—he gestured at the bloody body in the stall—"making people think this could happen to them anytime they're alone, even in places like an elevator or the john."

"Maybe that's the point," Jon said, then backed away from the victim and looked around the room one last time. "Where are the trash cans?"

"Taken back to the lab at HQ, along with all the other possible evidence from the other scenes."

"Then that's where I wanna go next," Jon said.

5

When they reached the Flatiron Building and parked the car in the garage behind it, Halladay insisted that they walk around the outside of the building and stand in front for a while before going inside. He wanted to show Jon a "visual picture" of the politics of New Manhattan, comparing and contrasting some of the important buildings around Madison Square Park.

What Jon noticed first about the park were not the buildings around it, however, but the fact that unlike most of the city, it was actually filled with living grass and trees. Because this district was now so central to what remained of the island, and to the politics of the city because of who occupied the buildings, the park was lit by industrial-strength UV lamps, and had been heated by warmers to melt the snow before the temperatures had warmed recently at the coming of Dayfall. The UV lamps seemed to be the primary cause of the odd-colored, otherworldly glow that emanated from the area, though there were also two large TV screens positioned at the north and south ends of the park.

Despite the recent warming, it was still cool enough that Jon could wear his black leather trench coat, with its long belt tied around his waist and its collar turned up. It was an inexpensive one made by Navarre, with an Italian Stone Design pattern, all he could afford on his police salary. But it was lightweight enough to move around in and didn't elicit ridicule from his coworkers like the tan one he had bought at first, in an attempt to dress like Philip Marlowe. He never even tried to wear a fedora, because of the same problem, though he would have liked to. Halladay, for his part, wore a shorter leather jacket, beat up and brown.

"The Flatiron was the first skyscraper built in New York," the older cop said, gesturing at the building they were standing in front of. "Which is one of the reasons, along with its central location, that the King picked it. She wanted to connect her post-flagger regime with old New York . . . 'a symbol of our enduring past,' I think she called it. So Darth Render went and picked another old building for his base, right across the park, obviously for symbolic reasons of his own."

Halladay pointed across the east end of the park at a thick, imposing-looking structure that sat to the left of one with a taller and thinner tower topped by a large lighted clock. The tan stone facade of the building on the left was terraced and buttressed in an almost martial fashion, and the top seemed to be abruptly truncated rather than decorated with a tower like the one adjacent.

"That's Eleven Madison, known as the Metropolitan Life North Building," Halladay continued. "Because the one next to it with the clock was the first one built for MetLife. They say the

North was supposed to reach a hundred stories and be the tallest building in the world, when it was designed back in the 1920s. But then the stock market crashed and they only ever got to thirty floors."

I guess that explains the truncated look, Jon thought.

"I think Render said it represents something," Halladay added, "like how he's been rebuilding the city but isn't done yet . . . something like that. Maybe he'll finish it when he's in charge."

"We can ask him when we go to see him," Jon said, eliciting a puzzled look from the bigger man. "Will he be there later today?"

"Either there or where he lives. That's the other building I wanted you to see."

Halladay turned to his right and gestured in the direction of an insanely tall and thin skyscraper with glass for walls, which was a block away on the same street from the Flatiron and obviously much newer than any of the surrounding buildings.

"That's One Madison, finished in 2010, sixty stories of some of the most expensive real estate in Manhattan. Render owns the top four floors." He gestured with both hands at two of the three of buildings he had described. "What I want you to see is the difference between the headquarters of Gotham Security, and the one the cops and Mayor are working out of."

Jon looked again at the fortress-like stone building across the park, and then at the Flatiron. From where they were standing in front of it, the latter only looked like a tall thin column. He knew that was just an optical illusion, because the city's original skyscraper widened progressively toward the rear, and the buildings behind it had been co-opted for offices and parking. But he got the idea of how the private company of Gotham Security seemed to have a lot more resources than the city government itself.

"Now look at where Render lives," Halladay said, gesturing again at One Madison, and then pointed to the other side of the Flatiron Building, across the street from it. "The Mayor lives in that old building with the cool gold dome on the top." He turned to face Jon. "All of this'll show ya how the Mayor is facing some tough odds, but also why a lot of people are still betting on her. You've got the big, impressive properties of GS, because they care about utility and security and power. Then you've got the Mayor picking buildings because they've got history and artistry."

The contrast between Render and King seemed to be further confirmed for Jon when he accompanied Halladay inside the Flatiron Building to the crime lab and met Amira Naseem. On the way, Halladay told him that she was one of the few police they could know for sure wasn't in bed with Gotham Security in any way—because she was a Muslim. Gar Render was reportedly opposed to Muslims even being allowed in the city, so he likely would never have one on his payroll.

She was on the tall side, with a medium build, and wore her white lab coat over the typical black attire Jon had seen on other Muslim women, with a long top and loose pants below it. An attractive olive-green head scarf framed a face that was not strikingly beautiful, but her eyes were, and the scarf itself was ironically much nicer than the white mesh nets that other lab workers had to wear on their heads. She looked to be in her thirties.

"Princess Jasmine," Halladay said when he saw her, reminding Jon that the mercurial cop had a nickname for everyone, and worrying about what his own might be. Then he found out, when Halladay added, "Meet my new partner, Diaper Dandy." Jon didn't know whether this just meant that he was young and new, or whether Halladay somehow knew about his pissing incident in the cemetery. He hoped it was the first.

"I'm Jon," he said to Amira, shaking her hand.

"The Princess here will get us everything we need," Halladay said, "And we'll *only* work with her." He looked at the woman meaningfully, making sure she knew not to involve others. "What do you want from her, DD?"

"You mentioned telling the research staff to find out who might make a custom jacket for serial killers, to hold knives inside." Jon said this to Halladay, but then turned to Amira. "What have you found out?"

"I was kidding," Halladay said.

"It's not a joke. We should be working every possible angle."

Amira said, "Good idea," while Halladay rolled his eyes.

"Any blood of another type that could be from the perp at any of the scenes?" Jon said this to Amira.

"No," she said. "Just a lot of the victims.'"

"Anything from the trash that could have been used to clean the knives off?"

"That we have, but it's a needle in a stack of needles."

"Show me," he said. "Please."

Amira retrieved a big plate of glass from the back of the lab with various pieces of refuse attached to it, separated from one another according to which crime scene they were from. Immediately Jon noticed several napkin portions with dried red stains on them, and gestured in their direction.

"Ketchup," Amira said right away.

"Did you examine them to see if there could be blood mixed in?" The killer could have been clever enough to cover his tracks in that way. . . . But Amira had thought of it and checked them.

"What's that?" Jon asked.

"Part of a towelette wrapper from Wednesday's killing in the Village. There were ripped pieces in a trash can a few floors down from the scene. It's a long shot, but I thought maybe he could have put them in his pocket, not wanting to risk clogging a toilet, maybe . . . then unloaded them on his way out, worried about getting pinched at the door or something."

"Can you find out who makes them, and where they're sold in the city?"

"Yes," the head-scarfed woman said, "but that will be a needle in a *mountain* of needles."

"Narrow it down to anywhere near here," Jon said, and when Halladay asked why, he answered, "Just a hunch."

"What's on the paper towels from today's scene?" Halladay asked.

"It's makeup," she answered. "They're from the women's bathroom, not from where he did the vic. But it was deposited near the time, so I used my imagination again and thought, 'What if he was in disguise somehow, went over to the other bathroom and took something off to make it easier to get out of the building?' Then again, a woman may have just been at the mirror somewhere around then."

"No, that's good thinking," Jon said. "Check to see if it's just normal makeup, or if there's anything unusual about it. If there is, run a search for where it's sold in the city and give us the results."

"Would she help us with the building access issue?" Jon continued, addressing Halladay now. "Or would that be someone else?"

"Normally it would be someone else, but in this case let's run everything through her."

"So I want to know every group in the city that could possibly finagle dropping someone on the roofs of these buildings, since that seems to be the only way they could have gotten in. Whether it's by helicopter, by parachute, whatever."

"Unlike the other leads," Amira said, "that's a very short list. Maybe someone from the police could manage it, but it would be hard, especially more than once. Even Gotham Security can't navigate by air around the city without us knowing it."

"I'm especially interested in how Gotham Security might have managed it," Jon said. "Or how someone in the police might have let them."

"There you go again," a puzzled Halladay said. "You seem to be really worried about GS. . . ."

"One Hundred Park Avenue is protected by Assure Security, which is one of the few remaining competitors of Gotham. Assured and Classic had to merge a few years ago just so that they could stay in the game, and barely. Maybe GS wants to 'assure' people that they can't protect them."

"You did your homework," Halladay said, "But not well enough. Two of the previous Dayfall killings were in buildings protected by GS."

"Oh," Jon conceded after an embarrassed pause, but then moved on persistently. "How about the chaos crimes? Do I talk to Amira about those?"

"No," Halladay said with an annoyed sigh. "That investigation's run by Airhead and Dickless. . . . I'll take you to them."

"More nicknames," the younger man observed to the older one as they said goodbye to Amira and walked away from her. "I'd rather you just call me Jon."

"Just be glad I didn't call you Piss-Pants," Halladay said with a smirk, confirming Jon's worst fears. "Yeah, I did some checking on you, too."

6

"I need to go home for a while after we talk to these guys," Halladay said as they headed toward the Chaos Crimes offices. "I've been on for twenty hours and I need some rest."

Jon didn't respond, but studied the two plainclothes officers who were talking in an enclosed office with a lot of glass on the front, until they noticed Halladay and him heading their way. One was an Indian man and the other a blond woman.

"You can ask them whatever you want," Halladay told Jon. "But don't give them anything. I wouldn't be surprised if they're on the take with GS."

"Is this the new blood?" the Indian man said as they approached.

"This is . . . Jon Phillips," Halladay said with a slight hesitation. "Jon, this is Airhead."

"Ari Hegde," the man said while shaking Jon's hand, not even bristling at Halladay's nickname for him.

"And this is Dickless," the older cop said about the blonde.

"Compliment," she responded, and then offered her hand to Jon: "Brenda Dixon."

"I'm surprised he doesn't have an insulting name for you yet," Hegde said to Jon. "He even called Amira 'Towelhead.' "

"That was before I got to know her," the big man replied. "Notice how I still call you Airhead. . . . That should tell you something."

"So . . . the chaos crimes," Jon interrupted. "What can you tell me about them?"

"Not much to tell, unfortunately," Hegde answered. "Random violence when the sun's been out, mass psychology of some kind, probably. Fights, arson, theft, some deaths . . . happened at random places around the city, heightened during the daylight."

"Random," Dixon added, and nothing more.

"No common themes or repeated perps? Have you made arrests?"

"Some, though it's really hard to respond to widespread panic like that. A few we brought in said they felt something affecting them, one or more said they weren't in their right minds, that sort of thing. They seemed pretty normal after being inside for a while."

"Halladay's theory," Dixon offered.

"Yeah, has Halladay infected you with any of his paranoid ideas?" Hegde said with a smile. "Like right wing radicals are behind the Dayfall chaos because they want Render to gain power in the city?"

Jon looked at Halladay, hiding his surprise, then asked Hegde and Dixon why they didn't find Halladay's theories credible.

"Because they've always turned out to be wrong," Hegde answered. "And besides, the government has too many other problems to be nosing into our business here."

"Ridiculous." This from Dixon.

"I suspect everyone and everything," Halladay explained. "That's what makes me a good cop."

"That's what makes you wrong so often," Hegde said.

"How many deaths?" Jon asked.

"Twenty-four to date, and a lot more injuries."

"Ballistics?"

"Only one gun death, and that was one of our arrests. Store owner who got scared of the people crowding into her store because they were scared of what was going on in the street. Told them to leave, one man came at her, to take the gun, she thought. . . . She shot him."

"The rest?"

"Blades, blunt instruments. People carry these things, they're gonna use them when threatened."

"Descriptions of the attackers from the ones who survived?"

"Uh . . . actually, the injured people were just from the fires and explosions caused by the fires. Shrapnel, burns, etc."

"No survivors of the manual attacks?"

"No, not that we know of yet."

"And not a single homicide suspect in custody?"

"Nope," said Hegde. "Boring job, actually."

After a pause, he added, "Are we done here?"

"Why, are you busy?" Halladay chimed in, seemingly more interested in Hegde's rudeness than anything he had to say about the crimes. "How *can* you be, if your job's so damn boring?"

"Have you checked for any civil lawsuits resulting from the mob crimes?" Jon continued, "to see if anyone brought forth evidence or testimony that might be pertinent?" He'd read that many Manhattanites made a living, or at least supplemented their income, by filing lawsuits when anything went wrong—and even when it hadn't. They needed the money, he guessed, so they could party all the time.

"That's an idea," Hegde said, "but what's the point? Even if we do tap someone, they were under the influence of whatever's happening out there, and probably protecting themselves from everybody else."

"So you buy the Dayfall idea, that something's coming over these people, something they can't control?"

"We wouldn't need this department if it wasn't true, though I can't say I understand it myself. You'll have to talk to the experts at NYU about that."

"Can I see what you have in your lab?" Jon asked.

"I guess we can't stop you, if you fill out all the forms and manage to get them signed. But last I checked, you were Serial Homicide and we're Chaos Crimes. Why don't you do your job, and we'll do ours."

Jon looked at Dixon, waiting for a word from her, but she just nodded.

"Nice meeting you," Jon said after studying them a little more, and turned to go.

Halladay flipped them the bird as he did the same.

When they were clear of the other cops, Jon asked his partner, "Did you ever do any investigation into the right-wing government conspiracy angle?"

"No."

"You don't believe your own theories enough to follow up on them?"

"No, because they've always turned out to be wrong," he said with a smile.

"Well, I want Amira to follow up on mine. Have her check into any civil lawsuits that have been filed as a result of the chaos crimes. I also want her to question some of the injured survivors."

"Really?" Halladay groaned. "She's already too busy with what you just gave her."

"And tell her to look for anything that even smacks of intentionality."

"I don't see the point," the big cop persisted, and Jon noticed the similarity to what Hegde had just said. "These crimes are different in every way from the ones we're investigating."

"Not in every way," Jon said. "They're both making people afraid of Dayfall."

Halladay grunted and fumbled with his phone as Jon followed exit signs, looking around at the police staff and wondering how many of them sympathized with Render. Did a lot of them agree that the Gotham boss would make the city safer if he was in charge?

They were back out in the long night, in front of the Flatiron Building, by the time Halladay was done talking to Amira on the phone.

"The Princess told me," the big cop said to Jon, using his nickname for Amira, "that she found some businesses who've bought those towelettes you asked her to check on."

"Anything near here?"

"Yeah," Halladay said with a puzzled look. "One's a bar only a couple blocks away."

"That's it," Jon said, causing the other cop's brow to furrow even more. "I want to check out that bar. But first we should talk to Render." He gestured at the two big buildings owned by Gotham Security—the stone fortress at Eleven Madison and the thin glass tower a few buildings to the right of it. "Where do you think he is right now . . . at work or at home?"

"I'd try work first," Halladay responded. "But listen, like I told you, I need to go home, see the family and get some rest. You'll have to visit Garth Vader by yourself."

"Come on, Frank. I really need an extra pair of eyes and ears for this. And time is of the essence, remember?"

"My time *is* the essence," Halladay said. "I'm going home."

"How about a compromise?" Jon said after a moment of thought. "Let's check out the bar first, we can get a drink or two, and then you can decide what you want to do."

"Okay," the big man said after a moment of his own. "Only because I would've stopped for one on my way home anyway."

"Great." Jon patted him on the back and gestured forward. "Lead on . . ."

"One more thing," Halladay said, "since we're making a deal. Take that bandage off the bottom of your chin—you look like a dick. It's not still bleeding, is it?"

"No," Jon said, feeling it with his fingers. "But it looks kinda gross underneath."

"Naaah. It'll make you look tough."

As Jon removed the bandage, Halladay led them north on Broadway, straddling the left side of the park and then veering away from it for a block until they reached the St. James Building at the corner of Twenty-Sixth Street. On its first floor, with an entrance on Twenty-Sixth, was a newish-looking establishment called "The Office." Jon chuckled at the name and followed Halladay in and up to the bar, where they took the two stools farthest away from the other patrons, just a few at this hour.

Before they even settled in their seats, both men couldn't help but notice the woman serving at the other end of the bar, whose beauty was not ostentatious but was still too obvious to miss. Everything about her was attractive, but what became most noticeable, as she approached their side of the bar, were her fair, slightly freckled complexion and shining ice-blue eyes. They contrasted strikingly with her dark shirt and hair, which was half-gathered so that wisps of it graced her forehead and accentuated those amazing eyes even more.

"Wow," Halladay said as soon as she stopped across the bar from them.

"Thank you," she said, as if she was used to it, with a medium-pitched and slightly coarse voice. "What can I do for you guys?"

Halladay grinned at Jon, who responded with a slight frown and shake of his head.

"I'll try to restrain myself," the big cop said, "and I'll just ask for a BrewDog ale. If ye have it." He turned up the brogue on the last phrase.

"Aye, we do," she said with a smile, then turned to Jon. "And for you?"

"Well, since it's my first drink in the city, I guess I'll have a Manhattan." Jon laughed nervously, half because of the woman's effect on him and half because he couldn't believe he was feeling it. He was usually too preoccupied with his work to even notice anyone.

When she left to get their drinks, Halladay turned to John and said, "Damn."

"I thought you were a family man," Jon said.

"I am. I'm thinkin' for you." He nodded at Jon and raised his eyebrows.

Jon looked back at the woman, who seemed about his age, and actually had to shake his head to clear it and remember why they were there.

"What's your name?" Jon said, when she returned with their drinks.

"Mallory Cassady," she said, putting her hand out.

"Jon Phillips," he said, and took it, feeling more sparks despite the fact that he was telling himself how ridiculous it was. "This is Frank Halladay."

She shook Halladay's hand, too, and said to him, "Speaking of names, yours sounds familiar. But I haven't seen you in here."

"Do you own the place?" Halladay asked, smart enough to know that if she was here most of the time, she probably did. And she was smart enough to tell that he had evaded her question, so her demeanor changed ever-so-slightly when he did.

"I do, along with my father. Why do you ask?"

"I really like the name."

"We're MPD, Mallory," Jon said, trying to be as straight up and nonthreatening as possible. But her demeanor changed noticeably this time, as if she felt threatened anyway.

7

"You're not a suspect," Jon said, "if you're worried about that."

"I'm not worried about anything," Mallory said, almost convincing him.

"We're wondering about those little wet naps, actually," Halladay said, pointing to the small bowls of them at two spots on the bar. "Has anyone suspicious taken any of them recently?"

"No," she answered, a little too quickly. "Like . . . what do you mean by 'suspicious'?"

"Military or ex-military, maybe?" This was Jon, and Halladay looked at him strangely again, wondering what he was on about.

"There's a serial killer on the loose," Halladay interrupted. "As I'm sure you know. And sometimes you can just tell when you meet them, that there's something not quite right."

"Huh. I can't imagine." Then she said "Excuse me for a minute," and left to tend the other end of the bar again. Jon wasn't sure whether he saw anyone come in, or signal for her, or not.

"I'd like to interrogate *her*," said the family man, draining the rest of his beer. "I'll just say I was at The Office. Heh." Then he looked at Jon, who had barely finished half of his small drink. "Why did you say, 'Military or ex-military?'"

"A hunch," said the younger man.

"If you're implying GS again, because they have a lot of those types, forget about it. The Princess told me on the phone that she checked into it, and there's no way a GS copter could have dropped someone on top of those buildings. The Mayor keeps strict tabs on their aircraft. The only possibility for an entrance like that would be MPD or maybe a private company across the river. But there's too much surveillance on top of other buildings even for that."

"We get a very boring clientele here," Mallory said as she returned. "Hardworking, well-off people from this district. And they're usually pretty happy while they're here, even if they didn't come in that way. So no serial killer types."

"Probably not," Jon said. "But we'd like to get a copy of your security tapes, just in case." He gestured with his head toward a camera that was barely visible in the top corner of the room, and she stood a little bit straighter.

"Okay," she said. "But I don't have anything to copy them onto. Not here, anyway. . . . I have some flash drives at my apartment across the park that would be big enough." She leaned down closer to Jon. "You can provide some public service and walk me over there, keep me safe from that killer you're looking for."

"Hey, am I chopped liver over here?" Halladay said. "What about me?"

"You could walk me home later, when my shift is done."

"What time?" the family man said, but Jon interrupted him.

"It's tempting," Jon said, and meant it. "But we're very short on time. Frank, would you please call Amira and have her bring a flash drive to you halfway, so we can get on with this?"

The big man grimaced, grunted, and murmured something like "Damn right it's tempting" as he stepped off the stool, pulled out his phone, and headed for the door.

"Can you show me where the cameras feed into?" Jon asked when Halladay was gone.

When she'd led him into a small back room with two screens, and their bodies were pressed close together in the confines, he had to admit that he wanted to walk her home. This was the last thing he'd expected to happen on the first day of a new job in a new city, especially in this current situation. And worse, he knew that the faculty of reason he relied on so much could be adversely affected by feelings like this. He knew that he should get out of that dark room as soon as possible, but he had to wait a few minutes for Halladay to return, so he tried to use them to his advantage.

"If you're worried about the police," he said softly near her ear, "I can protect you from them. I'm a cop . . . but I'm not from here."

"Why don't you come back at two when I get off?" she said at his ear, leaning into him as she did. "You can pick up the tapes then, and you can walk me home."

Jon couldn't help but make a mental note of the time she mentioned, and think to himself that he might be alone for a while around that hour, if he couldn't keep Halladay from going home and wasn't allowed to go with him. But Jon's commitment to solving the crimes was still overriding any other considerations, no matter how appealing they might be.

"I'll take them now," he said, "when my partner returns." But he didn't comment about the two o'clock proposal. "Is there some reason you don't want us to have your security videos?"

"No, we don't have anything to hide," she said, again too quickly, but then added, "I mean, sometimes when a customer's had too much, I don't give them change. I figure it's their fault, you know. And I only did that in the early days. Now that we're doing better . . ."

"I wouldn't worry about that," Jon said, and she remained quiet for a while until Halladay clambored through the half-open door, and looked around in the cramped, dark quarters.

"What're you two doin' in here?" he said with a chuckle.

"Pulling up the files," Jon said, and held out his hand for the high capacity drive that Halladay had brought with him. He gave it to Mallory, telling her how far back he wanted her to go and that he would test the files before he left to make sure they had been copied. No one said anything in the minute or two this all took to happen, but finally the bartender spoke up as the men turned to leave.

"See you later," she said. "I hope."

Outside the bar, Halladay shook his head and said, "If you don't get some of that . . ."

"You will, I suppose?" Jon said.

"I was gonna say you'd be a fool," the sandy-haired cop answered.

"Did it ever occur to you," Jon said, frowning at him, "that she might have ulterior motives?"

"Nah." Halladay shook his head and pointed to it. "I wasn't thinking with this."

On the walk back to the Flatiron Building, Jon was ruminating on what it must be like for people to live in a city of endless night, never seeing the sun for more than ten years, when they passed a small "health store" that wouldn't have existed before the darkness fell. There were signs on the front windows with pictures of vitamin D products like fortified milk and orange juice, several kinds of fatty fish, and the usual bottles of pills. Others advertised the psychiatric medications that were only available by prescription in other places, but were allowed to be sold over-the-counter here. The signs indicated that D deficiency was known to cause depression, memory loss, and even schizophrenia.

Jon glanced over at Halladay and wondered if his partner was taking any of those drugs, or whether he should be.

When they reached the lab at headquarters, they gave the external drive to Amira and asked her to run facial recognition software on the customers who took wipes from the bar. And Jon told her to scan the staff, too. When she told them how long it would take, Jon said he would wait in the shooting range and motioned for Halladay to follow him as he headed out of the lab.

"The range is in the basement," he said. "Right?"

"Yes," Halladay answered, but then stopped in the hallway. "Damn me if I didn't forget because of that bartender . . . but I need to go home."

"Don't you want to know if anyone interesting turns up on the tapes?" Jon asked.

"I'll find out when I come back in."

"When's the last time you've been to the range?" A stab in the dark. "I made a vow that I'd practice with my left for a hundred hours, since it almost got me killed."

"It's been a while," the big man admitted.

"Wait . . . you didn't practice up for when the daylight started breaking through, even though you knew it might be dangerous?"

"I wasn't working when that happened."

"Where were you?"

"At home, where I need to go now."

"Nope," Jon said, shaking his head and pulling on the big man's arm. "You definitely need some preparation. In less than twenty-four hours, we'll have almost a full day of sunlight, and we'll have to be out there working. No hiding from this one. Come on . . ."

Halladay reluctantly went with Jon, probably because he knew there was some truth to what he said, but also because he actually *was* tired—almost too tired to argue with the persistent younger man. They practiced at the range for a while, then took a break outside of it at the snack machines when they realized Amira hadn't called yet. While they were hanging out, Halladay said hello to a man who walked through from the custodian's office nearby, and introduced him to Jon. His nickname was "Poppy," and Jon asked how he had come by it.

"My father was the super here before me," the man said, "His name was Sunny, spelled with a 'u,' but people thought it was Sonny, like someone's son, ya know, so they started calling me Poppy. Thought it was funny, I guess."

"This is a cool building to take care of," Jon said.

"Yeah, well, it was a lot cooler before you guys moved in. . . .

No offense. Now we have all this extra security. Used to be able to fix shit right away ourselves, now we got all this fuckin' red tape. Used to be able to show people around, like tell 'em about the fancy restaurant that was down here way back, or the big old boiler room thirty feet down with the big old generators, looks like some kinda movie set or something."

"I read that the Flatiron used to have hydraulic elevators," John said. "Water-powered, right?"

"Yeah, that old generator's down there, too. A lot of the buildings in the city had that. My dad said it used to break sometimes, water would gush out into the elevators and offices up there. Heh."

"What do you think about Gotham Security?" Jon asked him. "And what do you hear from others who work here, and around the city?"

"How ya mean?"

"Oh, I don't know, it seems that someone like you might have his ear to the ground. Have a good sense of how the vote will go on Tuesday."

"Still got a thing for GS, huh?" Halladay said to Jon.

"Huh?" Poppy said.

"Nevermind him," Jon said, "What do you think the chances are that Gar Render will be running this city in a couple days?" The man looked hesitant, so Jon added: "You can be honest. . . . We don't have a dog in the hunt."

"Well, I want the Mayor to win," he said, looking around. "She's been good to us here, and I think she means well. But if more people die when the Dayfall comes, I don't think she has a fuckin' chance. People are scared. . . . They know that the Big Man re-built the city, and they think he can keep 'em safe. A lot of 'em think that the only reason he hasn't stopped the killings is because his hands are tied, with the rules against his cops and all."

Jon thought it was interesting that Poppy conceived of Render's private army and the police as merely two different sets of "cops." That fact alone was probably a guarantee that his grassroots prediction would come true.

8

Amira finally called them, and Halladay went back up with Jon to the lab out of curiosity to see the results from the facial recognition software. She told them that there were only four customers who were found to be in the government database they were using, and one was inconclusive because she was obviously a woman but had come up under a male name. And none had a criminal record for anything worse than traffic citations. Jon put pictures and info for all four on his phone and told Halladay that it was time for them to talk to Gar Render, the Gotham Security boss.

Now that the big man's curiosity had been slaked, however, he insisted on going home ("For the last time!").

"You can go talk to Render alone," Halladay said. "Or wait until I've gotten some rest and come back on duty."

Seeing that his partner was more resolute this time, Jon played his best hand.

"If you go home before we talk to Render," the younger cop said, "I'll have to go with you."

"What?" Halladay said, then added, "You don't want to let me out of your sight, do you?"

"I told you," Jon said, "I really need two pairs of eyes and ears on this."

The clear implication was that if Halladay went with him to meet Render, Jon would let him go home, by himself, in peace. The young cop let him think that for reasons of his own, and the older one agreed. So they started across the park to the Gotham Security Building.

On the way, Jon noticed that the blue-green wash of UV light was more pronounced near the grass and trees in the middle of the square, since the industrial lamps were attached to the sides of the tall light poles there. He also noticed the proliferation and variety of the environmental masks worn by many of the adult pedestrians, and most of the few children he saw, who were probably coming or going with their parents from the playground at the north end of the park. Jon also noticed a street vendor who had set up a small portable table in front of the statue of William H. Seward and was hawking "Dayfall survival equipment" like protective glasses, head-to-toe plastic ponchos, and extra door locks. Halladay swerved a little out of their way to flash his badge at the man, who promptly folded up the table and moved deeper into the park (where he would probably set it up again, if no other competitors were there already).

"It's funny. . . . They used to sell all kinds of stuff related to the darkness," the older cop explained. "Like drugs and light-trackers for your health, and rip-off glasses that are supposed to help you see in the dark, but really don't. Now they're pushing sunlight stuff."

"Supply and demand," Jon said.

"Sometimes they'll have guns and knives underneath," Halladay said, apparently unconcerned whether that one did or not. "Or at least they'll have business cards telling people where they can get them."

"I guess some things are always in demand," Jon observed, then he asked, "Gun control is another big difference between the Mayor and Render, right?"

"Yeah," Halladay answered. "When people get scared they want to be able to protect themselves, or think they can anyway. That will get him a lot of votes, especially if tomorrow's a bad day."

The Gotham Security headquarters at Eleven Madison seemed even more formidable up close, definitely a symbol of both strength and a connection with the New York past, as opposed to the Flatiron, which was only the latter. But despite its fortress-like appearance, Jon was surprised to see that there wasn't much security at the main entrance, other than some ex-military types in suits stationed near the doors. Perhaps there was some kind of hidden surveillance equipment, or invisible scans running, but no one confronted the two cops about the guns they wore underneath their coats, and they walked freely into the interior of the building. Jon wondered if this was intended to make GS seem more open or secure than the relatively inaccessible police headquarters. But when they got inside he realized that Render probably wanted to show off the amazing lobby of the historic building to those who visited.

The Art Deco interior of the sprawling lobby gleamed gold,

from the period lighting on the marble walls and floors and the gilded paint on much of the elaborate metal and stucco trim work. Jon and Halladay proceeded down a spacious hall with a very high ceiling and large portraits of famous men punctuating the walls. These included Chester A. Arthur, John Pierpont Morgan, Cornelius Vanderbilt, Thomas Edison, William Cullen Bryant, and others whose names Jon didn't recognize, as the big hall opened into an even bigger one with an even higher and more elaborate ceiling. The main cavern of the lobby did have some security turnstiles (stylish in themselves) leading to four alcoves with banks of elevators on one side. Above each alcove and on the adjacent walls there were words like THRIFT, INDUSTRY, and SECURITY carved into the marble in large, prominent letters.

No one was manning the turnstiles, but there was a semicircular marble counter attached to one of the huge marble pillars in the center of the lobby, with two of the suited ex-soldiers standing behind it. Halladay approached them, showed his badge, and said they were here to talk to "Darth Render."

He's got no sense of appropriateness whatsoever, Jon thought to himself, *but at least he's consistent.*

They were told to wait, and before too long a somewhat short and very thin man, meticulously dressed, approached them from one of the elevator alcoves. Though he looked slightly familiar, Jon knew this man wasn't Render, because he had seen pictures and video of the GS boss.

"My name is Nelson Gant," the man said, offering a semi-limp handshake to both of them. "I am Mr. Render's Administrative Assistant. What can I do for you?"

Jon recognized the name—this was Render's childhood friend,

who had accompanied him throughout his rise to wealth and power. Jon didn't remember for sure whether it was a literal fact or a metaphor, but he had read somewhere that in high school Render was a state champion wrestler, and Gant was the nonathletic friend who held the towel for him. There had been some of the inevitable tabloid rumors about a romantic relationship between the two men, of course, though the GS boss was married. But Gant himself was not, if Jon remembered correctly.

"You can let us talk to him, Mr. Gaunt," Halladay said with irritation. "*That's* what you can do for us."

Jon noticed how "gaunt" the man actually was, now that he was close to them. His face had a skull-like quality to it, drawn and angular, and his thin black hair was perfectly cemented in place. "Death's head" was the term that came to Jon's mind, and stayed there as they interacted with the man.

"Mr. Render isn't here right now," he said, "but I would be willing to share any information that is public and necessary to an investigation."

Jon was impressed, because the man managed to frame and limit any discussion with just one sentence. Halladay, for his part, was smart enough to know he was being handled, but not smart enough to know exactly how.

"What kind of legalese crap is that?" the big cop said with disgust. "You might as well just tell us what you're hiding before we pull it out of your ass with pliers."

Gant smiled, and the effect was even more unsettling than his previous rawboned frown.

"Officers Halladay and Phillips," the thin man said, surprisingly knowing their names and again making an important statement with just a few words, "surely you understand that there are protocols we must follow anytime we communicate with law enforcement. It's nothing personal, and we have nothing to hide."

"Where is Mr. Render?" Jon asked.

"He is at his private residence," Gant answered. "And would prefer not to be disturbed."

"Would he prefer to be disturbed by you," Halladay said, "by telling him we're coming? Or should we just walk over there and disturb him ourselves?"

"I'll tell him," Gant said, after a few moments of mutual staring. He stepped away from the cops and put an earpiece in to make a call.

"Administrative Assistant my ass," Halladay said to Jon, lowering his voice only a little. "He's the Big Man's number one henchman, his right-hand fan, would do anything for him. They grew up together. . . . Render's literally a big man, was an athlete, has the looks and charisma. This little worm attaches to the friend he wishes he could be; the Big Man loves him because he's so loyal. Classic."

"Oh, so you're a psychologist now?" Jon said.

"Mr. Render will see you for a few minutes at his home," Gant said, returning to them. "But please keep in mind that he hasn't been feeling well, and so he might need to cut the interview short."

"Yer talkin' pish," Halladay said, resentful of being handled again and waving his hand at the well-dressed man. "We'll interview him as long as we want." At that, both he and Gant turned to leave in opposite directions, but Jon stepped after the thin man to ask him one more question.

"Mr. Gant," he said, softly enough that Halladay wouldn't hear. "My partner thinks you would do anything for Mr. Render." Gant just looked at him, so he continued. "Would you carry out an order to kill, maybe even a lot of people, if you thought it would get him elected?"

"Mr. Phillips," Gant said, matching his soft voice. "Gotham Security exists to save people's lives, not take them. And that's why Mr. Render doesn't need any help getting elected."

"Thank you," Jon said, nodding, and shook his somewhat limp hand again. Then he turned and followed Halladay out of the building.

When he was back outside, Jon noticed that there was an enclosed walkway about ten stories high between the GS building and the next one over, which had been built in the same era with the same type of stone, but was taller, more streamlined, and topped by the thin clock tower. He had also noticed while inside that there were steps at the side of the lobby going down to an underground passage that led to the companion building. He knew that many years ago both buildings had been owned by Metropolitan Life, so that explained the walkways, but he asked Halladay if GS owned both of them now.

"Not yet, I don't think," Halladay said. "They rent part of it, but don't need more than that, so there's other businesses in there."

They passed in front of the old building with the clock tower and soon found themselves at the very end of Madison Avenue, looking up at the much newer tower of glass called One Madison, which was so tall and thin that it made Jon think of kids' games where they tried to stack LEGOs or blocks as high as they possibly could without them falling over.

Two more of the muscled men in suits stood waiting for them at a private entrance to the left of a retail store on the ground floor, and walked them into the building's lobby from the back. A couple of residents were coming in the front door as they waited for an elevator, and another man came out of the one they got in. As they rode up the fifty-plus stories with the two bodyguards, Halladay proved again that he wasn't shy about speaking his mind around anyone.

"Asshole owns the top four floors," he said. "The penthouse on the top three alone is worth about seventy-five million. Right place at the right time. The flagger hits, the river rises, and his construction company is right there, ready to cash in on it. And now his security company is right there to capitalize on our newest problems."

"You don't like him?" Jon asked, glancing at the stone-faced security soldiers.

"I don't like anyone who's power hungry. I don't like Nazis."

"Well, he can't be *that* evil," Jon said, and now gestured at the suits standing next to them. "These guys haven't killed you for talking bad about him. Yet."

"Let 'em try," the Scotsman said.

When they reached the fourth floor from the top, the elevator stopped and all four men stepped out into what had once been one of the building's "normal" apartments, but had been renovated into a meeting and office area for the Big Man, where he could come down from his deluxe penthouse to greet visitors. But even this floor was stunning, with high ceilings and breathtaking 360-degree views of the city surrounding enough inner rooms to house servants, bodyguards, or others who might need to stay near the GS boss for whatever reason.

Gareth Render soon appeared out of another, smaller elevator next to the one they had arrived in, which Jon assumed was a private one connecting this floor with the penthouse. The older man was even taller than Halladay, and was definitely more muscular, though he had much less hair. He wore the kind of simple, casual clothing that might be seen on a construction company owner who had to visit the job site sometimes. And he was immediately and unquestionably hospitable to the two policemen, which to Jon actually seemed sincere. But the young detective had been fooled before.

"Ah, my brothers," Render said, shaking both their hands in a way that seemed even more firm and genuine when contrasted with the way his assistant had greeted them. "Anyone who serves to make this city safer is a brother to me."

"Nice place you have here," Halladay said.

"Thanks a lot," he answered. "But I actually live up there, on the top three floors."

"Can we see it?" Halladay said, and both Render and Jon looked at him. They kept looking at him, so the big cop shrugged and explained himself. "I figure this is the only chance I'd get to be in a place like this—might as well take a look at it."

Realizing Halladay was actually serious, Render "hmmmed" for a moment and then said, "I don't see why not. The Mrs. is out shopping. Come on up."

He led them back to the elevator they had arrived in, presumably because it was the only one big enough to hold all of them at once.

"I'm sorry it's necessary to have these guys with us," Render added, gesturing at the suits. "Frank here has been around a while, but you're new here. . . . I'm sorry, what's your name?"

Jon told him, and then fought hard to keep his mouth from gaping when they walked out of the elevator and into the penthouse.

9

The elevator opened into a small foyer adjacent to the great room that Render then led them into. It was two tall floors high and half as wide as the building, the transparent walls with huge panes of glass on two sides affording a vertigo-inducing view of the north and east ends of the city. The nearby MetLife Clock Tower, which was brightly lit and the same height as the penthouse, dominated the north side, while the Empire State Building was behind it and slightly to the left. The more famous skyscraper looked smaller than the first, because it was a half mile in the distance.

To their left was a bronze spiral staircase that wound through the upper two floors and was visible all the way up to the third floor, because the second was partial to allow for the high ceilings of the great room. The furniture and decorations were obviously expensive, but also rather sparse and generic.

"Three floors, as you can tell," Render said, gesturing to the spiral staircase. "Almost seven thousand square feet, five bedrooms and baths. Another private elevator beside the stairs there, just for these top three floors." He looked directly at Halladay, wearing a little smirk. "Did ya wanna ride it to my bedroom on the third floor, or have you seen enough?"

He said it nicely but it irritated the big cop anyway, and caught him off guard—so much so that he forgot his newfound manners toward Jon, and awkwardly deflected the attention to the younger man.

"Yeah, this is enough for me," Halladay said. "But Country Boy here might want to check it out. I don't think he's ever been in a building this big."

"Definitely the nicest view I've ever seen," Jon said, gazing out of one of the tall, transparent walls.

"The only disappointment is," Render said, gesturing at the dark city skyline, "I've never even seen a sunrise or sunset from up here. I sit out on the terrace with that fancy UV light on, pretending it's daytime and getting some rays. Do you want to go out there?"

"No," Jon said, "I just have some questions for you."

"Okay," Render said. "Have a seat." They did, on the couches in the center of the big room. Except for the two bodyguards, who stayed standing in strategic spots. "Would you like something to drink?"

"It won't take that long," Jon said. "But thanks."

Halladay leaned back and sprawled out on the plush pillows, but Jon sat up straight on the edge. Render did something in between on his.

"I'm wondering how much you want to be the Mayor of Manhattan," Jon said.

"I don't want to be the Mayor," Render said, seemingly puzzled by the question. "I would prefer the title 'Protector,' but we couldn't legally word the referendum that way. Once I'm elected, I'll reorganize and give others most of the responsibilities of a Mayor, while I devote myself to making sure the city is safe. Along with my Builders, and any current police officers who can buy into what I'm trying to do."

He looked meaningfully at the two cops, as if offering them a job—with some major conditions.

"'Builders' are what you call the members of the small army you've put together," Jon said. "Right?"

"Right. I initially hired many of them to provide security for our rebuilding projects around the city after the flagger . . . the *first* time we hammered impending chaos into lawfulness. The second is about to happen. I decided to keep the same nickname for my employees once the material rebuilding was done, because I realized that we now need a spiritual rebuilding . . . to provide peace of mind for the people of the city."

"So that's how you went from the construction business into the security business."

"They're so related," Render said, leaning forward and getting into it more. "Have you been to our headquarters down the street?" The two officers nodded. "Maybe you noticed the words carved into the marble above the elevator halls?" Now only Jon nodded. "We had our offices there years ago when my father was still alive and running our construction company—one of the reasons I bought the building. But when I worked there, every day I would walk under the word SECURITY into elevator bank D, to get to my office. So every day I was reminded that buildings were about providing security for people, especially in a scary place like Manhattan.

"When the flagger hit," the GS boss continued, "our company replaced the ruined structures with new ones that could keep the city safe. And now we have to finish the job by replacing the ruined infrastructures of a liberal Mayor and soft law enforcement. What good will it have done to build a place where we can live, if we can't live in peace and safety?"

"You're definitely running for Mayor," Halladay said, with a look of bored dissatisfaction. "You've got all the talking points down perfectly. But you're like all the other Nazis. . . . You just want to be in charge, plain and simple."

"You should be grateful, Frank, like most of your fellow officers are." The big bald man sat back again while he said this, and then directed his next comment toward Jon. "According to the technicalities of the law as it stands now, my men aren't allowed to work on the streets. They do anyway, of course, because it's the right thing to do. But they give the credit officially to the MPD officers who arrive at the scene. . . . It's good for the city and it's good for the cops."

"Yeah, and that's why you have so many of them in your pocket," Halladay said. "But I'm my own man . . . so, sorry if I don't kiss your Nazi ass like everyone else."

"I know why you don't like me," Render said with a smile. "It's because you know that when I'm in power, I won't let you continue your little arrangement down on Lexington."

Halladay shifted in his seat, but didn't reply, so Jon redirected the conversation.

"You didn't answer my original question," he said to Render. "About how much you want to win the vote on Tuesday."

"How do you mean?"

"Well, you just admitted that you break the law to accomplish what you think is best for safety on the streets. Would you be willing to do that to get elected?"

"Within reason, I guess." The big old man knitted what was left of his brows and sat up again. "What are you suggesting?"

"Well, it seems to me that the murders we're investigating make people feel unsafe, and if more of them happen tomorrow during Dayfall, that would make people more inclined to vote for someone who says he can keep them safe."

Render stood when he realized what Jon was implying, and unleashed a stream of profanity that said "construction foreman" much more than "Mayor." Jon stood, too, responding with "Leave my mother out of this," and the two bodyguards stepped toward the two men, who were now about a foot apart. Jon was much younger, but he was also much shorter and not built as powerfully as Render . . . so it wasn't clear whether the guards would have to intervene on behalf of their boss or not. Halladay didn't move from his spot on the couch, but his mouth was hanging slightly open.

"My goal in life is to protect life, of any kind, at all costs," Render said through clenched teeth. "I would never take it or allow my men to take it, unless it was necessary to protect others' lives."

"Maybe you think it's necessary in this case," Jon said with equal conviction, not backing down from the argument or the staring contest, "so you can get elected and 'save more lives.'" He put the last three words in quotes with his fingers.

"No," Render said, actually considering what Jon was saying. "That's a line I wouldn't cross. I've offered to help the police in any way I can with the Dayfall killings, and that offer stands."

"Why don't you guys just sit down?" Halladay said. "You look like two fighters before a boxing match . . . except from two really different weight classes."

Jon and Render took his advice, because they both knew any further escalation would do nothing good for either of them.

"I guess it's more sad than anything," Render said, genuinely seeming to feel that way now, and obviously thinking about something as he spoke. "That you or anyone would ever think I would be involved in murder. That's what I'm trying to stop, along with other hurtful crimes that thrive in the city because this Mayor is more concerned about diversity, civil rights, and philanthropy than she is about security. But you *can't have one without the other.*" His tone was pleading now, the talking points seeming more personal than the two cops would give him credit for.

"Besides," the old man continued, regaining his composure quickly, "Dayfall doesn't need any help to be as dangerous as it can possibly be. Have you talked to Gunther and Carter at NYU about their research into the scientific and psychological effects of it?"

Jon remembered these names from his reading before coming to the city—they were the foremost experts on why the emerging daylight would make people go crazy.

"Not yet, no," he answered.

"You should. I don't think the MPD is nearly prepared enough for what will happen, and it's only about twenty-four hours away." He gestured at the top half of the transparent wall and the starless sky beyond it. "I'm not a scientist, but I can tell you something's cooking in the atmosphere just by being this high up, and surrounded by metal maybe, I don't know. I've noticed a bunch of, what do they call them . . . anomalies . . . right here in my place. Especially when the sun has broken through."

"I just have a couple more questions," Jon said, and Render nodded. "Would you be willing to hand over all the flight records and any other information we request about aircraft you own or work with, so we can establish that GS hasn't transported anyone to the buildings where our crimes took place?"

"Absolutely. Anything you want."

"And I was curious," Jon continued. "There's an impressive lab tech at the MPD who is a Muslim, and I understand you wouldn't hire her because of that."

"That's right," Render said without hesitation. "No disrespect or judgment about her personally, but this city saw what people of that religion can do to us. I know a lot of 'em are more moderate, but you've got the law of averages and there's always gonna be some degree of suspicion. I'd rather be safe than sorry, and not roll the dice, and I believe a lot of the people in this city share my feelings."

"Okay," Jon said. "Or not. . . . I'm not saying that's okay. But you know what I mean. Thank you."

Render said the same, but only offered his hand this time to gesture them toward the elevator.

"Man, you really have something against that guy," Halladay said, this time waiting until they were out of the lobby and out of earshot. "And what's with the 'mother' issue? You were almost out of control."

"I don't know," Jon said. "I can handle any other kind of insult, it really doesn't bother me at all. But that one really does." The younger man shrugged as he pulled his coat together in the front. "What can I say? I love my mother, despite our differences. And I'm the only one allowed to cuss her out."

"Yeah, well, I love my family, too. And right now I'm going to see them, and get some sleep, no matter what you say."

"I'll come along, then," Jon said, realizing he wouldn't be able to change the big man's mind this time. "Like I said, I haven't slept in a long time, either."

"Okaaay. . . . Well, we do have a number of beds in the old homestead," the older cop said with a mischievous smile.

10

They got Halladay's car from the garage behind the Flatiron Building and headed northeast to the older cop's "homestead," both sitting in silence during the ride. Jon studied the streets as Halladay
drove, noticing the irony that there was some kind of club on almost every other block, but also about an equal number of those
"survivalist" vendors and stores advertising similar merchandise in
anticipation of Dayfall. The lines at some of the stores were as long
as those at some of the clubs.

Before too long they reached a rather nondescript, older brick
apartment building in the Murray Hill section of the city, and
Halladay pulled the car into a "No Parking" spot in front of it. Jon
followed him inside to a smallish lobby that was more like a wide
hallway, with a black-and-white checkered floor and a reception
booth at the far end of it. As they traversed the lobby toward the
booth, Jon could see that it was manned by a middle-aged Asian

woman and a younger Asian man who sat behind her watching a TV. Halladay stopped before they reached the booth to check a mailbox in a bank of them along the wall, and Jon found himself standing between two wide doorways on either side of the hall. He was able to glance each way just long enough to see that they both had small but well-stacked wet bars, and several men of various ages were hanging out by the bars or on the furniture nearby. Jon saw only one young woman, who was dressed normally, sitting by herself on a couch, but then he saw another one, dressed provocatively, walk into the same room and approach one of the older men.

"Country Boy," Halladay said, "this is Bai Liang, better known as 'Betty.'"

Jon shot a disapproving glance at him for the nickname, then turned a smile toward the Chinese lady and said hello to her.

"Don't let her cherubic face fool you," Halladay went on. "She can be a real bitch if she needs to. And Pan back there is a martial arts badass. . . . Don't get him mad at you. Come on, I'll show you *mi casa*."

They proceeded into a hall behind the booth with two elevators and waited for one to arrive. As they did, a giggling blonde in a low-cut evening gown pulled a nervous teen boy into the alcove from one of the rooms Jon had been checking out. She was stroking his hair as the two cops stepped through a door that opened, and Halladay gestured to the blonde in a way that indicated they would be riding alone and she should get the next elevator.

"What is this place?" Jon said.

"You don't want me to call you Country Boy, but you deserve it if you can't tell what this is. What, you don't have many brothels in F for Fart, or whoever you're from?"

"Ephrata," Jon said. "And last time I counted, I think it was exactly zero."

"Well, there's a few here, but this one's unique. Officially it's known as 'Three Hundred Lex,' but people call it 'Hetero House,' because Betty won't allow any gay sex at all. She's a born-again Christian, considers it her job in life to keep people biblical, you know. So she provides these . . . services, for teens, especially. A lot of them are sent by parents who want their first experience to be hetero, to put 'em on the right path from the beginning, they think. You'd be surprised how many people around here are worried about that, at least privately, though they might be really tolerant in front of everyone else. And Betty obliges them. . . . 'Screw 'em straight,' that's her motto."

"Only in New York," was all Jon could mutter before the elevator stopped at the top floor, which was the eighth, and Halladay led them to a door with a police badge taped next to the number.

"There's something else unique about this establishment," Halladay said as he turned a key in the door. "It's protected. They don't have to move around or worry about getting shut down by the cops . . . as long as they let me and the missus stay up here." He opened the door and took Jon inside to show him a modest but nice living room. "Ta da. A little 'penthouse' of my own. . . . It's not One Madison, but I like it." He cupped his hand to his mouth and yelled, "Yoohoo . . . anyone home?"

Both men stood quietly, lost in very different thoughts, until out of the far hallway there appeared a young black woman, with a hint of Asian, pulling a robe around her. Her hair was messy, but she was still quite attractive. Halladay sprang toward her and started kissing her.

"What time is it?" she said, gently pushing Halladay away.

"What difference does it make," the now red-faced cop said jokingly, "when it's always nighttime?"

"I was sleeping."

"Well, you'll have to take a little break, 'cause your man's here now. Jon, this is Nina Cobra, my main squeeze. Nina, this is my new partner."

"Nice to meet you," Jon said, and looked at his partner. "Where did that nickname come from?"

"It's not a nickname," Halladay said. "Believe it or not."

"It's my work name," Nina said.

"It *used to be* her work name," Halladay corrected her. "When she used to work here." The tall older man looked down at the short younger woman, and pulled her closer. "Before I saved her."

"Yeah." She hugged him back. "He saved me from everybody else."

"So she's taken," Halladay said to Jon. "But Betty can get you one. . . . What kind do you like?"

Jon shook his head and laughed nervously, but then answered, "I guess I like the same kind you do—the kind you don't have to pay for."

Halladay and Nina looked at each other, not sure whether that was a compliment or an insult. So John changed the subject.

"Do you have children?" he asked, expecting a 'yes' because of Halladay's references to going home to see his family.

"Are you kidding?" was all the big cop had to say about that.

"Okay, well, I'm gonna get some R and R with Nina . . . literally, but in reverse order. You can raid the fridge and crash on the couch if you want—the other rooms in this building aren't available for just one person. Sorry if any noises make it hard to sleep, though— the walls are a bit thin." He winked at Jon and pulled the woman down the hallway and out of sight.

After standing in the same position for a little while longer, Jon shook his head and stepped over to the kitchen area of the big open room. He opened the refrigerator and immediately won- dered if Halladay's reference to "raiding" it was an intended or un- intended pun, because along with some food and drink it contained various kinds of illegal drugs, with no attempt being made to hide them. There were conspicuous amounts, too much for just the woman or the two of them to ingest, so Jon assumed that this was Nina's new source of income. She probably provided them for the hookers and their customers, keeping them here because it was the most protected place in the building.

Jon didn't see anything he wanted to eat, and his appetite was also stunted by the sounds that were now floating out from the back room, as advertised. Along with some rather loud music there were squeals of delight, which Jon found mildly amusing at first. But then he felt increasingly uncomfortable and knew he would indeed have trouble getting any rest here. So he checked the time on his phone and stared for a while at Halladay's keys, which were beckoning to him from the coffee table. Finally, he snatched them up and headed out of the apartment.

As he passed by the older Chinese woman and her cubicle in the lobby, she asked if he was leaving without sampling the mer- chandise.

"It's free for you," she said in a thick accent.

Jon stopped in front of her briefly, curious and with plenty of time to spare before his 2:00 P.M. date.

"I heard you won't serve me if I'm gay," he said.

"Right," she said. "Straight is natural, gay is not natural. Says that in the book of Romans."

"How can you get away with that," he asked her, "with the discrimination laws and all?"

"We're illegal already," she said.

"Hmmm, I guess that makes sense," Jon said, to be polite, and then added, to be honest: "Or doesn't."

He smiled awkwardly at her, waved goodbye, and headed out to the car.

It took him longer than expected to get back to the Flatiron District, because the GPS on his phone stopped working a few times along the way and he had to guess which direction to go in. When he got there, he found a parking garage not far from The Office—not wanting to test Halladay's illegal parking methods without the older cop there—and then walked to the bar. He had made it with just ten minutes to spare before 2:00 P.M.

Mallory was still working behind the bar, as was a good-looking young man with bright gold tips in his short dark hair. She saw Jon when he was about halfway across the room, and moved to make sure she would be serving him when he took a seat.

"I hope it's not a coincidence," she said, drawing as close as the bar would allow, "that you came when I'm about to get off."

"I definitely wanted to catch you before you left," Jon said, letting her possible pun go. "To show you these pictures."

Jon needed to gauge whether his plan for the next few hours

was even necessary, though inwardly he was hoping that it would be. So he pulled out his phone and showed Mallory the photos of the four recent customers from the security tapes that had been identified by the facial recognition software at police headquarters. He asked her if any of them might be suspicious in any way, or if she thought there was any possibility one of them might be the killer they were looking for. He watched her closely as she looked at them, and then went back through them a second time to observe her reactions further. She laughed out loud at two of them as she said "No way," and didn't recognize a third, but her laughing from the prior one modulated involuntarily when Jon switched to the photo of the female who had mistakenly come up under a male name. And the second time through the pictures, Jon noticed that Mallory seemed to make an extra effort to compose herself when she denied recognizing the short, round woman.

"Aren't you going to ask me what I want to drink?" Jon said, giving her an opportunity to compose herself by putting the phone away and flashing his nicest smile.

"Oh, yeah, sure," she said. "Whaddaya want?"

"I'll take a Link Up."

"Okay," she said, thinking. "That's American whiskey and Russian vodka, with lime juice, right?"

"Usually Southern Comfort, I think."

"Okay. I'll be right back."

As Jon sat on his stool, admiring Mallory while she made the drink, he realized that his secret wishes for the next few hours were coming true, and so were his worst fears about her.

11

"You won't have much time to drink this if you're gonna walk me home," Mallory said when she returned with the cocktail. She was completely composed again by now.

"That's okay," Jon said. "I don't ever drink the whole thing anyway. I only take a few sips."

"Really? Why's that?"

"To tell you the truth, I don't really like the taste. It's just a hobby for me, 'cause I love a series of books by a guy who drank a lot, and his detective character drank a lot. So it's kind of a way to be like him. I know it's weird. But I also can't afford to be off my game mentally at all. . . . I like succeeding at what I do, and I'm pretty much working all the time."

"That's not weird at all," Mallory said, and seemed delighted to hear this from Jon. "Well, maybe it is, but I'm weird, too." She lowered her voice. "I'm a bartender, but I don't actually drink my-self. Not a drop."

"Hmmm. Why's that?"

"I'm like you, I don't really like it. But also my dad, who bought the bar with me . . . he has to have it all the time. Can't get to sleep without it, gets irritable without it. It's sad."

"Is he the man sitting over there in the corner?" Jon said, and Mallory looked surprised and asked how he knew. He responded, "Pretty basic detective work." Then he changed the subject, not wanting his job to be the center of this conversation.

"So when you leave—and it's almost two, by the way—I'm guessing the number of men in the bar goes down considerably. You're the biggest source of business, I imagine."

"Not really. They like Bree, too." Jon realized she must have been referring to another bartender who was not currently working.

"And him, over there," he said, nodding toward the young man with the gold tips, "he brings in the female crowd?"

"Some, and men, too. Most of the women come for the men who come for me and Bree."

"Ahhh," Jon said. "I think I followed that."

As if on cue, another attractive girl with dark hair appeared behind the bar from the rear entrance. She was a lot shorter than Mallory, but like her boss also made the most of a similar black outfit, utilitarian yet classy.

As Mallory said, "Ready to go?" to Jon, and came out from behind the bar with her purse and coat to walk with him to the door, both Bree and the male bartender stopped what they were doing, wearing surprised looks at the sight of their boss leaving with a customer. Apparently that didn't happen very often.

"My place is on the other side of the park," she said as they hit the night air, which seemed to be warmer than Jon remembered it.

"Do you usually say goodbye to your dad when you leave?" Jon asked as they were walking.

"Uh, yeah, I do, actually. I forgot this time."

"You're distracted."

"It's your fault," she said, after thinking for a few seconds. "Asking for a drink named Link Up. . . . That was really subtle."

"At least I didn't order a Screaming O. Though I thought about it."

"You could have had a Flirtini. . . . That would have worked."

"Nah, I like to skip right past the flirting, and go straight for the Screaming O."

Jon almost winced at this theatrical banter, which sounded more like Halladay than himself. But it was a part of the role he felt he had to play to get more information from Mallory. He also was aware, however, that she was doing the same thing for reasons of her own.

They both laughed half-sincerely at the jokes they continued to make as they traversed the park, bathed in the otherworldly light of the UV lamps. By the time they had reached the other side of it, they had both taken off their coats and were each holding them in one hand, because it really *was* getting warmer out. And their other hands were clasped together.

Her apartment was a couple blocks beyond the park, on Twenty-Third Street, and shortly after they reached it they had taken off a lot more than their coats, and a lot more than their hands were clasped together. The words "dream girl" floated across Jon's mind as he saw and felt more of her, and when he apologized for the various wounds and bandages on his body, she even said that she liked them. ("They'll leave some major scars, and I've always loved men with scars.")

In any other situation Jon would have seen this as a sign that they were meant to be together, but in this situation he knew that neither of them could trust anything the other said. In fact, before they fell asleep next to one another afterward, to get the rest they both needed, Mallory had made sure her phone was password locked before she put it on her nightstand, and Jon had stuck his under the pillow on his side of the bed, along with his gun.

They both woke at the same time after a few hours, as if neither could allow the other an advantage, and the conversation was nothing like what lovers usually share in such moments.

"Are you sure you don't want to change your story?" Jon said, while stroking her hair gently.

"Why would I want to do that?" she said with a puzzled look, resting her hand on his hip.

"I wouldn't want anything to come out that would keep me from being able to walk you home again . . . because you were locked up somewhere."

"I have nothing to hide," she said, gently moving her hand up and down his side. "And you wouldn't do that anyway."

"Maybe I wouldn't. But somebody would."

"But you wouldn't let them."

"Maybe I would."

At this Mallory pulled her hand away and rolled onto her back, so her hair was now out of his reach.

"I'm hungry," she said. "You want something?"

He said, "Okay," and they each dressed in silence on their own side of the bed. Then there was a lot more silence as she made some eggs and toast in the kitchen with him sitting on a stool on the other side of a bar, not unlike the way they had met a few hours earlier.

"What's with the kids on the fridge?" Jon asked. There were several pictures of young children with obvious disabilities. One little boy was severely bow-legged, and another's smile showed her obviously diseased teeth.

"They're children in the city who have rickets," Mallory explained, "because they've never had any sunlight and their parents didn't give them the nutrition they need. I sponsor them so they can get help."

"How could people who live here not give their kids vitamin D?"

"Welcome to humanity," she said, spreading her hands. "A lot of them are single parents, and they're sick themselves with addiction or depression or whatever."

"Why don't they just leave?" Jon was about to say "this hell-hole," but then stopped himself when he realized who he was talking to, and added, "Why haven't you left?"

"My dad doesn't want to," she answered with a shrug, "and we have the bar. Every year we think the sun might come out again."

"But didn't the scientists say how long it would take?"

"Yeah, but I never know what to believe. Plus, it might sound trite, but this is our home, so why shouldn't we try to make it better and not just give up on it?"

"Hmm," Jon said, nodding. "Well, I think it's cool what you're doing for those kids."

She looked at him thoughtfully for a few moments, and then said, "I'm thinking this might not be the time to play games with each other."

"What do you mean?"

"I feel like something really bad is going to happen tomorrow when the day comes. It seems like the end of the world, at least around here."

"Is this just a feeling," Jon said, "or do you have some reason—"

"I've read some of the stuff that's been written about it, seen some stuff on the news. But my dad says that's all bullshit, or conjecture at least, so I don't know who's right about what exactly will happen and why. But I just have this . . . intuition or something, that it'll be bad. And if it is, isn't that a game changer?"

"I remember my father," Jon said, "quoting some famous person who was asked, 'What would you do if you knew the world was ending tomorrow?' And he said, 'The same thing I was planning to do today.' I think he even said, 'plant an apple tree.' I understand the first one; not sure I understand the apple tree thing."

"Well, I don't know about that," Mallory said. "But it just seems wrong to keep covering up, to play games with each other, like I said, when we might be dead tomorrow. I don't even know if I should keep the bar open after tonight. . . . I don't know if it'll ever be open again."

"So where are you going with this?" Jon asked, abandoning his breakfast and watching her beautiful ice-blue eyes. They looked away and then back at him.

"Would you be up front with me if I was totally honest with you?" she said.

"How have I not . . . ," he started, but then stopped when he saw her shoulders droop. "Okay, I guess so. This has been a day of firsts for me, why not another one?"

"Okay, I'll start," she said, seeming invigorated. "I don't want to tell you everything I know about my customers, because I trust Gotham Security more than the police."

"Go on."

"Long story short . . . my boyfriend—he was my fiancé, actually—disappeared and was found dead two years ago. The cops were utterly useless, but it was Gar Render's people who broke the case. They found Tom's killer—it was a carjacking—and they avenged us."

"They killed him?"

She nodded resolutely, and said, "No one ever deserved it more. And that was something else the cops could never do, even if they had found him."

"Were you involved in the . . . execution?"

"No, they just told me about it. But I was, and am, eternally grateful. So I signed up to be a 'Friend of Gotham,' as they call it. I do what I can for them, because I think they're what the city needs, to keep us safe."

"What have you done for them?" Jon asked.

"Your turn now," she said, poking him in the chest. "Are you gonna be one of the cops who works for GS when they take over, or are you gonna be exiled by them because you've been a bad cop? Are you a part of the corruption they say has been the most abiding tradition among New York police, or will you be a part of the new force that actually cares about the city?"

"Well, first of all," Jon said, taken aback by her idealism, "re-member I've only been here a day." His first instinct was to tell her what she wanted to hear, so he could get any information from her that might help in his investigation. But then he thought about his promise to her, and his heart strangely warmed to it. It was somehow becoming more real to him than when he had first said it.

"So I haven't had enough time to sort all that out," he said. "But I'm not convinced that Gar Render really loves the city as much as he wants power over it."

"I'm sure there's some of that in there," she said. "But I've talked to him personally, and I really think . . . there's that intuition thing again . . . that he's mostly on the level."

"Funny, I felt the same thing with the Mayor."

"Oh, she might be sincere, or at least *mostly* sincere, like Render is. But she's sincerely wrong . . . taking money away from law enforcement to put into the arts and such, tying the hands of the police by limiting how much force they can use. Render will fix all that, like he fixed my problem."

The references to the law and Render made him think of a question he was curious about. "What do you think about the city employing Muslims, like in important jobs with security access?"

"I don't have a problem with it per se," Mallory said quickly, having obviously thought about the issue before. "But only if there's a thorough enough background investigation, etc., to establish that the person's not a risk, and I'm not confident Mayor King has the balls to do that."

"Yeah." Jon smiled. "I'm pretty sure she doesn't have any balls."

She laughed, then said, "So if I tell you what I've done for GS, will you drop it and trust me?"

Jon thought for a few seconds, then answered, "If it's not pertinent to my investigation."

"Oh, it's not. In fact, it's about GS doing your job for you, and better. Because they can't do police work legally on the streets yet, they have to do it on the sly. So the management gives lists of people who need protection or other help to a middleman like me, and we pass them to one of their agents. In my case they come into the bar, of course. Render doesn't want the police to know because they're resentful of someone working on their turf, and I don't want any of you to know the details, so there'll be no hindrance to them helping others like they helped me."

"So you're not going to tell me who the GS agent is," Jon said, "the one that comes into the bar?"

"No."

"I thought we were being honest."

"We are being honest. I'm honestly telling you why I'm not telling you."

"Okaaay," Jon said, shaking his head. "Can I see one of the lists you passed on?"

"Don't have them," she answered. "They're on a piece of paper."

"Can you take a picture with your phone and send it to me, the next time you get one?"

"Why?"

"So I can make sure there's no relevance to my investigation."

"I'll think about it."

They sat and stared at one another, their breakfast long forgotten and this particular conversation apparently over.

"While we're being honest," Jon finally said, "were you actually attracted to me when I first came into the bar?"

"Not really. Not any more than other good-looking guys who come in."

"So the invitation to walk you home?"

"Self-protection," she said, pondering it. "I got scared, knowing what I do for GS and having two MPDs asking questions. I didn't want you to ask more, and maybe get in the way of what they're doing, so I used the only tools I have to try to get you to forget about it, and not take it any further."

Jon nodded cheerfully, but inside he was disappointed, despite the fact that he had already known what she would say, if she was truly being honest.

"What about you?" she asked him. "Would you have walked me home if you didn't want information from me?"

"No," he said, part of him wanting to stick it to her in return. But then he remembered his promise of honesty. "Not while I'm in the middle of something like this, anyway. But at some other time, I might. I would . . ."

He let the thought trail away because she was looking at him differently than she ever had previously. And then she took his face in her hands gently and started kissing him. He responded and did the same, and they continued for several minutes, slowly and affectionately in contrast to their frenzied physical passion when they had arrived in the apartment. This time they didn't even give a thought to things like phones and guns—until they were interrupted by Jon's phone beeping with a message from Amira, which said that another avenue of investigation had yielded a suspect.

Jon apologized and pulled himself away, but he was thinking on the way out that those few minutes on the tall seats, fully clothed, were way better than anything that had happened earlier on the bed. The feeling of dread was still somewhere inside him—the one that was saying he had been brought to this city to fail at his job. But now there was another emotion bubbling up with the faint hope that there might be another reason for him to be here.

12

Halladay wasn't answering his cell phone, so Jon couldn't tell him from the car what Amira had said, nor could he warn him that he was coming back to the apartment. When the young cop arrived at Three Hundred Lex, the lobby was busier with hookers and clients than it had been a few hours before. Initially Jon thought this might be because it was around eight o'clock at night, but then he remembered that it was always night in Manhattan and so time probably had very little to do with the cycles of activity in the brothel.

He banged on the door to Halladay's apartment and rang the doorbell, but there was no answer, so he located the house key on the chain he had taken and let himself in. The living room was as he'd left it, and the same type of music was still playing loudly in the back room. He called Halladay's and Nina's names as he proceeded in that direction, but no one answered, so he opened the door gently and peered inside. The music was even louder than he thought it would be, which explained why they couldn't hear anything, and they were both sound asleep on the bed.

Jon stepped softly to Halladay's side of the bed and grabbed the gun off the nightstand next to him, to test the older man's cop instincts and make sure he didn't get shot if they were good. Sure enough, Halladay woke up and furled his thick sandy eyebrows in Jon's direction.

"I hate to interrupt your nap," Jon said, leaning down close to him. "But we have a suspect."

"Wait out in the living room," Halladay finally said after climbing back into full consciousness.

Jon left the bedroom, but took the gun with him to make sure the tired older man didn't just roll over and go back to sleep. In a few minutes Halladay appeared from the back room, fully dressed. Jon handed the gun to him and they made for the car.

"Amira did a search through the depositions of civil lawsuits connected to the chaos crimes, like I asked," Jon explained as they headed west across the city. "She found one where a junkie who got hurt in a panicked mob tried to sue the city for not keeping him safe, and as a part of his testimony saying how terrified he was, he mentioned a 'big hairy guy' who he saw knifing someone in the crowd. Seems he recognized the guy because he buys drugs from the same dealer at a club, and—you know how these people talk—he's heard rumors that the guy kills for hire to pay for his meth habit. The junkie's testimony is all over the map, but since that slice fit my criteria, Amira questioned him and found out the name of the club, the name of the dealer, and even the name of the big hairy guy."

"Which is?" Halladay said.

"Shinsky. So Amira looked it up and, sure enough, there's a guy with priors who fits that description. He was a football lineman when he was younger, so he shouldn't be hard to recognize by his size, but here's his picture." Jon held out his phone to the yawning Scotsman.

"Yeah, he's big," Halladay said. "And hairy. But that's hardly a crime, and this junkie doesn't sound very reliable. Did you really have to wake me up for this?"

"If you have a better lead, let's hear it. Dayfall is about ten hours away."

"He's also too big to be the perp from the office building," Halladay said. "The one we saw on the video was a lot shorter."

"So there might be two killers—at least. Fits a theory I have."

They drove on in silence in the darkness of the Sunday evening, with Jon thinking about what might happen in the next ten hours, during the heavy thunderstorm that was predicted to roll in through the night and dissipate enough of the dense cloud cover for the sun to shine all day on Monday.

Another kind of shine was emanating from their destination when they reached it. Lit up like a carnival, Party Row was one of the hottest spots in the post-flagger economy of Manhattan. It stretched for a whole block on both sides of Twenty-Ninth Street in between Ninth and Tenth Avenues, club after club jammed in next to each other in two large industrial buildings that had been abandoned by businesses because they were too close to the water after the River Rise for the tenants to feel safe enough there. The only thing between them and the Westside Wall, in fact, was the truncated stretch of the High Line that still remained because the Wall was built along the outer side of that elevated train platform, which had been made into a public park before the flagger.

The businesses that formerly occupied these buildings could never have dreamed of raking in as much money as the thirty-plus establishments that had taken their place. The never-ending night of New York brought continual waves of partiers to the Row, and the light emanated from bright signs lining the streets on all sides of the massive buildings, and from spotlights and UV lamps shining from their rooftops. There were too many pedestrians and taxis on the streets for Halladay to do his parking trick here, so they had to take a spot in an adjacent garage and walk to the club where Shinsky's dealer reportedly worked the crowd.

The Starlight was on the east end of the block in the north building, farthest from the High Line and the Water Wall. While some of the clubs in the Row were rather narrow or sat on top of one another, this one was a single large atrium room that stretched from the ground floor all the way up to a transparent ceiling at the roof. Jon figured that the stars had never actually been visible through the roof, because the club was built after the black clouds had descended, and they probably never would be due to the preponderance of light in the area. But the owners obviously *were* concerned with the sun coming through the next day, because when Halladay flashed his badge along with a picture of the dealer to various employees and managers, they all said something about how they were asking for a heavy police presence during Dayfall. This was the first evidence Jon had seen that the fears about it had definitely taken hold at the street level.

None of the employees were helpful in any way—they had probably been told not to assist the police in finding anyone, especially someone like a drug dealer who provided a commodity important to the club experience. But in response to directions from a random customer they questioned, the two cops made their way up some stairs to one of the raised balconies surrounding the main dance floor. As they did, Jon realized that the Starlight apparently had a sci-fi theme, with otherworldly lighting and some replicas of movie spaceships hanging from the walls. And the dealer they were approaching seemed to fit right in with the theme, because he looked like a vampire.

"Balo Spenser?" Halladay said to the white-skinned man sitting at the table.

"Call me Éric Le Boursier please," he responded. "That's my sang name."

"Well, Fanny Baws is your Scottish name," Halladay said, "so I'll call you that. But we're looking for a big hairy guy by the name of Shinsky who buys from you. Has he been here recently, Fanny, or is he coming by anytime soon?"

"The only illegal purchases I'm involved in," Spenser/Boursier said, "is for the blood I need to survive." He fingered a brightly colored button that was attached to his lapel in the middle of a collection of Gothic pendants—it said RIGHT TO BUY on it. "Because the government you work for discriminates against us by not allowing it to be sold in stores."

"Oh, so you're a real vampire—whatever the hell that is." Halladay looked at Jon, nodding his head and pursing his lips. "This is a nice development, actually. Squeezing you about your drug business won't get you to tell us anything, because you're smart enough to not keep anything on you, and you send your buyers to another room to get it . . . maybe even to another club."

As he said this he glanced over to the wall to the left of them on the balcony, where there was an interior entrance to the next club over, with a sign saying SWEETS above it.

"But I think we do have some leverage here," Halladay continued, "because the bags you have in your refrigerator at home are still illegal in New York, and what you just said is enough for us to get a warrant and send a car over there while we make sure you stay here and don't call anyone to hide them. And that's not to mention the assault charges that we'll bring after an investigation into your 'bloodplay.'"

"We only feed by mutual consent," the man said, agitated now and maybe even a little scared.

"Yeah, right. Tell me you're gonna completely give up one of the biggest appeals of your new identity. We'll find and interview everyone who's been bitten by you, Fanny, and we'll see if they all wanted you do it."

"Okay, okay," the dealer said, waving his pale hands with their long black fingernails in front of him, then flashing a fanged smile when he saw something behind the cops. "Oh, looks like I won't actually have to tell you anything."

He nodded ever so slightly toward what he was looking at, and the two police turned around to see Shinsky coming in the direction of the table from the other end of the balcony, literally head and shoulders above the rest of the crowd. Unfortunately, the big hairy suspect noticed them looking at him and veered off to the left toward the entrance to the adjacent club called Sweets. Jon and Halladay immediately headed that way themselves.

Just inside the entrance to the other club, they were greeted by a bouncer asking for the cover charge and their online invitations.

The cops flashed their badges and confirmed that Shinsky had just passed through, asking the bouncer how he got in if an invitation was required. The man said that Shinsky had a "universal card," which they took to mean a pass that allowed him to get into any and all of the clubs on Party Row.

"He could go into any of the series of clubs in that direction," Jon said to Halladay, "or circle back this way without having to go out to the street. And he could exit on either side of the street. So I doubt calling for backup to cover exits would do any good."

"Who would we call, anyway?" Halladay said, as he moved forward into the second club. "Let's just find him." But Jon grabbed his arm to slow him down.

"Be careful," the younger detective said in his ear. "We know he's killed in public, and if he has a gun he could just wait for us to turn a corner and open fire. Let's keep our distance from each other so he couldn't take us both out as easily, but not so far that we get separated."

Halladay nodded, and they both stepped out onto a balcony similar to the one they had just been on in the Starlight club, with the main dance floor ahead of them and down on the ground level. The ceiling was not nearly as high as at the former club—in fact, it was just above them. But when they moved closer to the railing, staying about ten or fifteen feet apart from one another, they could see most of the club from there, so they both stood still for a while and scanned the crowd for the suspect.

This club was better lit than most, and after a few moments of checking out the clientele, Jon found out why. He had noticed that the couples talking or dancing with each other were almost all older men with much younger women, and the few exceptions were older women with much younger men. The people who were not paired up yet were all young and attractive, or older and not, seemingly without exception.

"What is this place?" Jon yelled across to Halladay, over the noise of the music and conversations. He had to yell loudly enough that some of the customers milling around them stopped what they were doing and gave him a nasty look.

"It's a Sugar Daddy club," Halladay shouted back. "Old farts with money come to get some young fud, and the young fud come to get the old farts' money. Just another modern version of the oldest profession."

Now they were *really* getting some looks, and the surrounding crowd started slowly parting from them. Apparently they didn't like how the big Scotsman's frank description cut through whatever mental spin the customers had used to justify what they were doing there. But the cops stopped talking, realizing that they were drawing attention to themselves and wasting precious time, and went back to scanning the crowd. There were a lot of men who were older, like Shinsky, but not very many as big, so it wasn't long before they spotted him on the bottom level dance floor, moving toward the entrance to the next club over. This move on the perp's part made sense, because Sweets was too wide open for him to hide effectively. It was also too well lit, because the clientele had to be able to see the merchandise.

The next establishment in the Row, into which Shinsky disappeared and the cops pursued him, was the exact opposite when it came to lighting, and that was even reflected in the name. It was a sex club called Dark Desires.

13

"In here we have to worry about a knife," Jon said after they wove through the crowd at Sweets, flashed their badges at the entrance of the sex club, and saw how dark it was inside. "He could be hiding anywhere in here."

He had noticed a bed near the entrance, which was only slightly partitioned off by three small temporary walls, and he could vaguely make out others like it in the darkness ahead.

The two cops proceeded farther into the club, spaced like they were before but with guns drawn now, and Jon noticed that there were a variety of places that couples could choose. In addition to the cubicles, there were doors to private rooms along the outside walls and mattresses lining the floor in between the doors. The rooms were obviously for those who preferred privacy, the mattresses for those with an exhibitionistic streak, and the cubicles for those somewhere in between.

There seemed to be only one other exit from the big room, in addition to the door they had entered. Even though it was on the far side, Jon could see that no one was entering or leaving it currently, because the stairwell going up behind it was more brightly lit. He could also make out direction signs pointing up the stairs that said, BAR, DANCE FLOOR, and EXIT.

Jon knew that Shinsky might possibly have run right for the stairs as soon as he'd come in, and disappeared up them before he and Halladay had gotten there. But the big killer could also have found a good place where he could hide, hoping that the cops would go straight through the room and allow him to escape by circling back. Or, as Jon had suggested to his partner, he could have found a good spot for an ambush and planned to take each of them out under the cover of darkness. So Jon kept his eye on the exit, but bore to the left behind one of the cubicles to spread out the search more. As he did, he started to notice the smell of sweat that was mixed in with that of the many scented candles that were burning at various places in the room, but not really doing the trick.

As he was passing a second cubicle closer to the left wall, two men suddenly stepped out of it, fully clothed and obviously finished with whatever they'd been were doing in there. This made Jon jump slightly, but the men were much more frightened themselves when they saw his gun. They instinctively raised their hands and then backed away from him toward the exit when he gestured that way with the weapon. There were two couples on an oversized mattress along the wall as he continued farther, and they were completely naked. But Jon didn't find this stimulating in the least, first because he could only glance at them briefly and second because it only took that brief glance to see that they were not very attractive people. All four of them were seriously out of shape, to put it nicely.

Then Jon jumped again, and much more violently this time, because the overhead lights abruptly flashed on and illuminated the whole room. After waving his gun around during the initial startled screams and shouts, he saw Halladay at a bank of light switches near the exit, smiling from ear to ear. The noise died down when the big cop held up his badge and people throughout the room saw it and started to dress and file out, even though he'd never told them to do that. Jon noticed that the plague of unattractiveness wasn't limited to the two couples he had seen on the mattress—it seemed that it was true of almost all the people there, except for a few, whom he surmised might have been prostitutes.

"Reminds me of the old saying about nude beaches," Halladay yelled across the room at him, either reading his mind or thinking about the same thing. "Those who *should* don't and those who *shouldn't*, do. That's why they keep these places so dark—nobody wants anyone to see their bodies."

Some of the people filing out of the room between the two cops grunted and scowled at Halladay, and Jon was amazed at how accomplished the big Scot was at offending even total strangers.

After a minute or so of scanning the customers and checking any possible hiding places, which was much easier now that the room was awash in light, they concluded that Shinsky wasn't there and pushed their way up the stairway to the next floor, which turned out to be the main one. They talked briefly with a woman in management who told them she had seen someone fitting Shinsky's description linger in the lobby for a few minutes but then take off into the next club in the Row—presumably because there wasn't a big enough crowd in this one in which to get lost. The killer made a big mistake, however, when he tried to hide in the next club.

It was called Continuum, and they entered onto a balcony like they had with the first two. But this one was different in that it stretched across parts of the whole top floor in a seemingly random pattern, leaving some large holes through which the bottom floor could be seen. Jon and Halladay took up positions at the railing in two different spots that they thought would afford the best combined view of both floors, and started panning them for Shinsky.

The club was more crowded that any of the other three they'd been in, but even before they spotted him, Jon knew that the big hairy guy wouldn't be able to hide for long in this place. That was precisely because he was big and hairy—especially the latter— since it became apparent after a few moments of scanning the customers that this was a "pan-gender" club. Everyone there was as androgynous and sexless as they could possibly make themselves, except for the perp, who had taken a seat in a crowded area at a downstairs table in an attempt to hide his height and bulk. But he looked so unlike the constituency that they probably thought he was a cop himself, and started giving him a wide berth. It was only a matter of time before Jon and Halladay identified him by the expanding circle of space around him, and then he himself realized it was a bad hiding place and took off for a doorway nearby.

"Not the sharpest tool in the shed," Halladay said with his patented smile, as they pushed their way down the stairs to go after him.

The doorway led into a large, unused industrial kitchen on the north side of the building, and after running halfway through it with their guns drawn again, the two cops could see a door standing open on the far side. They ran to it and through it into a short alley, at the end of which they could see people milling on the brightly lit Thirtieth Street.

"Wait," Jon said, holding Halladay back from running down the alley. He turned back to the open door to the kitchen. "Why wouldn't he close the door? He had time."

Jon slowly moved to the left so his view extended farther into the kitchen, even as far as the doorway through which they had entered it from the club. Sure enough, as he watched, a silhouetted figure flashed into view from somewhere on the side of the kitchen and went back through the door into the club.

"Come on," Jon said, and they both ran back through the kitchen, reaching the door in time to see Shinsky exiting the club through the side door that led into the next establishment. He was obviously sticking to his plan of trying to lose his pursuers in one of the long row of clubs. But there couldn't be too many more on this block.

And as it turned out, the next establishment in the Row wasn't actually a club. It was Jayne's Day Care—an ironic name, given the endless night—and it provided a place for people to drop off their kids while they partied.

"Only in New York," Jon muttered under his breath again, but he didn't have much time to marvel at this, because he and

Halladay stumbled into a scary standoff when they ran inside the day care's main room, which was populated by a few inflatable slides and trampolines, and a lot of now-screaming kids being herded to the corners by staff members.

Shinsky had pushed his way through and grabbed a little girl as a hostage when the security guard at the door pulled a gun and told him to stop. When the two cops arrived, the killer and the guard were about twenty feet apart, both pointing their guns at each other. Shinsky held the preschooler effortlessly in front of his chest with his other hand. She was one of the few kids in the place that wasn't screaming, possibly because she was in shock.

Now that there were three guns trained on him, the big man backed slowly toward the exit behind him, which according to a sign led into another club called The Jungle. Jon and Halladay moved forward at the same pace to where the stationary guard stood, and Jon motioned to him to remain there, noticing a Gotham Security patch on his uniform.

"Don't come after me," Shinsky shouted, "or I'll kill her."

He backed through the door and disappeared while the two cops continued to move slowly forward, but when they got close to the exit they stopped and looked at each other, unsure of what to do. Then a couple shots rang out from inside The Jungle, and that settled it. They rushed inside, fearful of seeing a little girl's bloody body, but instead they saw an older man lying on the ground, clutching his wounded gut. He was dressed in a uniform that looked like a safari outfit, and it became obvious that Shinsky's universal card wasn't enough to get him into the club while holding a little girl hostage.

Speaking of the girl, she soon stepped out of the shadows nearby as other staff arrived to help the wounded man. A relieved Halladay told them to take care of her, and the two policemen proceeded with caution into the interior of the club. It was huge and elaborate inside, which made Jon think that it was likely the last club in the Row, because it would make sense that the end properties were reserved for big businesses like the Starlight and this one. All throughout the massive room there were large and small trees, which looked real to Jon, and UV lamps high up on the ceiling that seemed to confirm his guess. There were various food and drink stations made to look like grass huts, and even one in a tree house built into the upper branches of one of the bigger trees, with a wooden staircase that led to it spiraling around the trunk.

They progressed quickly but with caution on the path Shinsky had almost surely taken, judging by the ripples in the crowd, and Jon noticed that the owners of the club had truly spared no expense—or excess—to achieve the atmosphere they wanted. Jon passed a large tank with a Burmese python lounging next to a small pool and an even bigger cage with some brightly colored macaws sitting on perches and periodically letting out their unique screams.

He and Halladay had made fun of Shinsky's intelligence, but neither of them realized how smart a move he'd made when they heard a couple more gunshots ahead of them. They thought he had shot another person, or maybe fired into the air to cause panic in the crowd and slow them down, but what he actually did was far more clever. He had shot the lock off a cage of monkeys and opened the door, letting the little animals out to terrorize the customers. By the time Jon and Halladay got to that part of the club, people were slamming into them to get away, and one screaming woman even had one of the critters attached to her shoulder, holding on to her hair and obviously enjoying the ride.

This was fairly effective in slowing down the cops in their pursuit, and Shinsky's next trick was even more so. The shrieks of fear on the far west side of the big room, close to the exit, were even louder after three or four more shots rang out and *everyone* on that side of the club ran past the cops to get away from whatever had been released this time. Jon and Halladay rounded some bushes and now faced a dark, empty section of dance floor, the music still thrumming and the colored lights still flashing. On the far side of the floor was the biggest cage they had seen yet, with the words BAGHEERA THE BLACK PANTHER shining from a sign above it.

Jon soon realized that the dance floor was not really empty, because when certain lights flashed on it, a dark shadow with two bright eyes became visible. A big Indian leopard was moving toward them across the floor.

"This is a new one," Halladay said.

"You go around to the left," Jon said after briefly surveying the scene, "and I'll go right. Hopefully it's been fed recently and isn't hungry, but worst case scenario . . . one of us might have to shoot it."

"Worst case scenario is we lose our suspect," Halladay said, and promptly put about five bullets into the panther.

Jon looked at him incredulously, but the big Scot just shrugged.

"Nooo!" yelled a safari-clad female employee who was arriving behind them and was probably a caretaker of the cat, because she ran to its side while Jon and Halladay ran past it toward the exit.

The door was an external one leading out to Tenth Avenue, and it wasn't hard to spot Shinsky as he made his way rather clumsily through the crowd on the adjacent Twenty-Ninth Street, and then ran up the stairs leading to the High Line. The two cops didn't have much time to wonder why he chose the elevated park rather than the city streets below it, where it would be easier to find a place to hide, because they were already running after him.

14

The High Line was an elevated train track platform, formerly part of the West Side Line, that was disused for many years and then transformed by the city into a park in a "rails-to-trails" program. The park was first opened in 2009, completed in 2015, and ran all the way from Thirty-Fourth Street in the north to below Thirteenth Street in the south. But as a result of the River Rise and construction of the Water Wall, the only part left was a stretch from Thirtieth to Twenty-Third Streets. The Wall was built right next to the outer edge of that section of the High Line, making it the only place in the city where residents and visitors could "walk the ramparts" along the Big Apple's newest architectural wonder.

When Jon and Halladay reached the top of the stairs, it wasn't hard to tell that Shinsky had gone south on the narrow parkway. There was a decent-sized crowd, and the big perp was bumping into enough of them that the cops could see the ripples of offended and off-balance pedestrians he'd left behind in his wake. Jon noticed the same eerie blue-green glow up here that he had seen at Madison Square Park, from the UV lamps that lined the path and kept the plants growing.

"I guess he's done hiding," Jon said, puzzled at the level of desperation the big ex-athlete had apparently reached. But he and Halladay just shrugged at each other and took off after him, making their own waves through the walkers and bicyclers. NFL linemen weren't very fast even in their heyday, and Shinsky was older now, so the two officers were soon gaining on him. They even lined up their guns a few times when they caught an unobstructed view of his fleeing figure, but there were too many people in the park for them to fire on him. Plus, they wanted him alive for the sake of their investigation, and there weren't any good angles to go for a wounding shot.

When Jon estimated they were about a block from closing on him, both the big man and the ripples in the crowd ahead suddenly disappeared. As the two cops reached the spot where they had lost sight of him, they found a small stairway that was on the Wall side of the path, unlike the others used by most of the people for access to the street level. It seemed their prey had descended this smaller stairway because of where the crowd ripples ended, and because of the wordless communication from a few bystanders who nodded and pointed that way. So Jon bolted down the stairs himself, noticing that they were half built into the Wall itself and therefore had been added during the newer construction.

Just a few feet away from the bottom of the steps there was a big steel door set into the inside of the Wall itself, and because Jon didn't see Shinsky running away from it toward the street, he instinctively stepped over to it and looked for a handle to open it. He found none, only a small mechanism built into the door requiring some kind of key, so he turned around and starting moving through the smattering of cars parked underneath the roof formed by the elevated train platform above. It was extra dark under there, so he and Halladay stepped around the cars carefully with their guns drawn, as they had done with the beds at the sex club. But Shinsky was nowhere to be found.

They scanned the nearest street, which led out to Tenth Avenue, but there was no sign of the big man, nor any indication he had gone that way. It didn't seem to Jon that the perp had been far enough ahead of them to have cleared that street, or the buildings on the other side of the High Line. So he had to rethink, and soon found himself sprinting back to the stairway and running up it, his older partner huffing and puffing as he tried to keep up.

When he got back up to the High Line, he made Halladay's heart beat even faster by jumping onto the railing on the Wall side of the stairway entrance, and then propelling himself up onto the top of the parapet itself, which was about six or eight feet high.

"What the hell are you doing?" the Scotsman said between heavy breaths.

"He could have climbed up here and jumped," Jon answered, peering over the wall into the darkness of the river below and listening for any sounds of swimming, or a boat, or whatever. He heard none.

Meanwhile, Halladay was using his still considerable vocal strength to ask people if anyone saw "a big hairy guy" jump, or go down the stairs, or anything else. But no one responded, presumably because the park was designed for walking and biking rather than loitering, and everyone who been here earlier had moved on by now.

The sound of MPD sirens arose from the bottom of the stairway, so Jon and Halladay descended it again and found three police cars had pulled in near the parked ones. Officers Ari Hegde and Brenda Dixon, of the Chaos Crimes division, had exited the lead one and were approaching them.

"Well, if it isn't Airhead and Dickless," Halladay said, still breathing heavily.

"You sound like you're about to have a heart attack, Frank," said the Indian cop.

"I'm fine," Halladay croaked. "What are you doing here?"

"We got reports from people who thought a chaos crime was going down."

"I thought they only happened in the daylight," Jon said, putting his gun back into its holster.

"Apparently they do," Hegde said, "because the only chaos I see here is Frank's shirt coming all out of his pants."

"Hilarious," Halladay growled. "Why don't you do something useful and head out onto Tenth and see if you can find a big hairy guy who's probably sweating even more than me."

"Wait a minute," Jon interjected. "Before you do anything else . . ." He motioned for the three cops to follow him in the direction of the big steel door built into the wall. "What's this?"

"What do you mean?" Hegde said. "It's a door."

"Can we get it open? The city must have keys for it, right?"

"I don't know," Halladay said, "but I assume GS would, because they built the Wall."

"I'll make a few calls for you," Hegde volunteered. He turned to go back to his car, followed by Dixon.

Jon and Halladay waited for Hegde to return, but after a couple minutes his car and the other two just backed out and pulled away.

"What the hell?" Halladay said, and dialed Hegde's number on his phone. Jon took it from him while it was ringing.

"Hegde," the Indian man answered.

"Where'd you go?" Jon asked.

"Oh, we're looking for your perp, like you asked."

"We're standing here waiting for you. You said you were gonna check on the door."

"Oh, sorry. Yeah, MPD doesn't have keys for Wall access points like that. . . . No one does. Render built it, and GS provides security for it. You'd have to talk to them. Sorry."

Jon ended the call and handed the phone back to Halladay, who just shrugged when the younger cop shot him a puzzled look.

"Do ya think he jumped?" Halladay said as they walked back toward their own car.

"Could be," Jon said. "Why would he go up onto the High Line just to run back down again?"

"Maybe because there are a lot of people."

"There's a lot of people on the street, too. But going down those stairs would have taken him away from the crowd and given us a clear shot."

"Maybe he knew we didn't want to shoot him."

"What if there was some way to get in the Wall from outside it, by jumping at that spot? Or he had a way to get in that door we saw? He could have been heading for that spot all along. That would explain the desperate sprint, if he knew he could disappear somewhere."

"Yeah," Halladay said.

"I want to talk to Render again," Jon said. "But first let's visit the people at NYU."

"Can't we just make calls?"

"Always better to talk in person, if you can. That's what Philip Marlowe says, anyway."

"What?"

"Raymond Chandler's detective, in his books—"

"I know who he is," Halladay said as they reached the car and got in. "I'm not completely illiterate. But why would anyone give a flyin' bawbag what a fictional character says?"

"Truth is no stranger to fiction," was all Jon had to say as they pulled out onto the Manhattan streets.

"What about the hot bartender?" Halladay asked. "I'm surprised you don't want to question her now, since we got the info from the cameras there. And I can understand why you'd want to do that in person."

"Already did, while you were having your family time."

"Oh you did?" Halladay looked surprised. "You questioned her, did you? In person. How'd that go?'"

When Jon didn't respond except to smile slightly against his will, Halladay was even more surprised.

"You dog!" the big Scot said. "I thought you Amish didn't go in for that kinda thing."

"I'm not Amish."

"I guess not," Halladay agreed, now seeming more impressed than surprised.

"There was . . . ," Jon paused, still serious, and looking for a word, "a connection."

"Yeah, I gathered that." Then Halladay himself turned more serious. "While you were, uh, connecting, did she have anything to say about the pictures?"

"Not much. Nothing helpful, yet."

"Maybe I should question her, then."

"No," Jon said, not sure whether Halladay was still being serious, then added in a lighter tone, "I don't think you're qualified."

"Oh, believe me, I am. Did I tell you my ancestors, the Halladays in Scotland, had a family motto? 'The fourth to health.' You know what that means?" He raised his eyebrows conspicuously as he said the last sentence.

"No, I don't know what that means," Jon answered. "And I don't care. You don't exactly deal with things in a gentle way."

"Me? Whaddya mean?"

"You shot Bagheera, Frank."

"Hey, that's the first time you've called me 'Frank.' Does that mean we're friends now?"

Jon said nothing.

They didn't talk for a few minutes, because Halladay was concentrating on driving and Jon was on his phone looking at a few internet pages about the two experts at NYU who were predicting that Dayfall would be a disaster. Then he looked at the MPD database, which had nothing about them except their phone numbers and addresses.

"The man looks familiar to me," Jon said.

"Of course he does. You've been looking at pictures of him."

"No, it's something else. And they both have PO boxes, with no physical addresses listed in their file. Is that typical?"

"Welcome to New York," Halladay answered. "You're not in Fart-Town anymore. We have to call the post office to get a residence address."

"No one could take the trouble to find them and put them online?"

"Actually, I think it's by choice. One of the few things I don't like so much about our liberal Mayor. Privacy concerns, you know, dating back to the Patriot Act and all that."

"Whatever," Jon said, and simply called the two professors' phone numbers. He reached the first, and told her to meet them at her office in a half hour. When the other didn't answer, Jon called the school and found out he was in class, so he left a message telling him to come to the other teacher's office when he was done.

"Don't you want to talk to them separately?" Halladay asked.

"We already know they have the same perspective," Jon answered. "I want to see if they have a relationship with each other."

"Another hunch of yours?"

Jon just smiled, and then called Amira and asked her to look for any pattern in the violence of the daylight chaos crimes that might point to a single perpetrator. He also told her to check to see if there were subway tunnels, used or not, near the buildings where the Dayfall murders had taken place. And then after some more Web browsing he called her once more, this time asking her to find out as much as she could about Mallory Cassady and the circumstances surrounding her boyfriend's death.

15

DAYFALL MINUS 8 HOURS

Since Columbia University had been lost to the River Rise, along with the rest of the Upper West Side, New York University was now without competition as the premiere higher educational institution on Manhattan Island. This virtual monopoly gave the thinkers there a tremendous amount of influence on the citizens of the city itself, and on the outside opinion of it—which explained how seriously the theories of Peter Gunther and Turnia Carter were taken, though they had been espoused by almost none of their peers around the country.

Gunther, a science teacher, was currently in class. So the detectives were meeting Carter, a social psychologist, in her office, which was on Lafayette Street in the Puck Building, a handsome historical landmark made of burgundy brick, with two gold statues of Shakespeare's mythical character on its exterior. One sculpture of the mischievous sprite graced a corner of the building and the other was above the front doors, framed by two sets of four high Corinthian columns. According to a directory inside the entrance, a significant portion of the building was taken up by NYU's Wagner Graduate School of Public Service, and a stop at the front desk inside the main entrance sent the two cops one story up on the lobby elevator.

They stepped out of it and into the most unique office area Jon had ever seen, though his experience was admittedly limited. A huge space that had probably once housed a factory was now converted into multiple levels of partial floors that seemed to hang in the air, following no uniform pattern, connected by numerous metal staircases that were painted a pristine white, as were all the walls and ceilings, contrasting with lightly colored hardwood flooring throughout. Above the offices and running through some of the higher ones were long stretches of visible iron pipes, which looked like they were part of the original architecture but were meticulously preserved and painted in a rich scarlet color that was matched by some of the furniture on display. The look was visually arresting.

"Cool place to work," Halladay said as they entered Carter's office, which sat on the corner of one of the partial floors and had a nice view of several others and the high space in between them.

"We like it," Carter said. She was an almost-middle-aged black woman who was noticeably taller than she looked in pictures, and seemed hunched over a bit because of it. "How can I help you gentlemen?"

"We're trying to find the Dayfall Killer," Jon said, "And we'd like to hear firsthand why you think everything is about to go to hell in this city."

"I can't help you with your murder investigation," she said coolly, "because I don't know anything about it except what I see on the news."

"But your theories about the effect of the daylight on people here, couldn't they apply to the murderer?"

"No, because my theories are about an effect that occurs involuntarily in people, and is exacerbated in groups of people. Your serial killer works alone in a premeditated fashion. He seems to have chosen daylight, rather than the daylight affecting him."

"What about Dr. Gunther's scientific angle . . . might that apply? Will he be able to help us when he arrives?"

"Our theories are similar in that way." She had no noticeable reaction to the news of him coming to the office. "But you can certainly ask him."

"Tell us about yours anyway, while we wait."

"Well, I like to use the illustration of what happens when a caver or spelunker shines a bright light into an underground nest where hundreds of bats are roosting. The bats panic and lash out violently toward anything around them, including one another. The same dynamic can occur with the human animal, given the right set of circumstances. So the Dayfall Effect is really based on some simple primal psychological and social forces that are inherent to our nature. I call them 'The Four Phobias.'"

"And they are?" Jon said.

"The first is metathesiophobia, or the fear of change. Many of the people in this city have known nothing or almost nothing but darkness for many years. To be exposed to full sunlight tomorrow, if they insist on being outside to welcome it, will by any definition be a trauma for at least most of them. They will respond emotionally in the various ways trauma victims do, and that will make human communication and conflict resolution problematic, to say the least.

"The second phobia is more subtle and controversial, but I've become convinced of it the more I study and observe. It's a form of photophobia, or the fear of light. There's something about light in particular, in contrast to darkness, that creates a feeling of exposure and guilt in humans. The major religions—Buddhism, Judaism, Christianity, Islam—all speak repeatedly of the dark as a place where people can hide what they don't want others, or the gods, to know. For example, the Bible says people love darkness rather than light, because their deeds are evil, and they won't come to the light for fear of being exposed by it. And you have many similar references in all the so-called 'holy books.' I'm not a religious person myself, but such a ubiquitous idea in the sacred records of so many cultures has to reflect something in reality."

"Hmph," Halladay grunted. "I personally like to leave the light on when I'm sinning."

"But those religious references are metaphorical," Jon said, ignoring his partner.

"Yes, you're right," Carter said, "But why did they choose that metaphor in the first place, instead of, say, the other way around? Because more crime clearly takes place at night, and the morning is when we have the hangovers, the walk of shame, et cetera."

"Interesting. What's the third?"

"Ochlophobia, the fear of mobs. The feelings of panic that will occur because of the traumatic psychological effects of the Dayfall are contagious, if you will—they will increase exponentially in crowds."

"Maybe everyone will stay inside," Jon interrupted, "and be careful to just venture out at intervals until they get used to it."

"Do you really think most people will do that? If so, you're ignoring some other basic and enduring elements of human nature, like how we stare at traffic accidents."

"Point taken. But what about the fact that you're saying these things so loudly, and they've been broadcast so widely? The guy from Harvard who criticizes you made this point—that it's like the opposite of a self-fulfilling prophecy. What's it called . . . ?"

"A self-defeating prophecy." She nodded.

"Right. People are talking about it so much that they'll prevent it."

"Let's hope that happens," Carter said.

"The more you say something's gonna happen, the less chance of it happening, right?" This was from Halladay, slow on the uptake and even slower in his understanding of statistical probability. "Like me and Nina never talk about winning the Lotto, because then it won't happen."

"I don't think it actually works like that," Carter said with a condescending smile, and then responded when Jon brought the conversation back to the point by asking about the fourth phobia.

"The last one is thermophobia, fear of heat. This is the one that's related to Dr. Gunther's theories, though I'm more concerned with the psychological effects than the physiological causes, which are his bailiwick. The ionization in the atmosphere that occurs during Dayfall will raise air temperatures considerably—this is already starting to happen as the clouds are thinning—and it will raise body temperatures also. Any New Yorker will tell you what happens in this city when it's really hot in the summer. . . . People's irritation levels are way up and tempers flare so much faster. This will start to happen within hours, or maybe within minutes of full sunlight, depending on how fast it snowballs."

"I think you just mixed your metaphors," Jon said. "But seriously. . . . Could you be wrong about all this?"

"Anybody can be wrong about anything," Carter said. "But if by some chance my theories don't hold up, I think Dr. Gunther's alone ensure that we'll have at least a minor apocalypse."

"You think his hard science is more reliable than your social psychology?"

"I trust Peter's expertise," she said confidently. "I fear that the physical effects of Dayfall combined with the psychological will make it even worse than anyone has imagined."

Then, as if on cue, the slightly older and graying man appeared in the office door, carrying a beat-up briefcase that seemed out of place in the pristine modern space.

It didn't take long for Jon to feel confirmed in his guess that the two professors had some kind of relationship with one another. They didn't give overt clues or evidence, but they also didn't seem to be going out of their way to act like they were merely coworkers. This contributed to the overall vibe he got that they were guilty about something, but in their minds it wasn't that bad or they weren't worried about any consequences.

To observe the dynamic between the two of them, and to build a bridge to what he really wanted to find out, Jon asked Gunther to summarize his theories as Carter had. His explanations were even further over Jon's head than hers had been—so much so that he found it difficult to interact in any way with the man. And Halladay was even more lost in the barrage of scientific terms and ideas. The older cop's only comment along the way was "In English, please," and that didn't help much, because Gunther's way of simplifying was to point out that the term "neurological" came from a basic element of electricity called "neurons." After that, Gunther steamrollered along in a lot of academese that amounted to incomprehensible gibberish in the ears of the two cops.

Jon did think he was able to decipher the basic idea, however, which was that the UV rays from the sun would mix with the otherwise harmless traces of radiation in the air, which had traveled there from the site of the flagger. This would produce an atmospheric ionization that would affect the way people's brains worked (because they worked by electrical impulses involving the "neurons" he had mentioned). And the primary effects, as had been proven in the recent stretches of daylight, would be panic and aggression. So in one of his more lucid moments in the conversation, Jon asked if this effect would occur in anyone who breathed the air during the day, or only in those who were exposed to the sunlight. Gunther said the latter, because the ionization would dissipate quickly where there were no UV rays.

One of the reasons Jon didn't follow the professor better might have been that he was distracted by the continuing sense that he'd seen the man somewhere since he'd come to Manhattan, which only increased the more time he spent in his presence. But Jon couldn't place him, so he eventually gave up and moved on to the questions he really wanted to ask.

16

"I'd like to know more about the nature of your relationship with one another," Jon said to both of them.

The two professors looked at each other, then Gunther said, "How so?"

"How would you describe it?"

"Professional admiration," Carter offered after they looked at each other again.

"How about collaboration?"

"We read each other's material, and we've talked about it, if that's what you mean." She shrugged. "But we're in different fields."

"But you've reached similar conclusions, which are unlike most other experts in your fields. Did you collaborate on that?"

Gunther and Carter didn't look at each other this time, like they were trying not to, but just stared at Jon for a few moments as if considering how to answer.

"Where are you going with this, pardner?" Halladay asked.

Jon weighed whether to go all in with the big Scot, as he had been considering doing for some time, and this direct question tilted him that way. He also looked at his phone and noticed there were only seven hours left until Dayfall.

"I know what you're doing," Jon said to the two teachers, who both continued to look straight at him. "I know that Gar Render is paying you to create a panic about tomorrow."

"Whoa . . . wow," Halladay reacted.

"You need to admit it to the public now," Jon continued. "Tell people not to worry, and save this city a lot of trouble."

"Why would we do something like that, and put our careers at risk?" Carter said. And Gunther added, "Preposterous."

"It's a win-win situation for you," Jon said. "If it happens to hit the fan like you say, you'll be prophets. If it doesn't—"

"I've had enough of this!" Gunther interrupted, lifting up his old briefcase to his lap as if he was about to leave.

"Shut up and let him talk," Halladay growled.

When Gunther did shut up, the sandy-haired cop gestured to Jon.

"If it doesn't happen," Jon continued, "you can say your warnings prevented the problem. And either way you'll be rich. And famous, which you've already become by making these predictions."

"I won't say it's preposterous," Carter said, looking sideways at Halladay as Gunther defiantly grunted. "But I can say it's not true. What are you thinking Mr. Render would gain by paying us?"

"People here will clamor for more security, of course, and that's what GS offers. 'We will keep you safe' is his motto, right? Render will win the referendum vote and take charge of the city."

"But," Carter started, her PhD brain at work, "the referendum is *after* the Dayfall. If what we predict doesn't happen, we'll be discredited and Mayor King will look good. There won't be any need for people to vote for Mr. Render."

Halladay looked at Jon, as if to say, *That's a good point . . . isn't it?*

"I don't think you'll be discredited," Jon answered. "Because of how you can spin it. And I thought about the timing issue. . . . The vote was originally scheduled for earlier, when your articles started being published, and then it was postponed. At that point Render still wanted you to continue, because he *wants* the city to go to hell tomorrow."

Jon sensed his partner shifting in his seat, but he pressed on anyway.

"Render wasn't only relying on your propaganda to ensure panic in the city. Like any good builder, he's been very thorough, even to the point of sending a killer into the city when the sun has appeared. And he'll do the same tomorrow if we don't stop him. That's why you need to admit that he paid you, so we can expose him and stop the referendum. This is a bad man, one who should *not* be in charge of your city."

"That's all very interesting, though I find it hard to believe." Carter said this without much hesitation. "But we can't admit to something we didn't do. We are *not* a part of your problem, or your case."

"Preposterous," Gunther said again, and thrust his middle

finger at Halladay—rather awkwardly, like he didn't do things like that very often.

"I think you should leave now," Carter finished, "and find someone who actually knows something about your killer."

Jon studied them for a moment, then said, "Okay, if you're innocent, then you wouldn't mind us looking at your bank accounts, credit cards, et cetera, right? Just to make sure you're not making or spending an inordinate amount of money since your articles came out."

"Fine with me," Gunther said, surprisingly.

"Do you need our permission to do that?" Carter asked.

"If you don't give us permission," Jon said, "we'd have to get a subpoena from a judge."

"Screw a subpoena," Halladay said. "I don't need one."

"It would be a lot easier for us if you gave us permission," Jon continued. "Then we could just check you out and clear you quickly. Just say it into my phone, and we're gone."

Jon turned his camera on and pointed it in the direction of Gunther, who only temporarily hesitated before giving his permission. But when he turned it toward Carter, she hesitated a lot longer and eventually said she needed to check on something and would get back to him with an answer. Jon gave her his number and told her to text him within an hour, or he would be forced to get the subpoena.

The two cops left the office and the building, and didn't speak to one another until they were alone in the car.

"Okay," Halladay said before he turned on the ignition. "Spill."

"Does Gunther look familiar to you?" Jon asked.

"No. Can you just tell me what the hell is going on?"

"I'll tell you everything when we have some more verification," Jon said, "Head back to Madison Square. But in the meantime, did you think they were telling the truth?"

Halladay needed a moment to get over his frustration at Jon's clandestineness, but only a moment because he actually didn't care that much.

"I thought when you started accusing them," the sandy-haired cop said, "the conversation took a slight but noticeable turn. Before that they seemed only mildly nervous, like anyone would be when talking to the cops. But then they got cagey when they could tell they were under suspicion in some way."

"They still didn't seem nervous enough to be guilty in the way I suspect," Jon said.

"Or maybe they're not that worried about being caught."

Jon called the Gotham Security offices to find out where Gar Render was, so they could visit him again, but after several transfers was told by Gant that his boss was having dinner with his wife and daughter uptown. Jon said it was urgent and asked for his cell number; Gant said, "I'll see if he can call you."

"I thought that Marlowe guy always wanted to talk in person," Halladay said.

"He did," Jon said. "But we're running short on time. Keep going past the Flatiron, to the part of the High Line where Shinsky disappeared."

"Another hunch?" Halladay asked, and Jon nodded.

When they reached the High Line, Jon told Halladay to park underneath it near the locked door that seemed to provide access to the lower parts of the Water Wall.

"It keeps getting warmer outside," Halladay said as they waited for a return call, and took off his coat. Then he pointed above them, to the underside of the elevated track platform. "The heaters for the grass up there aren't even on anymore. They're not humming like they usually do."

"You've been here before?" Jon asked.

"Hmmm?" his partner said, looking around. "I don't think so, not before today."

"Then how did you know that about the heaters?"

Halladay cocked his head at Jon, as if to say, *Why the suspicious questions?* But all he said was, "I've lived in this city a long time."

They sat in silence for a few minutes, until Render called and Jon answered.

"What do you want, detective?" the Gotham Security boss said, obviously irritated. "I'm having dinner with my family."

"Your company not only built the Water Wall," Jon said, "but secured the subway tunnel system after the flooding started, right?"

"Yeah," the older man responded. "Why?"

"Are your people able to move around down there, under the city, conduct operations?"

"Yeah, we did some engineering to prevent more flooding, and to travel underground if we needed to. We also built some rooms down there—we call 'em 'Belows'—to use as posts just in case. We haven't needed them much so far. This isn't some big secret, though we don't broadcast it. Why are you asking?"

"We want you to unlock a GS door for us along the Water Wall, below the High Line, and send us a map of the underground."

"Why?"

"Because we have a suspect, and we think he might be hiding down there."

"Why didn't you ask Gant when you talked to him? He could have taken care of that."

"Because I wanted you to be the only one who knows. And I wanted to see what you would say."

"What the hell?" Render said, even more irritated now, but Jon just let the question hang in the air.

"Is the suspect a Gotham employee?" Render asked.

"Not officially. But he could be using your tunnels to move around and hide."

"If he's not our employee, then he would've had to steal a key, or find one that was lost, which isn't likely."

"Unless you hired him unofficially."

"What?" Render asked. Jon couldn't tell for sure over the phone, but the GS boss seemed to be genuinely perplexed. "Oh, right, your theory about me being involved in these crimes. I don't know what else I can do but tell you I would never in a million years do something like that."

"You can come down here yourself and open this door for us, and give us a map."

"What would that prove?"

"It wouldn't prove anything," Jon said, "but it would help us to believe that you're not involved."

"How's that?"

"If you make us get in some other way, and we can't find the guy, then we'll think maybe you warned him so he could get away. But if you come here yourself—"

"I hate to tell ya," Render interrupted, "but that doesn't prove anything. I could warn him on my way there. Look, I told you I want to cooperate in any way I can, and I want to know myself if someone is doing this, Gotham employee or not. It's just that there are other good reasons for me not to drive over there right now, like *I'm having dinner with my family*. So let's do this. . . . I'll personally call one of my agents who's in the area, tell him not to talk to anyone else, and have him open the door for you and search with you. I won't even tell Gant, though he'll be pissed when he finds out I didn't."

"Okay," Jon said. "I guess that's the best we can do right now. What about a map of the underground?"

"I'm sure the MPD already has one."

"Would it have all of your modifications and additions?"

"Probably not," Render admitted. "So I'll send you a link to ours, right to your phone. And if you find your guy, you'll know I'm not involved in these murders."

I already know you are, Jon thought.

17

The link to the map arrived almost immediately, and the agent Render had promised not long after. When Jon forwarded the map to Amira, she said that it would take a little while to adapt it for use on their phones, but Jon figured they could do without it right now because the man who arrived from GS would presumably know his way around down there.

Or woman. Jon couldn't tell which it was until she introduced herself and said her name was Natalie, and was still a bit confused because the voice definitely seemed male. The shapes under her higher-level "Builder" uniform seemed rather ambiguous as well, and John had heard stories of how many ex-military men (especially Special Forces, for some reason) were transitioning after they completed their service. He had even read an article online about some controversial psychological theories suggesting why this was happening so often—one was that they had reached the pinnacle of masculinity and found it unsatisfying, and another was that they carried guilt from all the killing they did in their macho job and tried to escape it by creating an entirely different identity for themselves. But all that really mattered to Jon right now was that Natalie had the much-needed key, which turned out to be a thumb-sized cylinder attached to a flat square.

"It's a magnetic code locking system," she explained as she opened the door, when she saw Jon looking at the key. "No electronics were allowed because of the water threat, so the locks can't be controlled remotely. You need one of these keys to get through any of the entrances to the underground, and to move around once you're down there. And they are *very* carefully guarded, impossible to copy by anyone but us. That's why it's very unlikely that the person you're looking for went in here." She led Jon and Halladay inside. "But we'll look anyway."

On the wall inside the door there were some industrial flashlights sitting on shelves. One of the shelves was empty, but Natalie didn't seem to notice that when she pulled one down for each of them.

"We didn't hook up any lighting in the halls or tunnels," she said as she turned her flashlight on and locked the door behind them. "The cost would've been prohibitive, and we don't use them that much."

"What about the rooms you built down here?" Jon said. "What are they called again?"

"'Belows.' Yes, they have light and power. And cell phone signal boosters and Wi-Fi routers that are left on for when we do come down." She shook her phone at Jon and thumbed its screen as she led them down a hallway, which Jon figured was built into the Water Wall.

"So there's a Below near here," Jon said.

"Uh-huh," she said. "We'll check it out."

"We should be quiet," Halladay whispered, "in case he's in there."

"If you insist," Natalie whispered back.

They continued in silence down the dark hallway, which was more like a narrow tunnel, and then turned left away from the Wall into another passage that sloped downward. That one, apparently excavated by the Builders, led to a wide stairway that even an outsider like Jon recognized as part of the subway system. When they reached the bottom of the stairs, they turned right onto an abandoned train platform. As Jon swung his flashlight around, it revealed that the tracks in the tunnel below the platform were covered in water. He also noticed a bad smell and heard Halladay make a disgusted noise.

"We weren't able to close up all the tunnels before they flooded," Natalie whispered as she also shined her light on the small river over the edge of the platform, where the trains used to run.

At the end of the platform there was another narrow passage, obviously created by GS engineers to run parallel to the flooded subway and to provide access along it. Jon wondered why it had been less trouble to dig this tunnel rather than clear the water out of the already existing one, but he didn't have much of a chance to think more about it, because they soon arrived in front of a closed door set into the side of the passageway. Natalie abruptly shut off her flashlight and motioned for the two cops to do the same. They could see a very thin line of yellow around the edges of the door—indicating that there was a light on inside.

Jon caught a whiff of strong perfume when Natalie moved close to him and whispered in his ear that she would go in first, in case there was a GS employee in there. Then she moved quietly over to Halladay and did the same thing. Both cops drew their sidearms, but Natalie didn't, apparently still confident that there would be no one dangerous in the room. Instead she pulled out the underground key, opened the lock with it, stuck it back in her pocket, and pushed open the door.

As she and the cops stepped inside, a big figure was only about ten feet way, moving toward them in the middle of the room as if he had heard the door opening and was coming to greet them.

"Hello?" said Natalie.

Shinsky's face filled with puzzlement at seeing Natalie, but then with panic as his eyes fell on the two detectives behind her. He immediately dove into the woman like he must have done in his football days, driving her back explosively into Jon and Halladay and scattering them like bowling pins back through the door and into the tunnel outside it. Shinsky simultaneously fired his handgun into Natalie's midsection as he drove her body back, and though blood from the exit wounds sprayed onto the two cops, none of the bullets hit them.

By the time they gathered themselves and figured out that the blood on them wasn't their own, Shinsky had disappeared into the darkness down the tunnel, in the opposite direction from which they had come. Jon located and picked up the flashlight he had dropped in the melee, and Halladay did the same for his gun, and they took off down the passage after the perp.

After about thirty feet Jon skidded to a stop, realizing that he could only see what the flashlight was shining on, and that Shinsky could easily wait for them in ambush, or even just turn around and shoot them from beyond the range of their lights. So he experimented quickly by turning the flashlight off, with Halladay following his lead, but then they couldn't see anything ahead of them. Their prey must have had a light as well, otherwise he wouldn't be able to see anything, either. He had probably turned a corner or was too far ahead, because there was no sign of him except a far echo of footsteps.

Jon turned the flash back on and decided to keep it pointed low so that they would be able to see Shinsky's light ahead of them if it came into view. He was trusting his ears at this point, in the belief that the big man was fleeing ahead of them and not waiting around a corner to take them out.

There was a corner that turned to the left about a hundred feet up the passage, and Jon peered around it cautiously and shined his flashlight into the flooded subway tunnel. A makeshift bridge consisting of a long metal girder stretched over the water to the left end of a service platform on the other side of the tunnel. Shinsky had obviously crossed it, because he was now on the far right end of the platform, climbing down into what looked like a small inflatable boat.

"Police! Stop!" Jon yelled as he stepped out from behind the corner and trained both his flashlight and gun on the perp. The big man started firing wildly in his direction while continuing to situate himself in the little water craft. Jon ducked back behind the corner and heard Shinsky starting the motor, but the sound was drowned out by Halladay stepping out from behind him and firing about five rounds right next to his ear.

"Frank!" Jon shouted, batting at his partner's arm and pulling his shoulder backward. "What are you doing?!"

"Shooting the bastard," Halladay shouted back. "Whaddaya think I'm doing?"

"You're too far away to ensure a wound shot, and we don't want to kill him."

"I do," the bigger cop said, glancing down at the blood on his shirt.

"We need him to talk."

Jon pointed the flashlight around the corner again just in time to see the little boat passing out of view down the flooded tunnel. He and Halladay both stepped out into the opening at the end of the bridge and shined their lights around to see if there was another craft like the one Shinsky had taken. There wasn't, so they gave up on any pursuit and headed back down the passage to the Below, which was easy to find because the yellow light from inside the room was still shining through the open door.

They checked Natalie's body for any signs of life and found none. Shinsky had put at least three rounds into her.

A brief inspection of the Below revealed that it had obviously been serving as Shinsky's headquarters for the crimes he had committed during the brief stretches of daylight, and for whatever he was planning to do when Dayfall arrived. In addition to the cell booster and wireless router in the corner of the room, there was a

TV hooked up to the router, a stock of food and water, a cot for sleeping, and meth paraphernalia in one of the tall lockers along the back. In another there was some clothing, including a long leather coat like the one worn by the killer they had seen on the video from the office building murders, with custom slots inside to hold an array of knives and other cutting weapons. A third locker contained the weapons themselves, an impressive collection containing everything from switchblades to bowie knives to even a couple of small axes.

"Look at this," Halladay said from next to a small card table in the middle of the room, where Shinsky had apparently been sitting when they arrived. The big cop was flipping through a sketchbook with elaborate drawings of trees, flowers, animals, and other innocuous subjects. "He definitely ended some people, but I don't get the impression he was into it like the killer at the office building. That one mutilated the women and threw the guy's junk across the room."

"Maybe the other one enjoys killing," Jon said. "But this one is just doing his job, so he can pay for the drugs. The question is, who's he working for?" He looked at Halladay. "Let's see how well the cell booster works."

He dialed Render's number and found the signal was good enough to reach the GS boss.

"What'd ya find out?" Render said when he picked up.

"One of the killers was using a Below as his base of operations."

"What? Was he one of mine?"

"Apparently not," Jon said. "An independent hiring himself out to support a meth habit."

"Did you get him?"

"No, unfortunately he escaped, using some kind of small boat to travel in the flooded subways."

"A dinghy," Render said thoughtfully. "We put them down there, but they require the same key as the doors." The older man paused for a few seconds. "And you're not insisting that he's working for me?"

"He didn't know we were coming," Jon said. "He was surprised. So you didn't alert him, like you said you wouldn't."

"Damn right I didn't, and I didn't tell anyone else, either. Hold on a second."

Jon heard the click of the phone as Render made another call, then came back on the line.

"Gant doesn't know anything about this, either," the GS boss said, "but he was pissed about me not informing him, just like I said he'd be."

"You've earned some trust from me, sir," Jon said. "But we'll need more of your help. Is there anyone else who has access to the keys for the underground?"

"Hmmm . . . I'm not sure, but I think part of the deal when we secured it was that we had to give some to the Mayor's office. That's all I can think of right now, but I'll check on it."

"Thanks, and one more thing," Jon said, after thinking a little. "I'm sorry to say that the agent you sent to meet us was killed by the perp, so you'll have to send another to let our cleanup crew in."

"Awww . . ." Render responded, swearing under his breath. "He was a good man."

Jon hung up, noting the male reference and figuring that Natalie's transition was a recent event. He knelt down and felt through her pockets until he found the underground key that had been used to open the door. He put the key in his own pocket and noticed again the blood from the shooting that had sprayed onto his shirt and neck, making it look like the wound below his chin had reopened. He and Halladay, who was also wearing some un-wanted red, washed themselves off in the Below's bathroom and borrowed a couple of shirts from Shinsky's locker. The one Jon put on was obviously several sizes too big for him, but he really didn't care at this point.

They left their stained clothing on the floor for Amira, whom Jon texted about cleaning up the scene and gleaning any further evidence from it. He also asked her to check Gunther and Carter's bank and credit accounts for anything suspicious, because he saw on his phone that Carter had sent him a text giving permission to do so.

While he was sending these instructions to Amira, another message came through, this time from Mallory. It said:

> I got a new list from my GS contact, and took a picture of it like you said. You'll have to come here to The Office to see it, though, I don't want to send it. And come alone.

And then another one from her:

> You won't believe whose name is on it.

18

"You need to go back to the Flatiron," Jon told Halladay when they were in the car. "Work with Amira on that map of the underground and any chaos crimes video she can get access to. Now that we know our witness was right about Shinsky knifing people in the crowd, and we also know he's been moving around in the underground, we can piece together how many of the deaths could have been caused by him or his buddy from the office building."

"Where will you be?" the older cop said.

"Drop me off at The Office, so I can talk to Mallory a little. I'll walk to the Flatiron when I'm done."

"Without me?" Halladay said with raised eyebrows. "Is there an apartment behind that bar or something?"

Jon let that ride, because Mallory hadn't wanted Halladay to be there, so she probably didn't want the big Scot to know why Jon himself was going.

"You wanna tell me finally," Halladay said after a while, "why all the focus on Render and Gotham Security? I'm figuring you had some information you didn't share with me, and that's how you knew what direction you were going in from the start."

"The Mayor told me something when she hired me," Jon said, ready for Halladay to be all in—or mostly in, at least. "She told me that Render was behind the crimes, sowing panic so that he could win the referendum vote on Tuesday. She said she knew that the two professors at NYU were on his payroll, though she couldn't prove it. She wanted me to get the evidence to expose Render before the vote, and stop the killings before Dayfall so that people could feel safe without him."

"Ahhh," Halladay said. "Why didn't the King just give me the info she had? She knows I like her, and she knows I don't like Darth Render."

"That's why. She needed an outsider who could be believed, not someone who owes something to either side."

Halladay thought for a moment, then said, "But now you're having second thoughts . . ."

"Why do you say that?"

"You called him 'sir.'"

"I was surprised that Shinsky was still there, that Render didn't warn him off. But I'm sure there's an explanation for that—the evidence all still points to GS. The Mayor hadn't even thought about the underground transportation angle, which I bet you'll find is something that ties the Dayfall murders and the chaos crimes together."

"Makes sense to me," Halladay said, then both men sat in

silence for the last few minutes of the ride, until Jon got out at The Office and the older cop continued toward MPD headquarters a couple of blocks away.

Jon felt a surge of adrenaline as he entered the bar, knowing he was about to get some new information for the case, but also because he was going to see Mallory again. He felt even more exhilarated when those ice-blue eyes looked up at him, her full lips smiling at him, the dark wisps of hair on her forehead moving as she gestured for him to meet her in the back room. She opened the door ahead of him, and pressed against him in an embrace once they were both inside. He kissed her tenderly, forgetting completely for a few moments about the case and the threat of a coming apocalypse.

As he hugged her tighter, he moved his face to the left to nuzzle her neck, and as he did his eye was caught by the top of her one small tattoo, peeking out from beneath her shirt collar just below her right shoulder. Jon moved the edge of the shirt down with his hand so he could see the small green-and-black figure of a four-leaf clover—except it was only half of one.

"I like your ink," he said as he studied the unusual shape. "It's . . . different."

"I went to get it when I was a teenager," she said. "Felt pressured by my friends, and then I didn't like some of the stuff the guy was saying when he was working on me. So I got up and left in the middle."

"Why didn't you ever have it finished?"

"I don't know," she said pensively. "I guess I like that's it unique, and kinda represents how broken and incomplete I've always felt."

She seemed on the verge of tears, but then a thin smile creased her lips. "Except for with Tom. . . . He said that when he looked at it he saw the whole thing."

John looked harder at the two leaves of the green-and-black clover and tried to imagine it with four, but it remained half-finished to his eyes.

"I wish I could," he said softly, and then into her ear: "But I like it."

"I like *your* beauty spots, too," she said, putting her hand up to the wound under his chin and gently touching it with her finger. It must have been visible to her because he had been craning his head to study the tattoo.

"So you really meant that?" he asked, snapping upright again and looking into her eyes. "When you said it before?"

"I did," she said.

Jon pulled away from her slightly, smiling, and asked about the picture of the list. She pulled out her phone and found it, holding it out for him to see. He didn't even have to expand the view, because there were only three items on the list. The second was "Bear," the last was "Whoever you can at Dayfall," and the first item on the list was "Detective Jon Phillips."

"Hmmm," he said. "Did you pass this on?"

"Yes, the recipient usually comes in right after. But I took the picture first like you asked." She smiled broadly, then added, "You're in some kind of danger, aren't you?"

"I don't know, but . . . you're happy about that?"

"I'm happy that I can prove to you that Gotham is the good guys." She pointed at the phone. "See, you're on their protection list. You must have talked to Gar Render like you said you were going to, and he wants to keep you safe. Did you talk to him?"

"Yeah . . ." Jon said, thinking about how it did seem to fit together. Apparently this list arrived sometime after he had talked to Render about the perp using the underground, and maybe even after they'd been attacked by Shinsky.

Jon's phone buzzed and he paused to read a text message from Amira. Her first perusal of the NYU professors' accounts didn't yield any connection with Gotham Security, but there was a recent $10,000 deposit in one of Dr. Carter's accounts that she was able to trace back to the Mayor's office. John texted back to her, "The Mayor? Are you sure?" and she answered "Yes, don't know what that means, though."

Jon was starting to think he knew what that meant, and he turned back to Mallory.

"So you said that they use these lists to do police work without the police knowing," he said, and she nodded. "Do you think they also might be protecting some of these people *from* the police?"

"They could be. That's why I didn't want you to bring what's-his-name along with you. I don't trust him, or anybody in the existing government. That's why we need a change of the guard, and thank God that'll be happening on Tuesday."

Jon felt even more attracted to her because she cared about something bigger than herself—unlike a lot of beautiful women. But he still didn't register most of what she said, lost as he was in a new paradigm of thought about what might be going on in this city. He was thinking about what all this might mean for the Mayor, and even for his seemingly glib and apathetic partner.

"What?" Mallory said, after a little span of him staring into space.

"I have to go," Jon said, snapping out of it. "I'm not sure anything is going to happen when the sun comes out in the morning, but until I know more about it, you should probably close the bar and lock yourself up in your apartment. Just in case."

"Can't do that," she said, shaking her head. "A lot of customers told me that they plan to be in here drinking to the Dayfall, or maybe so they won't have to worry about it. My dad says he wants to be here then, too, so even if something does happen, I want to be with him. I'll go home once everything calms down or turns out okay, 'cause that's the end of my shift anyway."

"Okay. . . . Well, maybe I'll make sure I'm patrolling this block at that time, and stop in to keep an eye on you. Have a drink ready for me. . . . How about a Tequila Sunrise? That'll be appropriate."

"I already stocked up on orange juice. . . . I'm sure you won't be the only one with that idea."

She flashed that killer smile again, which was half-innocent and half-experienced, and Jon wanted to stay. But he briefly kissed her goodbye and then tore himself away.

Outside, it had started raining, and gathering storm clouds were visible overhead from the light of the city. Jon used his coat as an umbrella, since it was now warm and humid enough that he would have been sweating inside of it. Thunder boomed and lightning flashed a number of times during his walk to the Flatiron Building, a portent of the tempest that would clear away the remaining canopy of darkness overhead during the rest of the night, and make it possible for the daylight to break through in the morning. But it also provided a fitting soundtrack for the gloomy thoughts that were racing through his head about what he was preparing to say to the Mayor when he reached her office.

19

"Why isn't Halladay with you?" Mayor King said after she dismissed a couple of aides and allowed Jon to enter her office, at his insistence. "I just talked to him on the phone a few minutes ago."

"Because I don't know what you're saying to him," Jon answered, taking a seat across the desk from her.

"I was just checking up on you," she said, puzzled. "Seeing how you're doing, since I haven't heard much."

"You told me that you were too busy for me to report in unless I had something substantial."

"That I did. But Dayfall is only five hours away. So hopefully you have something now?"

"I think so," Jon said. "But you're not going to like it."

"Oh?"

"You told me that you brought in an outsider like me because I was impartial and people would be more likely to believe me if I found out Render was behind the murders."

"Yes. And he is, right?"

"I'm thinking you also brought in an outsider like me because I wouldn't already be impressed by Render like so many people in this city are, including a lot of your own cops."

"In a way, that's true," the Mayor said, still visibly puzzled about where he was going with this. "You're more objective, so you'd be able to see what he's doing more clearly. . . ."

"Or believe lies about him."

"What are you trying to say?"

"Knowing that I didn't have much time to investigate, you prejudiced me against him and planted enough evidence that I would conclude he was behind the chaos and the killings. Then this 'outsider' would accuse him, and you hoped that the suspicion it created about GS would be enough to at least even the ground going into the referendum."

He paused for effect, as her mouth slowly opened in disbelief.

"The worst part is that you actually instigated the chaos and the killings so Render could be blamed for them, because it would be easy for people to think he had the most to gain by them. If I bought into that idea and accused him of it, the city would be suspicious of him and feel safer, which benefits you in the vote. If the panic happens anyway, the city eating itself alive is a small price to pay for you staying in power."

"Hmmm," she said after a moment, finally closing her mouth. "You're right." But after Jon nodded proudly, she added: "You're right that I wouldn't like what you're saying. Because it's ridiculous, and I'm really disappointed in you. But I'm really at a loss to know what to do about it. So let me ask. . . . Why do you think this? You must have some kind of supposed evidence. I'm not sure it's worth even a few minutes of my time right now, because I don't think you'll be working for me after this, but maybe I can show you the holes in your thinking."

"Fine. I'll walk you through it," he said.

"Make it quick," Mayor King said, looking at her watch.

"Gar Render *is* rather impressive, actually, and he's fully coop-erated with our investigation, right down to allowing us to corner a suspect and proving the guy couldn't have been working for him."

"Why's that?"

"Because if he was, and we caught him, it would have impli-cated Render. There's no way Render, if he was paying him, would have even taken a chance of him being arrested."

"But you didn't arrest him," King said. "I know that from talk-ing to Halladay earlier."

"Not Render's fault," Jon said, and King had no response, so he continued. "Then there's the fact that at least one of the killers has been using the underground to move around, and you're the only one other than GS who has access to the keys needed to do that."

"Hmmm," she said again. "Well, I haven't given any of those keys away. I put them in a safe and haven't touched them since I got them. And you're assuming Render's innocence when there could be any number of explanations for your first observation. But go on."

"The suspect shot a trusted lieutenant of Render's, making it unlikely they were on the same team."

"Sometimes you have to sacrifice a pawn to win the game."

"Gotham Security gives its agents on the streets a list of people that need protection. I saw one of the lists and my name was on it, but Halladay's wasn't."

"Meaning what?"

"GS thinks I need protection from someone, and it's not them, obviously, because they're trying to protect me. The only criminals I've encountered that might want to take me out are ones who are working for someone else, and you're the most likely candidate. Halladay, on the other hand, has no love lost for GS, but he seems to like you. And we know whose payroll he's on."

Rialle King laughed. "You think Frank Halladay can be bought?"

"Maybe not in the conventional way, but you're looking the other way on some things that Render wouldn't, if he was in charge. That could be enough to make Halladay prejudiced towards you, and maybe even do some dirty work on your behalf."

She laughed again, but Jon went on.

"The last nail is that there's ten grand in Turnia Carter's account that we traced to your office. You told me Render was paying them to create panic about Dayfall, but the money trail leads to you."

"Well, that I can explain," she said, nodding and sitting back in her seat. "Turnia Carter is a college friend of my daughter Ria, and they've kept in touch since then. She confided in Ria that she was feeling guilty because she was being paid to slant her research— she was torn because the pay and notoriety are great, but she knows this could hurt her friend's mom. It was all pretty vague but I could tell what was going on from talking to Ria, who did *not* want Turnia to get into any trouble. She made me promise that I wouldn't let the cat out unless it was absolutely necessary. So we tried to offset whatever GS was doing for her by Ria giving her the ten thousand, which was the most I could manage to earmark for research from my budget without raising red flags. But it hasn't been enough to turn her, obviously. It was like a bidding war, and I lost."

"If this is all true," Jon said, thinking she was a very good liar if it wasn't, "why didn't you tell me about it?"

"I was trying to keep my promise to my daughter. I was hoping you would discover the GS bribe and deal with it, so she wouldn't blame me for whatever happened."

"And if I discovered your bribe?"

"Then I would explain it to you, like I just did." She made a gesture with both hands that said, *It's as simple as that.* "In fact, I knew you would probably find out, because after you interviewed Turnia, she called me to ask if it was okay with me to give you permission to look at her bank account. I just thought you were a better detective than to assume the worst about me."

"Halladay could have told you all this when you talked to him," Jon said, "giving you time to come up with your story."

"It all can be verified," King said. "You can talk to Ria if you must, though I'd rather not involve her if we can help it. But I think something else Halladay told me is more pertinent to what's going on here."

"What's that?"

"Well, speaking of being prejudiced, he was concerned that you seem to have fallen under the spell of a GS sympathizer, who also happens to be 'hot as shit,' to use his words. Love is blind, Detective Phillips, and sex makes you stupid. . . . There's a reason for those clichés."

"Is that what you think?" Jon said, caught a bit off guard.

"I think you're young, and like a lot of young cops, you can rush to judgment too soon. But you're talented, too, so as stupid as some of your ideas are, you're probably on to something with the others." She sat up in her chair and leaned toward him. "I'm going to give you another chance, if you promise to think this all through some more. But if you don't get your head straight in the next few hours, I'll have no choice but to take action."

"Are you threatening me?"

"You're damn right I am. And you can make use of the door, please—I've got work to do."

Jon nodded and left the office, more off-kilter now and not sure what else to do.

He felt like he needed to get his bearings and think through all of this before talking to Halladay, Amira, or anyone else, so he walked out of the building and across the street to Madison Square Park. There were still plenty of cars on the street, but the storm had left the park almost deserted.

At first Jon used his jacket again as an umbrella, but then gave up and let the unusually warm rain drench him as he situated himself on a bench facing north about a third of the way into the park. The clouds above flashed and rumbled slightly more often now than during his previous walk, and the tops of the highest buildings around the park were hidden in the fog generated by the storm. Only the lighted clock on the Met Life tower to his right was bright enough to shine through, and it was just a dim yellow, moonlike sphere. He couldn't see above the first five floors or so of the Gotham Security base to its left, or the thin glass monolith of One Madison to its right. The whole scene was colored even more blue-green than before, because the light from the industrial

UV lamps was bouncing off the clouds, fog, and maybe even the rain.

Because of those features, the park seemed even more other-worldly than usual, an impression heightened by the two huge sculptures planted in the patch of grass to the left of Jon's bench. They were of similar shape and size, at least ten feet tall and a little less than five feet wide, and both obviously represented Manhat-tan because there was a solid ring like a wall around the bottom and a cityscape of buildings projecting diagonally up from the tall center columns above them. There were only two differences between the sculptures: the one on the left had a moon extending from the top and buildings that were well defined and recogniz-able (Jon could make out the Empire State and Chrysler Build-ings, for example); the other one had a sun at the top and buildings that were noticeably unfinished, looking almost like they were melting.

John became curious enough about the artist's meaning and the material used (bronze, he guessed) that he got up from the bench and walked toward the sculptures to get a closer look.

As a result, he didn't see the masked figure emerge from the cover of the street behind him and move purposefully in his di-rection.

20

At first glance, Jon thought the sculpture with the sun at the top was predicting doom for the city, because of the "melted" look of the buildings on that one. But when he got closer he realized it had a different meaning, because he could read the inscriptions on the solid rings around the bottom of each. The one with the moon at the top said, "What we are" and the one with the sun said, "What will we be?"

As Jon got close to the sculpture on the left, he could tell that his guess was right and it was made out of bronze. But he reached out to touch one of the semi-vertical buildings with his hand anyway, appreciating the detail in the metal. As he did, an unconscious instinct suddenly caused him to jerk his upper body slightly to the right, and a long blade flashed by his neck and slammed into the statue, sending sparks flying. Jon turned his whole body to the left and managed to pull back just enough that a backhand slash of the knife barely missed him. This only took a second or two, but even in that short time his brain registered that his attacker was the Dayfall Killer they had seen on the video from the office building, the one with the short "bowling ball" figure and the utilitarian black mask.

If the attacker would have simply slashed back the other way again with the knife, it probably would have connected. But fortunately he brought it to his waist in a stabbing position and lunged toward Jon, probably wanting to make sure the young detective wasn't only wounded by the next attack. The time it took for this adjustment, however, was just enough to allow Jon to roll his body around part of the big sculpture and put it between him and the killer.

Jon thought of fleeing toward the street, but his heart was already pounding from the shock of the attack, and he wasn't sure he could outrun the powerfully built man to the edge of the park. Just as he was about to try it anyway, for lack of a better plan, several gunshots rang out behind him and a couple of bullets sparked on the metal of the statue.

Jon glanced back to see Halladay walking calmly toward him across the grass with his gun extended, and then looked forward again to see that the killer had immediately taken off running in the other direction, keeping the statue between him and Halladay's gun, and quickly disappearing through some bushes into the busy street beyond. Now that Jon had seen how fast the little man could move, he was glad that he hadn't tried to outrun him.

"You all right?" Halladay asked when he reached Jon, who was breathing hard.

"Yeah, barely," Jon said. "Thanks to you."

Halladay holstered his gun and then smacked Jon upside the head.

"Ow," Jon said. "What the hell was that for?"

"I'm only here because the King told me what you said to her, so I went looking for you, to tell you what a fuckin' dumbass you are."

"Why?"

"For thinkin' the Mayor is crooked."

"I *know* she is now," Jon said.

"How's that?"

"I'm on the GS protection list, and sure enough, right after I confront the Mayor, an assassin tries to kill me."

"Och!" the older cop said, shaking his head. "Did it ever occur to you that your protection list might be a hit list?"

"Yeah, but—"

"But you're not thinkin' with your head right now, Casanova."

"The Mayor just threatened me, Frank. That's a fact."

"What did she say, exactly?"

"Something about taking action if I don't drop my theory about her."

Halladay raised his hand slightly, as if he was going to hit Jon again, but the younger cop moved backward a little.

"She was talking about *firing* you, Piss-Pants." He shook his head again, then turned around to head back to the Flatiron Building. "Come on, you need to hear the latest from the Princess."

The rain seemed even stronger to Jon, and the storm more menacing, on the brief walk back to headquarters. Or maybe it was just because he was more confused now than when he had walked out.

As he realized that he might be back at square one, a hopeless feeling began flooding over him in concert with the rain. He tried to buoy himself by remembering why he had taken this job in the first place, but that just made it worse. He had now alienated the Mayor, who was the one person who could give him the kind of recommendations he wanted for the future, and the motivation of catching the killer was ebbing because his chances seemed so slim. He remembered Anton Versa, the police chief in Philadelphia, talking about the "bigger picture" of helping the rest of the cities that would experience Dayfall, but right now that was being crowded out of his mind by the picture of a beautiful woman who, he suspected, was going to end up being a big disappointment for him. Anger at her was growing in him, mixed with anger at himself for letting his heart screw up the case.

The adrenaline from that emotion was enough to offset the feelings of hopelessness, and once he was back in the building, Jon washed his face and changed his clothes, and then went to join Halladay and Amira in the lab.

"What's up?" he said when he got there, trying to make a new start.

"A lot," Amira said. "We've got new info on the Dayfall murder locations, the chaos crimes, the NYU teachers, and your . . . uh, friend at the bar." She glanced at Halladay, who raised his eyebrows. "Which do you want first?"

"The order you just said," Jon answered, wanting to make sure he didn't allow Mallory to be the priority in his mind, and not wanting Amira and Halladay to think she was.

"Okay, the Dayfall murder locations," Amira began. "Now that we have the GS map of the underground, with all their modifications on it, I found out there's subterranean access into every building where the Dayfall Killer has struck. They're all near subway tunnels, used or unused, and they all have passageways from the tunnels to their basements put in by GS engineers when they were securing the underground. There are over a hundred such access points throughout the city, all below buildings because entrances on the surface would be too easy to discover. Where they could, they made use of already existing underground structures, like the floors below the library and the abandoned construction below Grand Central."

"So our ghost-who-walks-through-walls mystery has been solved," Halladay added. "The one who just attacked you was using them to sneak in and out of those buildings to play with his cutlery collection, and Shinsky could use them to disappear after working the crowd with his."

"Here's an overlay of the underground map and the fatalities and injuries that happened during the chaos crimes," Amira said as she brought it up on a nearby screen. "As you suspected, there *is* a pattern to them. . . . They all started with fatal wounds that took place near access points from the underground, and then spread out in concentric circles, with the nonfatal injuries happening as people panicked after the fatal ones occurred. And as you can see by the different times and locations of the circles, Shinsky could easily have caused almost all of this by himself. You can actually tell where he waded into a crowd, did his thing, then traveled to another place a little later via the underground and did it again. And here's what made it seem like there was chaos all over the city. . . ."

She added another overlay to the map that showed a bunch of red spots that were also near access points to the underground, but in different parts of the city than the ones before.

"These are the fires and explosions that took place when the sun came out briefly," Amira said. "This is obvious enough that it didn't take me long to figure it out once I knew what to look for, thanks to your suggestions. One wonders why the Chaos Crimes people don't seem to know it."

"Maybe they do," Halladay said, "but they're just not doing anything about it."

"So there's a third perp, one who's a pyro," Jon said. "The short guy carves up people inside buildings to scare the city, the big guy slashes people in crowds to create panic on the streets, and the third one does it by burning and blowing shit up so it'll look like the city's descending into chaos because of the Dayfall."

"All because Garth Vader wants them to feel unsafe," Halladay offered, "so they'll vote for him on Tuesday."

Jon looked at Amira, who nodded slightly.

"Or," the young cop said, "someone else who has access to the underground is behind it." Halladay reacted, but he went on. "Look, Frank, you can hit me in the head all you want, but Mayor King did make a payment to Carter at NYU. That's still the hardest evidence we have about who wants there to be fear in the city."

"She explained that to you, Piss-Pants."

"Stop calling me that!" Jon started to say, but Amira jumped in. . . .

"It could be precisely because Mayor King is well intentioned that her payment was so easily discovered. She doesn't know how to hide a bribe like criminals do, nor does she have as much need to."

"No offense intended, Amira," Jon interrupted. "But Gotham Security is prejudiced against your religion—they would never hire you—so don't you think that might make you biased against them?"

"No offense taken," the woman in the head scarf replied. "But one reason I like my religion is that it emphasizes justice, and I'm determined to be just in my judgments. My older brother was killed in a crime on the streets of New York when I was a teenager—that's why I wanted to be a cop in the first place, and I fought through a lot of obstacles to make it to where I am. I'm actually sympathetic to GS because it's true that the police are hog-tied sometimes, so I think I'm seeing this objectively." She paused and met Jon's stare. "So can I finish what I was saying?"

"Of course," he said.

"I took a closer look at the professors' accounts, and I realized there's something important that's *not* there."

"What's that?"

"Housing payments. I couldn't find any mortgage or rent."

"So you're thinking someone could be giving them a place to live as incentive to promote the chaos theories."

"Though it would have to be a really nice place," Amira said, after nodding, "to offset the amount of money the Mayor gave Carter."

"And we don't know where," Halladay said, "because their addresses are PO boxes, so we'd have to tail them to find out."

"That won't be necessary," Jon said, as a light bulb went on in his head. "I know where they live."

"Really?" his partner said. "How's that?"

"Remember how I thought I'd seen Gunther before? I just re-membered where. It was in the lobby of One Madison, where Render lives. He came out of the elevator in the lobby when we were going in."

21

"Wow," said Amira, "a free condo in that building is a pretty nice bribe, especially in a city where housing is such a big deal."

"And you have a pretty good memory," Halladay said to Jon, "for an incontinent."

"That's why we talk to people in person," Jon fired back, "instead of being lazy and calling on the phone."

"Even if we put all our biases aside," Amira said, "it seems pretty clear that Gareth Render is the only person who could have arranged for the NYU professors to live at One Madison. And with the way that's been done clandestinely, and what we heard from the Mayor's daughter, it seems pretty clear that their theories were invented to create panic under the Mayor's watch and give the impression that only Gotham Security can keep people safe."

"So Darth was making extra sure he would get elected,"

Halladay said, "just like the King suspected. If the experts spreading their lies didn't work, the killers spilling some blood would."

"It makes sense," Jon said, thinking about it for a few moments. "Except that Render doesn't actually seem like the type to me. It's just a feeling, I don't know."

"Don't let him fool ya."

"Researching the underground reminded me," Amira said, "how the homeless population down there basically disappeared when GS was securing it. It was reported that they were wiped out or driven to the surface by flooding, but the idea that it happened to all of them seems really far-fetched. There was a lot of whispering that Gotham Security actually killed most of them, but of course most people didn't care that much because it didn't hurt them personally. So there have probably already been examples of Gar Render sanctioning murder if he thinks it will benefit the city."

"Or his own ambitions," Halladay said.

"You said you discovered something about Mallory Cassady?" Jon asked, not really wanting to know.

"A couple things, actually," Amira answered, and Jon's heart sank more. "First, about her fiancé's death. I have access to police records and data that Miss Cassady doesn't, so my guess about what happened to him is much more educated than what she heard from GS. And as far as I can tell, it wasn't that he died in a random crime and GS avenged his death by killing the perps. The random part was that he accidentally witnessed one of their unauthorized law enforcement actions, when they executed three alleged criminals without legal process."

"How do you know this?"

"Because he reported it to the MPD."

"Why wouldn't he tell Mallory?"

"Maybe he was scared, maybe he didn't want to put her in any danger. But he only kept it secret for less than a day, because it looks like someone from GS was sent to kill him. Then they blamed it on the three dead perps and told her that they killed them in reprisal for his death."

"She said the MPD dragged their heels or something," Jon said. "Seemed like a while before she heard from GS."

"The bodies of the perps weren't found until months later," Amira answered. "They were put into the river, probably through a service hatch in the wall."

"Why didn't the MPD investigate GS and find this out?"

"Like you've already seen," Halladay jumped in, "it's a crapshoot whether the police who get a report are willing to investigate GS, or whether they'll just look the other way. Some of 'em will even doctor reports to help the bastards in a lie like this."

"I just sent the report on that case to your phone," Amira said, looking up from hers. "You can look at it for yourself, but I think you'll see the same thing I did."

"What else about . . . Miss Cassady?" Jon said.

"We think that list she showed you is an assassination list, not a protection list."

"Told you so," Halladay said.

"'Bear' could be a code name for Shinsky," Amira continued, "considering how he looks. And he may need to be knocked off, now that he's been identified by us and almost arrested, because he might talk if we get him. And 'Whoever you can at Dayfall' could easily be instructions for a killer to do the same things they've been doing the other times the sun has come out."

"Did she tell you anything about the guy who picked up the list?" Halladay asked Jon, who thought about it. He hadn't asked Mallory about that when she'd shown him the list, because previously she'd been adamantly against giving up any of her contacts. Plus, he had trusted her that it was a protection list, since he'd believed her to be sincere. Or maybe he'd just wanted her to be. He also realized she could simply be wrong, and misled by the people she was trying to assist.

He thought back through the review of the security tapes from the bar, and remembered that the facial recognition software had only flagged four customers, and none of those had any criminal record beyond traffic violations. He remembered that one of them was obviously a woman, but mistakenly came up under a male name when the software identified her. This made him think of Natalie, the transgender GS agent who'd died in the tunnels and might have exemplified the trend of Special Forces operatives creating a new identity for themselves when they left the service. Then he put two and two together and called up the pictures of the bar customers he had saved on his phone. He swiped through them until he got to the woman who had been identified as a man.

It was the Dayfall Killer, who had been captured on the video and had tried to kill him in the park. Jon was almost sure. She had the same round face and short round figure, but clearly looked like a woman without the mask, with makeup and long dark hair.

"This is why we leave no stone unturned," Jon said emphatically to Halladay and Amira, holding out the phone with the picture on it. His anger was swelling, probably because this was the last nail for any relationship with Mallory, but his excitement was also returning because this was a great development in the case. "I've been carrying this around in my pocket all day." He handed the phone to Amira. "Run the male name that came up for her. . . . She was a man before."

In less than a minute, there was little doubt left about the identity of the Dayfall Killer. The bar customer's name (at least before her transition) was Rogers Sturm. He was a Navy SEAL originally from New York who had been hired by Gotham Security after being discharged from the military, but let go by GS after less than two years. Apparently she'd transitioned while working for GS, because there were a few news stories on transgender websites saying that she claimed discrimination as the cause of her termination, but there were also some quotes from unnamed sources within GS accusing her of being "a loose cannon," "really unhinged," and "sadistic." One person interviewed even alleged that Gar Render himself had found out about some of the things she had done to criminals on the street, and said "he doesn't tolerate that kind of brutality at GS."

"To me," Amira said, "this likely paints a picture of the kind of unstable, violent person who would commit the Dayfall crimes. But what doesn't seem to fit is that she had been fired by GS."

"Maybe she's the kind of person they need now," Jon said. "Desperate times, desperate measures, and all that."

"She has no home address in Manhattan," Amira said.

"'Cause she's living underground in one of those Belows," Halladay said, "like Shinsky was."

"And if so, we can't just send MPD SWAT down there to find

her," Jon said. "We don't know if whoever does might be GS sympathizers and let her go."

"So what now, boss?" Halladay said to Jon, with a sneer. "Now that you seem to be back in the game."

"I was always in the game, Frank," Jon said with pride, which dwindled when he saw their faces. "I just . . . hit a few foul balls." They both smiled, and he felt confident they were still on his team. Whether the Mayor was, however, he was unsure. "We need the evidence that I was brought here to find. So we'll shake down the NYU teachers—at least one of them is bound to be in their condo right now because of the storm and Dayfall coming. But first we'll start at The Office, to confirm that Sturm was Mallory's contact."

"Better take me with you this time," Halladay said. "Or she'll have you thinkin' the Pope is behind all this."

"Don't worry about me—the blinders are off. Amira, while we're gone, do whatever you can to find Shinsky or Sturm. And see if you can find out anything more about the third perp, the pyro, now that we know what was happening there. And send us a map of the underground that's easy to use on our phones, please."

He and Halladay took the nondescript patrol car, even though they could have walked the three blocks to The Office, because Sturm was still out there somewhere and might possibly see them if they were on foot. Obviously knives had been her weapon of choice recently for stealth purposes, but a former Navy SEAL would be good with guns as well, and probably even a sniper rifle. There was also less cover than usual now that the storm had driven so many people indoors, to wait it out until the Dayfall. So Halladay kept his eyes open even while driving, as Jon scanned the rest of the report about Mallory's fiancé. He didn't have to read too much of it to see that Amira was obviously right in her assessment of the situation, and his disappointment with Mallory continued to mix with the newfound excitement at the progress in the case.

Along the way, Halladay asked him why they had to talk to her when they already basically knew that Sturm was the killer to whom she passed the names. Jon didn't respond to the question, but he knew the answer. He wanted to bring some closure to this relationship that had been extremely brief but nonetheless more promising than any he'd had before. And he wanted to find out, if possible, whether Mallory was intentionally deceiving him or just being deceived herself. He was still clinging by a thread to the hope of a relationship, because he had never felt as good as he did in the few times he'd spent with her.

22

They parked in the nearby garage, not wanting to draw attention to themselves by doing so illegally on the street, and made their way to The Office under a couple of umbrellas they'd grabbed at headquarters. Once inside, Mallory caught Jon's eye when they were halfway to the bar, but her initial smile faded when she saw his expression and the big Scottish cop accompanying him. The place was semi-busy, but they found two stools toward the middle and waited for her to approach after she'd finished serving another customer.

"Do you want a drink?" she asked, obviously wondering why they were here and sensing a bad vibe.

Halladay pursed his lips and shook his head no, but Jon said, "I'll take a Whisky Sour this time."

"You really want one?" she said. "Or is that just another metaphor?"

Jon tried not to notice how her ice-blue eyes flashed in lovely contrast with the dark lashes, brows, and wisps of hair on her forehead, and he held out his phone to her with Sturm's picture displayed on it. She reacted initially, but quickly gained her composure.

"What about it?" she said.

"Is this your GS contact, the one you give the names to?"

Jon could already tell that it was.

"I told you I didn't want to give you any more information about this," Mallory said, "because I don't trust the police." She looked at Halladay. "Why is he here?" She was asking Jon, but the older cop answered.

"I'm here to make sure he doesn't end up in the back room with his brain hanging out."

She looked back at Jon, her face flushed, and said, "Was it a mistake for me to give you that list?"

"No," Jon said, "but it was a mistake for you to give it to this person." He pointed at the picture on his phone. "You've gotten a lot of people killed."

"What are you talking about?" she said softly, then looked around a little to make sure no one was eavesdropping.

"Those lists were not people to protect," Jon said as he pointed at the picture, "they were people to murder. This woman is the Dayfall Killer. She's a vicious mercenary, hired by GS to brutally mutilate her victims in order to cause panic in the city. And there are two other killers on the loose, too."

"Gar Render would never do something like that," she objected.

"Gar Render also paid two professors at NYU to falsify research for the same purpose. We're on our way to get the evidence to prove it right now. And what's more, you were fed a bunch of lies about what happened to your boyfriend. We investigated it and found out that Gotham Security wasn't avenging his death—they were the ones who killed him, and then took advantage of your grief to enlist you."

"I don't believe you," she said after a moment, but she put her hands on the bar to steady herself, and her breathing was a bit uneven.

"I didn't want to believe it myself," Jon went on. "I wanted to believe *you*. But there's too much evidence."

"We don't have much time here, Jon," Halladay interjected, but there seemed to be a hint of compassion in his voice.

"Mallory, I need to know," Jon said. "Did you lie to me, or did you just not know this was going on?"

She clenched her jaw and looked at the floor, silent, and some of the customers from along the bar were starting to notice her discomfort. So was the other bartender at the far end of it—Bree was wiping at a glass but was obviously concerned for her boss. And Mallory's father had noticed, too, because he actually dragged his old, half-intoxicated body out of a chair in the corner and approached the two cops with a fist raised in the air.

"You damn goons get away from her," he shouted, waving the fist shakily. "Leave her alone!"

Before Jon could respond, Halladay jumped off the stool and faced down the old man with his gun out, pushing him backward toward the corner with his forearm extended. It was restrained enough that Mallory's dad stayed on his feet until he plopped back in his chair, but violent enough to startle everyone in the bar.

"And stay there," Halladay grunted, gesturing with his gun before he holstered it and headed back to where he'd been sitting.

"Get out," Mallory said, looking up—not loudly, but very seriously. "Get out of my bar."

"Come on, Casanova," Halladay said, grabbing Jon's arm. "Nothing else to do here . . . unless you want to arrest her for aiding and abetting?"

"No," Jon said, a bit stunned, but allowing Halladay to usher him out. "No, I don't."

Outside on the rainy sidewalk Jon was too preoccupied to open his umbrella, so the older cop started assisting him with it, saying as he did, "That went well." Jon jerked the umbrella out of his hands and finished opening it himself, heading down the street in the direction of the garage. The big Scotsman had to hurry to keep up.

"Did you have to do that to her dad?" Jon asked when they were back in the car.

"No," Halladay said. "But I enjoyed it." He laughed, but then the slight hint of compassion returned to his face and voice. "Look, kid, there are thousands of women who look that good on the internet that you can enjoy anytime you want, and they never argue with you." He paused for a moment. "Well, almost that good. But the point is—"

"Shut up, Frank," Jon said. "Just shut the fuck up."

Halladay seemed more impressed than insulted, and his only response was a brief nod.

Jon scanned some articles about Dayfall on his phone for a minute or so, then brought up a new subject.

"Do you think—now that we know the whole chaos thing is fabricated, now that we know there won't be any mass psychosis or atmospheric poison or whatever—do you think that the storm clearing the sky, and the sun coming out at six . . . all that might be wrong, too?"

"Naaah," Halladay said, "that's been said by a lot more than two experts, and people all over."

"Yeah, seems to be the case."

Jon texted Amira, asking her to give him her best guesses for the underground structures that the killers might be operating from. He knew that even a confession by the NYU professors about Render's bribe might not be enough for the Mayor to discredit him before the referendum vote—they would really need to find one or more of the mercenaries and get them to talk. And arresting them tonight would keep them from any additional murders they were presumably planning to commit when the daylight arrived. So sooner or later, they would probably have to brave the underground, where their opponents had some serious home field advantage.

As if on cue, Amira texted him back and included a link to her version of the underground map, designed for him and Halladay to use on their phones if they needed to. He opened it and checked out the area around One Madison, where they were now arriving, and he wasn't surprised to see that GS had constructed access points and passageways underneath both the newer skyscraper where Gareth Render lived and the older one nearby, where he worked, in the Met Life North Tower. He could move back and forth between the buildings without ever coming to the surface and worrying about being gawked at or stopped on the street by curious citizens.

Jon also noticed that there was a Below built under One Madison and another about a block away, and wondered if the killers might be using either of them. But he didn't have more time to think about it, because they arrived at One Madison and parked two floors down in the garage next door. Before Jon exited the underground map on his phone, he noticed that the access point to the passageways was between the garage and the basement of the tower, and not far from where they'd left their car. He was tempted to use the GS key he had in his pocket to see if he could get to Render's condo with it by entering the building that way, and confront the man, but he didn't want to tip his hand that much yet, considering the lack of evidence they had at this point. So they went into the lobby, flashed their badges, and talked tough to the attendant at the main desk, to find out where in the building Gunther and Carter were living.

They found out that the two scholars shared the condo on the twelfth floor (listed under two barely disguised names), that the attendant had seen Gunther leave the lobby recently, and that he thought Carter was still in. So they called her from the desk and she somewhat reluctantly agreed to let them come up. Jon wondered if she knew she could have refused them and forced them to get a warrant, but either way he was relieved when she didn't.

The twelfth floor was nothing compared to the penthouse at the top where Render lived, but it was still very nice, and definitely not something two NYU professors could ever afford on their own. Carter looked nervous as the cops entered, and Halladay immediately gave himself a tour of all the rooms, while Jon stayed with her and tried to greet her nicely and keep her as calm as possible.

"Going somewhere?" the big cop said as he returned to the living room from his tour. "Looks like you just started packing a suitcase in your bedroom." He looked at Jon, who was the primary intended recipient of his comments. "But there's nothing like that in your boyfriend's room. Or maybe he's not your boyfriend, since you're not sharing a bedroom."

"He's my roommate," she said. "Kind of a marriage of convenience." This was another sign of her nervousness—offering more information than was necessary.

"I guess it makes sense," Jon said, "that Render wouldn't give you both a floor in this building. Even what you're doing for him doesn't rate that much cash value."

"I . . ." Carter started, trying to act ignorant.

"We know he's paying you and Gunther to fabricate, or exaggerate, the effects of Dayfall, and that he's paying you with this place."

"And we already talked to Gunther," Halladay lied. "He confessed everything, so you might as well spill."

"But . . . ," Carter stammered, trying to get her bearings, "he just went out for some food. How did you—?"

"We know you told Mayor King's daughter," Jon interrupted, playing good cop. "And how you've had conscience issues with hurting her mom like this. But that's all over now. . . . You can just give us a brief testimony and we'll handle the whole thing, you won't have to worry about it anymore." Now it was Jon's turn to shade the truth. "We can even keep it all under wraps so you can hold on to your jobs at NYU. The Mayor can use the evidence to get Render to drop out of the referendum vote, and no one would have to know about your involvement. I just need permission to film what you say."

Jon actually pulled the phone out to provide some more power of suggestion.

"It's not my job I'm worried about at this point, but my safety," Carter said, "if the Gotham people find out I ratted on Render." She seemed resolved now to being open with the two detectives, but not with anyone else yet. "I've thought this through pretty well, because I almost blew the whistle a few times. 'Cause I do feel bad about it." She paused, making a final decision. "I'd have to be able to leave the city first, before I make a statement. Same for Gunther—he would have to go with me, too. I don't want him to be in danger."

"We could think about that," Jon said, sensing Halladay shift uncomfortably next to him. "But let's talk about what your testimony would be. Did Gar Render himself bribe you, or was it just a lieutenant?"

"No, it was him," she answered. "He invited both of us here to this condo, showed it to us, and made the proposal while we were here. There was one other man with him, though, a skinny guy. . . ."

"Nelson Gant?" Jon said. "His assistant?"

"Yes, that was him. He seemed uncomfortable the whole time."

"Like he didn't want Render to bribe you?"

"Yeah, I guess. He definitely didn't seem to like the idea."

"Hmph," Jon grunted, glancing at Halladay and mulling another idea for bringing down the Gotham Security boss.

23

"Look," Halladay said, moving closer to Carter in a threatening manner, "You might as well make your statement now. We have Gunther's already, and if you don't talk there's no deal for you. . . . It'll all be pinned on you if we prosecute."

"But if you have Gunther's and you're not arresting me," she responded, "then you're not planning to do it. Just let us leave the city first, and then I'll make a statement."

"What makes you think Render can't reach you outside the city?" Halladay asked.

"I don't think he has that much reach, and before he finds out he'll be in the process of being taken down by this stuff, right?"

"Would you reconsider doing it now?" Jon asked, waving Halladay off. "If we promise to keep your part quiet?"

"No. If you want me to go on the record, I have to be out of the city."

Halladay grunted and started closer toward her, but this time Jon put his hand on his partner's shoulder.

"I don't think she's gonna change her mind, Frank," he said. "Let's concentrate on getting her out of the city quickly, so we can get what we need sooner. Besides, I think we may have some bigger fish to fry."

Then he turned back to Carter, and talked to her about how and when they would be able to leave the city. She didn't know exactly when Gunther would be back, but she had to wait for him because they shared a car, which was parked in the same garage as the cops'. Jon told her that he and Halladay would follow them to the bridge or tunnel exit of their choice, to keep them safe on the way. And he would have Amira send a police pass to her phone, so that if the coming of Dayfall was causing a traffic jam at that exit, the two teachers could bypass most of it.

The two cops left the condo and took the elevator back down to the lobby desk. Jon told the attendant that he should notify Nelson Gant, and only Nelson Gant, that they were there and wanted to talk to him about the twelfth floor. Then they hung out in the lobby, not seeing Gunther come in, but not having to wait long for Gant to arrive, with two large Gotham Security bodyguards flanking him.

"Is there a problem, officers?"

"Could I talk with you alone for a minute?" Jon said, gesturing behind him to a spot well away from the bodyguards and the attendant. "Over here?"

"I suppose," Gant answered, after furrowing his brow and thinking for a few moments. He stepped past Halladay and followed Jon to the indicated spot. The big cop and the two bigger bodyguards stood exactly where they were, with Halladay staring at them defiantly in what seemed like a Scottish version of a pissing contest.

"We know everything," Jon said, quietly enough that he couldn't be heard by the others over the background music playing in the lobby. "We know your boss bribed the two professors upstairs to fabricate lies about Dayfall."

"I'm afraid I don't know—"

"Their testimony says you were with Render when he made the offer, so don't deny it. But they also said you seemed uncomfortable with what was going on. So I want to help you out."

"Are you intending," he said after a moment, in which his already sunken cheeks seemed to recede even farther, "to arrest anyone?"

"No," John said, "they have immunity as long as they send me a statement right after they exit the city. And I'm hoping you'll cooperate with us as well, so we can save your friend Render from the added responsibility and stress of running the government here."

"Political machinations are hardly a reason for disqualification from office," Gant said with a surprisingly toothy smile. "If they were, very few people would be able to serve."

"Inciting riots is more than just politics," Jon said, ready now to push all his chips forward. "And we have evidence that Mr. Render has been involved in inciting more than that. . . . We believe that he hired mercenaries to commit murders to increase the danger in the city, including the Dayfall Killer herself."

Jon watched to see if there was any reaction from Gant to the feminine pronoun, but there wasn't, so he continued.

"If you were uncomfortable with some fabricated science being spread around, you certainly wouldn't have gone along with that kind of . . . machination. So you would want to save your longtime friend from whatever corruption his power is causing, and we might be able to do that in a way that won't land him in jail, or get him mobbed in a riot directed toward him. The Mayor just wants him to get out of the race and out of her hair. . . . And with a statement from you we could do that."

Gant looked around a little and seemed to be considering what Jon said. But then he pursed his thin lips and said, "The only statement I want to make is what I told you the first time we talked, officer: Gareth Render doesn't need any help getting elected by the people of this city. Further, I might add that Mayor King doesn't need any help getting voted out. And Mr. Render would never be involved in the kind of illegal, violent practices you are describing."

"But he would pay two experts to lie about Dayfall?" Jon asked, though he already knew his play was going nowhere.

"That seems dubious to me, also," Gant answered, proving it. "Are Carter and Gunther still here?"

Jon didn't know how to respond to that question, so he just remained silent, trying to figure out where to go from there. Then Gant saved him the trouble, when the thin man reached toward his belt.

"Oh, excuse me," he said, "my phone is buzzing." He looked at its screen, then added, "I have to take this call."

Gant walked even further away from the others in the lobby, saying, "Hello?" into his phone and then conducting a brief conversation that Jon could not decipher. When it ended, he walked back toward Jon and then past him to his bodyguards, saying that he apologized but had to attend to an important matter at the Gotham base on the next block over. The bodyguards followed him out of the lobby entrance, and he was gone.

"Well?" Halladay said, as Jon just stared toward the door that Gant had exited through. When Jon didn't answer, he said it again, a little louder.

"I saw a TV show once where a guy had set up dates with two different girls at the same time, and the same place, too," Jon said, still staring at the door. "So when he was with the first one, he pretended to be getting a call on his cell, when he was really making a call to cancel with the second one."

"So? What the hell does that have to do with what's going on here?"

"I think Gant might have just done that to me."

Jon stepped over to the attendant's desk, and then behind it, to look at the security cameras there and to check out the ones showing the parking garage. He called up to Carter and used her help to locate the car that she and Gunther were going to use when they left the city, so he could see it on one of the screens.

"What are you doing?" Halladay asked.

"Remember how Amira said that one of the killers is an arson and explosives guy, and how some cars were blown up during the chaos crimes?"

"Yeah, what about it?"

"Well, that would be a way to get rid of the teachers if they wanted to. It would be too hard to find them driving in the city, or to get to them after they were outside of it. So I'm gonna watch their car until they leave to make sure nobody does anything to it.

You watch the elevators to make sure no one goes up to take them out."

They didn't have to watch very long, because Gunther soon walked into the lobby with a bag in his hand and headed for the elevator. Before he saw the two cops, Halladay started to move toward him, but Jon held him back, saying, "We don't want to spook him."

When Gunther realized they were there and recognized them, Jon said, "Talk to Miss Carter upstairs and see what she has to say."

After hesitating for a moment, Gunther took the advice and went into the elevator.

Less than ten minutes later, both professors came out of the elevator with suitcases under their arms, and merely nodded slightly at the two cops as they headed toward the exit to the parking garage. Jon and Halladay followed them into the garage, and both parties got into their cars and drove out onto the street, the unmarked police car following close behind.

The rain was still coming down hard, but there wasn't as much thunder and lightning anymore, an indication that the storm would be ending soon, as predicted. Some dark gray clouds were actually visible now, the sun having broken the horizon and started climbing in the sky behind the clouds, and the predictions about the black layer dissipating as a result of the storm seemed likely to come true as well. Jon couldn't tell the exact location of the sun yet, but he could definitely tell which direction was east from the side of the sky that was lighter.

His atmospheric observations were interrupted when half a block down the street, Gunther and Carter's car suddenly exploded. The force of the blast shattered the cops' windshield and debris showered down on the top of their car, including several chunks of flesh and blood.

"What the hell?" Halladay shouted, as a wet mass hit the hood in front of him. He raised his arm to the front of his face when some of the blood splashed toward him and mingled with the rain that was already hitting the dashboard.

Jon stared, unmoving, at the burning wreckage of the teachers' car, the same way he had stared at the door when Gant had abruptly left the lobby.

"I watched that car the whole time," he finally said, pointing at it limply and looking over at his partner. "From the moment I told Gant that they were gonna talk. There's no way someone could have planted explosives in it."

"What, you think it was an RPG or something?" the older cop said, looking around at the buildings nearby.

"That's a thought. Didn't look like it, though. . . . Looked like a bomb under the car, the old-fashioned way."

"Maybe it was already there," Halladay offered, "before you started to watch the car."

"What?" Jon said, then thought a moment. "Yeah, that could be it. They knew the professors might talk about the bribe and blow up their plans to take over the city, so they planned to blow *them* up during Dayfall. Makes sense. . . . That would get rid of them and also add to the chaos and sense of danger at the same time. I could see the headlines—'NYU faculty members who predicted apocalypse are killed in it.' I bet Render and Gant could see those headlines in their minds, too."

"But do we know that Gant was actually in on this?" Halladay asked.

"Whattaya mean?"

"Maybe he called Render to tell him, and Render made the move. Maybe Gant doesn't approve of this kinda stuff, like you were guessing when you talked to him."

Jon thought back to his conversation with Gant in the lobby, and had to admit it was possible. He wondered if they should confront Gant again and see how he responded to what had just happened.

"One thing's for sure," Jon said, looking at Halladay. "It's definitely not the Mayor who's behind this. I'm sorry for accusing her, Frank, and for doubting your judgment."

"Don't apologize to me, kid. I'm totally biased against Render, 'cause he'd probably mess up the deal I've got with the cathouse."

Jon stared openmouthed at his partner, as the sirens of first responders became audible for the first time. Then he asked, "Do you think I should apologize to the Mayor?"

"Naaah, I wouldn't talk to her until you have some hard evidence for her. You're not exactly on her good side right now."

John nodded humbly.

"On the other hand," Halladay added, "the same question I asked about Gant applies to Render: Do we even know he was in on it?"

"Who else would Gant have been calling?" Jon said, thinking it through. "Maybe just someone to detonate the bomb."

"Ya know what else is interesting. . . . They didn't blow it in the parking garage, which would have damaged the place where Render lives. They waited until the car got clear of it."

"Yeah, so the perp probably had eyes on."

Jon unconsciously began to drum his fingers on a non-bloody

part of the dash in front of him as it all came together in his mind but then retracted his hand when they hit some of the wet pieces of glass that had come to rest there. "The killers are our only chance at proof now—we need to find one of them."

"Forensics from that might turn up some leads," Halladay offered, pointing at the burning remains of the car.

"That could take days, which we don't have," Jon said. "Let's head back to base."

While Halladay started navigating the traffic jam caused by the explosion to make it the couple of blocks to the garage for the Flatiron, Jon called Amira and told her to comb all the surveillance footage available from the block where it had happened, in the hope that she might get a look at someone who was casing the street, and maybe even using a cell or some other device that could activate a bomb.

"You think he'd be that dumb?" Halladay asked after Jon ended the call. "The chaos killers avoided any cameras during their other attacks."

"Desperate times, desperate measures," Jon said.

Halladay suddenly braked so hard that Jon almost hit the dash.

"What?" Jon said.

"If the bomber did rig that car just now," the big man mused, "this one was sitting in the same garage. And you weren't even watching ours. . . ."

The two cops looked at each other, and then instinctively down at the floor of the car, and then back at each other again. A car door slammed next to them at the curb, making them both jump in their seats, and then chuckle nervously at each other when they realized what had happened. But both seriously thought about getting out and walking the rest of the way to the Flatiron, know-ing that might pose some significant dangers, too. In the end they decided to brave the brief car ride, figuring that they would already be resting in pieces like Gunther and Carter if their car had been rigged, too.

24

Not long after they reached the lab in the Flatiron Building and began watching Amira do her thing, she picked out a possible perp from the street cameras. She found a male figure mostly concealed in an unused doorway that provided a vantage point of the street, just prior to the explosion. She watched the footage of his movements before he situated himself there, and noticed that he might have been subtly scanning the area for a hiding place. She found the best angle to zoom in and lift a shot of his face, which was unremarkable except for a pair of wire-rimmed glasses and a receding hairline.

The facial recognition scan didn't take long. The military records database quickly identified the man as an Army explosives expert named Kevin Witwer. The data trail on him went blank after he left the service three years earlier, which was a classic sign of mercenary activity. There was no record of him ever being in

New York, let alone recently, but fortunately another name popped up as a possible identification by the software. This one was Kevin Williams, who entered the Homeland Security database when he had to show ID to purchase some materials that could possibly be used in the manufacture of EFIs or "slapper detonators." This Kevin had a current address near Times Square.

"Looks like the cameras today wasn't the only time he got sloppy," Halladay said.

"Lucky for us," Jon said. "Compare his address to the underground map, and see if there are any Belows near it."

Amira did, and she found one behind a subway platform in an unused part of the Port Authority station along the Eighth Avenue Blue Line.

"I would guess the main access point for that would be here," she said, pointing at a spot on the screen with one hand, and adjusting her olive-green head scarf with the other. "This is an entrance just beyond the north end of the used portion of the station, so to get to it they would just walk among the commuters and step aside into this hallway. No one would see them when they're opening the door, so I imagine if Williams and the other perps are using that Below, that's how they would get in and out of it."

"Is there another way to that Below?" Jon asked. "One they're not likely to be using as much, or watching as closely?"

"Let me look," Amira said.

"You wanna go there first," Halladay asked, "and not Williams's apartment?"

"Yeah," Jon answered. "This close to the chaos they're trying to cause, I doubt he'd be in his apartment. But he might be getting some bombs ready in that Below."

"Yeah, and if Render is behind all this then it could be rigged with some of those bombs, waiting for us to trigger them. Remember, he knows we have the map to the underground."

"Well, that's a chance we'll just have to take," Jon said, "'cause we need to capture one of the mercs."

He waited for Halladay's objection, and when none came, began to wonder if there was more to the big Scot than just self-pleasure and self-preservation.

"Okay," the older cop said, then returned more true to form: "But you're goin' in first."

"There *is* another way to get to that Below," Amira interrupted, pointing at the map on her computer screen. "One that probably isn't used much, if at all, because the access is through John's Pizza. Which is an interesting place . . ."

"Tell us about it on the way," Jon said, moving toward the exit. "Let's visit the armory to top us off, and get you something, too."

He gestured toward Amira when he said this, knowing they were going to need her help if they happened to get in a firefight with up to three murderous mercenaries, two of whom were ex-military. He didn't relish the thought of her in that situation, but he knew there was no one else they could trust enough to be involved.

"And then we'll get a new car," Jon added as they all made their way through the lab section.

"Why's that?" Amira said, stopping them momentarily.

"The one we had is a big mess from the bombing," Jon explained. "Plus it was parked in the garage with the one that blew up, and we were kinda on pins and needles driving it here."

"Hah," Amira laughed, "big policemen afraid of a little bomber?" Then she added, "We'll take my car."

Once they were headed toward the Times Square area, Amira told them all about John's.

"They say it's the biggest pizzeria in the US," she said, "though you sure wouldn't know it by looking at the outside. But what's really interesting about it is that it's in an old church building, with a stained-glass dome on the ceiling and all. It was built about a hundred years ago by a famous pastor named Simpson, who started a whole denomination. The passageway to the underground probably dated from his time, since a lot of the underground access is from old churches. Many of them were part of the Underground Railroad during slavery, but in this case I think it was immigrants. Simpson took care of the kinds of people who were hated and sometimes in danger because of xenophobia."

"Wow," Halladay said, impressed. "For a towelhead, you sure know a lot about other religions."

Jon winced at his partner's choice of words, but Amira didn't seem to care.

"Well, I'm an *American* towelhead," she said, right in stride, "and I have a friend who happened to grow up in that denomination and teaches at a college here in the city. He tells me a lot about Christian history."

"He?" Halladay said, and Jon winced again, knowing what was coming. "Sounds like the Princess has an admirer." He raised his eyebrows at Jon.

"He definitely likes me," Amira offered, not shying away from the topic at all. "But from what I gather, he can't go any further with it unless I convert to his faith."

"So it's a Romeo and Juliet kinda thing," Halladay said, whistling. "Which didn't end well, by the way, if I remember correctly."

"Is that a possibility?" Jon asked Amira, and when she looked puzzled, he added, "I mean the conversion thing."

"Well, I wouldn't get executed for it here like I might have in Pakistan," she said, "but my parents definitely wouldn't be happy."

"Then don't tell 'em," Halladay said predictably. "Just get some on the side."

"Well, neither of us believe in that," Amira said.

"Not much else to believe in, if ya ask me."

During the rest of the ride, Jon couldn't help but think of his own star-crossed love for Mallory, and was further plagued by the nagging feeling that he had come here to fail in much more than that relationship. The sense of dread was compounded during the latter half of the drive, as he craned his neck to look up at the sky above the buildings and noticed how the thinning clouds had grown an even lighter gray. Since he knew that the apocalyptic Dayfall predictions had been fabricated, he wondered why he would still have this negative emotion inside of him, and figured it was some kind of psychological hangover from before he knew the truth. He hoped the fears about himself were equally unfounded.

The outside of John's Pizza was as inauspicious as Amira had said—its frontage was no more than twenty feet wide and sandwiched between a theater on the right and an apartment building entrance on the left. But after they traversed a narrow hall inside the entrance, Jon saw why Amira was so impressed and fascinated by the restaurant. Beyond a smaller section housing the bar, it opened up into a spacious old church sanctuary with the large painted-glass domed ceiling that she had mentioned, and a few other pairs of ornate windows high up on several of the walls. Covering one whole wall from floor to ceiling, where the church's altar used to be, was a huge sepia-tinged black-and-white mural of Manhattan from the air, which looked like someone might have used oversized pencils or pieces of chalk to draw. There were at least twenty tables on the floor, in the middle of which a stairway wound up to a spacious balcony, where there were about ten more tables.

Many of the tables were occupied, which reminded Jon how accustomed to the endless night the citizens of this city had become. At this early morning hour, most people in the rest of the country would be eating breakfast food rather than pizza, but even dietary schedules here had been changed by the constant darkness. He wondered if they would return to normalcy after the daylight returned.

Halladay, who was much less interested in checking out the unique space than the other two cops, found the manager and got her to lead them downstairs into the ancient basement, where the restaurant's stores were kept. The dark metal door she showed them, however, was obviously a lot newer, and she explained that this access to the subway had been here since the tunnels had been dug, but for a long time had been sealed and inoperable unless someone had the right tools and a reason to open it up. Gotham Security had both, so when the River Rise occurred and GS was securing the underground and adding Belows to it, they'd replaced the old obstruction door with one of their shiny new ones, which could be unlocked by the master key Jon had in his pocket.

He asked if there were any other exits from the basement to the restaurant above, and the manager said there was another stairway on the other end of the basement, which led up to the far side of the ground floor. But there was no external exit on that side of the building, because of the theater jutting up against it.

The cops sent the manager away with their thanks and a warning to be quiet about this, and headed through the door into the subway with trepidation, because they knew they weren't very far from the Below where the mercs might be. They used their own police flashlights they had brought along, instead of the GS ones on a shelf inside the access door, because they were more familiar with them and wanted to approach the Below with as much stealth as possible.

They didn't have to use the flashlights for very long. After they emerged from a small anteroom onto the walkway along the unused subway tunnel, they could see some light from about a hundred yards up the track, on the other side of it. Jon knew the Below was there, from the map on his phone, so he also knew that the light probably meant it was being used by one or more of the perps. He turned off his own flashlight, gestured to the other cops to do the same, and whispered to Halladay that he should cross the track and use the walkway on the other side, so that they wouldn't be bunched up in case they were seen and fired upon. The fact that Williams was an explosives man made Jon think of how easy it would be for the killer to lob a grenade or something else at them, and take them all out in one stroke.

As they continued moving down the tunnel toward the light, Jon began to notice that there was no walkway on the other side of it, so Halladay was walking down along the track itself, hugging the wall on the far side. When they got closer to the light, Jon could tell it was coming from the ceiling of a small platform along the line, which seemed too small for a train stop and was probably used for maintenance. Not all the ceiling lights on the platform were working—just enough of them that he could see, on the far side of it, a closed door similar to the one in the basement of the restaurant. In front of that entrance, about twenty feet away from it and about five feet from the ledge above the tracks, were three large support pillars, equally spaced from one another.

Good cover for our approach, thought Jon, and whispered across the tracks to Halladay, telling him he should use the first one. Then he told Amira to go across the tracks to the middle pillar, but to hang back for a minute first, while he moved along the walkway to the other end of the platform. If someone was watching from the patches of darkness near the Below entrance, he wanted to make sure it was he who was exposed first rather than Amira.

25

No one was watching from the shadows on either side of the platform, but someone did appear from them when the three cops were almost in position behind the pillars. Halladay had climbed up and situated himself behind the pillar on the left, Jon had done the same behind the pillar on the right, and Amira was crossing the tracks toward the one in the middle when they all heard heavy footsteps coming down the stairs at the right side of the platform.

Jon gestured to Amira to get down, and she wisely took another couple of steps forward and crouched in the shadowed area near the platform where the light was blocked by the wall. Jon and Halladay stayed behind the big square pillars so that whoever was coming couldn't see them either, but Jon listened intently to the footsteps and got ready to move if they happened to come toward him. They didn't, but proceeded along the back wall of the platform to the door of the Below, which was in the center of it.

Then Jon risked a glance around the edge of the pillar and saw Shinsky using a key to open the lock on the door, and pull it open. The big killer didn't enter the room, however, but stopped halfway into the doorway when he saw who was inside.

"Sturm?" Shinsky said, obviously puzzled. "Where's Williams? He told me to meet him here."

"He'll be back in a minute." Jon could hear this voice from within the room. "Come on in. And thanks for not using those stupid code names."

Shinsky moved forward into the room cautiously, leaving the door open behind him.

"Really happy to see you," Sturm said menacingly, the whole tone of her voice changing suddenly.

"Aw, come on," Jon heard Shinsky say, and knew intuitively that Sturm had pulled a gun on the big man, even though he couldn't see what was happening in the room.

Jon stepped out from behind his pillar, his own gun drawn, and moved slowly toward the Below across the right side of the platform, knowing that he wasn't visible to the killers because of the angle and the door. Halladay and Amira, who had climbed up from the tracks, also moved out from their pillars toward the door, but they were a lot farther away than Jon because they had to be more careful not to be seen from inside the room.

"Williams isn't coming back, is he?" This from Shinsky, as Jon heard what sounded like the fastening of handcuffs.

"No," Sturm's voice said, "he's throwing a Dayfall party somewhere else."

"Can you please make it quick?" Shinsky said, as Jon moved

closer to the door and heard the sound of something solid being dragged across the floor.

"Now, where would be the fun in that?" Sturm said. "Sit down."

Jon imagined the bowling ball–shaped killer stepping aside to get some tape or rope to tie Shinsky to a chair, and figured this would be as good a time as any for the cops to rush the room. He also thought it might be good if Shinsky was still somewhat mobile when they did, because the big man could possibly become a distraction for Sturm. He wasn't sure about this, but had to make a decision, so he took the leap and gestured with his head to the other two cops behind him that he was making his move and they should back him up.

He was planning to kick the door farther open and assume a firing stance on the right side of the doorway, hoping Sturm might be partially turned away and would surrender, or at least that he could fire before she brought her own gun to bear. He thought that one of his two fellow cops would also have an angle, from behind him, if needed. But he didn't get a chance to do any of that, because before he could put his foot around the bottom corner of the partially open door, a grenade flew out past him and bounced into the middle of the platform.

A second later, Sturm pulled the door shut from inside and slammed it with a loud bang that Jon initially thought was the grenade exploding. When he realized it wasn't, everything seemed to blur into slow motion as he yelled and waved for Halladay and Amira to take cover and watched them rush behind the two pillars they had used before. Because Jon was farther away from that cover and actually had to run *past* the grenade to seek it, he made another split-second choice and decided to forget the pillars and just dive over the edge of the platform, trying to clear it as fast as he could so the shrapnel wouldn't hit any part of his body.

The grenade exploded at the same time he was going over the edge, and after he landed hard on the dirt and metal of the track, he thought he'd been hit because of the pain shooting through various parts of his body. But a quick inspection revealed that it was probably just a result of the impact of his violent fall, and he also realized he had dropped his gun in the panic. He pulled out the second one he had brought and pointed it over the top of the wall, resting his arms on the floor of the platform so only they and the top of his head were exposed.

The platform was darker now, thanks to the explosion, but at least one of the lights on the sides of it was still working. The door of the Below remained closed, and a quick scan of the platform showed it was empty except for the debris from the blast. So Jon relaxed just enough to look to his left and check on the other two cops, who were safe behind their respective pillars. The sides that had been facing the grenade were mangled, but they were obviously load-bearing and solidly built.

"How the hell did he know we were out here?" Jon said to them, but kept his eyes on the door to the Below.

"I don't know," Halladay said, an adrenaline-fueled smile on his face. "Special Forces are special."

Jon saw the door unlock and open slightly, and started firing on it, as close to the opening as he could get. Halladay and Amira joined him, but it became obvious that the bullets hitting the door were stopped by its thick metal, and any that got through the crack weren't hitting anyone inside.

The former soldier managed to throw out two grenades this time before pulling the door completely shut again.

The cops cowered behind their respective shelters, Halladay and Amira both hoping that neither of the grenades landed far enough out to reach behind the pillars. The whole tunnel shook twice as hard this time, and much more smoke filled it after the blast, but Jon could soon see that they were still okay.

He also could see that Sturm had opened the door again after the blasts, and was now running through the debris toward the stairway on the right with an almost superhuman dexterity.

"Hey!" Jon got his fellow cops' attention, gesturing toward the fleeing killer, because they were on the platform and closer to her, while he was still down on the tracks. "Get Sturm. I'll take care of Shinsky."

Halladay and Amira took off after the short woman, not moving nearly as fast as she had been, and Jon pulled his aching body up onto the platform. As he did, he realized that the wound under his chin had opened slightly again, and blood was trickling down and staining his shirt. He touched it with his hand to see how bad it was, then wiped the blood on his pants so that his gun grip wouldn't be slippery. Then he headed across the ruined platform toward the door of the Below, which was hanging open from Sturm's rushed exit. He was hopeful that Shinsky seemed the type who would give him the evidence he needed. He guessed that was probably why Sturm had been told to kill him—to keep him from talking.

Two police to chase the athletic and armed Sturm, and one cop to secure and question the handcuffed Shinsky. . . . It seemed like a reasonable plan. But as Jon rounded the edge of the door to enter the room, Shinsky charged through it like he had done earlier in the day and throughout his football career, only this time his hands were shackled behind his back. But the effect was the same—Jon went sprawling backward to the ground with his gun flying away from him, and the big perp took off across the platform and the tracks, clearly heading in the direction of the exit below John's Pizza.

It took Jon a while to find his gun, which had slid over the edge into the darkness of the train tunnel, and he moved after Shinsky more slowly than usual because of the injuries from his leap over that same ledge. And Jon couldn't shoot him because he needed him intact for questioning. As a result, he wasn't able to catch up to the handcuffed man until they got to the basement of the pizzeria.

After Shinsky stopped to unlock the door down there before entering, giving Jon the last few seconds he needed to close the gap, the big killer instinctively maneuvered behind a row of food stores to keep Jon from having a clear line of fire. And he kept going through the basement, apparently knowing there was a stairway up to the ground floor on that side. Jon was glad he had asked the manager about that, and even happier that he knew there was no external exit on that side of the restaurant. So he simply went up the stairs on the near side, to cut Shinsky off when he tried to cross the main floor. If he had followed him across the length of the basement, the big guy might have gotten out to the street and managed to escape.

But as it was, Jon waved his gun and badge around after he got to the main floor, so that the diners there left hastily through the bar and the front entrance. Then he greeted Shinsky with the gun and a smile when the perp tried to cut back through the restaurant, waved some more to get him to sit down on the floor, and cuffed his ankle to a post at the bottom of the stairwell leading to the balcony.

Now that his prey was finally secure in his custody, Jon looked around to make sure everyone had left the ground floor, and looked up to see that the diners and staff had cleared out of the balcony as well. As he did, the stained glass high up on the magnificent domed ceiling and the overall "churchiness" of the space reminded him of his youth, and the thought entered his mind that maybe the God he had put on the shelf long ago had delivered the evidence he needed to have success in this job, rather than the failure he had feared. But then he realized that he'd better question Shinsky and get that evidence before some crooked police or GS agents showed up in response to the evacuation, and somehow screwed up everything he was trying to do.

"Listen, Shinsky," Jon said as he crouched down closer to the large figure. His instinct told him that "good cop" was a preferable approach with the man, who looked more defeated than defiant at this point. "Your friends at Gotham Security obviously want to kill you, so the only way you can be safe is with us. You need me to help you with that, so I need you to tell me all about their plans right now, so we can stop worse things from happening. And I want you to say it into my phone, so I can give it to the Mayor and she can use it against your boss—you know, the one who gave the order to kill you."

Shinsky kept looking down and didn't answer right away.

"I'll talk on one condition," the big man finally said.

"What?" Jon said. Normally he wouldn't negotiate with criminals, but he was desperate to get what he needed from this one.

"You have to kill me afterwards, before anyone comes."

"Why?"

"I don't want to go to jail. . . . I won't make it without a fix. And I don't want to end up in Sturm's hands again. . . . He's a nutbag who enjoys torturing people. I'd rather die quickly at your hand than slowly at his, or locked up."

"That's a tall order," Jon said.

"It's easy. There's no one here. Shoot me and take the cuffs off. I'm really big, I rushed you. I've killed dozens of people in the last few weeks alone."

"Okay," Jon said, making another quick decision as the sound of a distant siren fell upon his ears. "Fine. I'll kill you."

26

DAYFALL MINUS ZERO

Jon pulled out his phone, turned on the camera, and asked Shinsky who had paid the NYU professors to create panic about Dayfall.

"That was Render," the killer said. "He truly believes that the city will be better off under his control."

"And who hired you and the other mercs to murder people when the sun came out, in order to create more panic?"

"That was Gant. Render didn't know he was doing that."

"How . . . ?" Jon reacted. "Come on. . . . How could Render not have been involved in crimes using GS resources?"

"Render trusts Gant, they've known each other since they were kids. And Gant's the brains of the outfit, he has access to everything."

"So Render wasn't complicit in any of the murders?"

"He wouldn't go to those lengths himself, because he really does care about the safety of the city. But he did create an atmosphere of . . . let's say, pride and prejudice among his underlings—an atmosphere that caused them to believe his power and protection should be promoted at all costs."

Shinsky seemed awfully intelligent for a hired killer, Jon observed, but then remembered the sketchbook they'd found in the Below, and the fact that a meth habit will degrade anyone's life.

"Render's actually said, more than once," the big man continued, "'We must do whatever we can to wrest control.' Gant took that very literally and seriously."

Jon heard a siren again, somewhere outside on the streets. He didn't know whether or not it was headed his way, and he knew most of the police would be positioning themselves to prepare for Dayfall, which was about to happen. But he decided that this was enough from Shinsky, so he called Mayor King.

"Ma'am," he told her, "I have video testimony from one of the killers that Gareth Render paid off the teachers to write that stuff about Dayfall, and that his assistant Nelson Gant engineered the murders and chaos crimes so the city would feel unsafe and vote Render in to take your place."

"And Render told Gant to do this," the Mayor said.

"No, I'm afraid not—not according to my suspect."

"But he must have known about it, right?"

"Maybe, but apparently he wasn't openly complicit. My suspect says Render wasn't prepared to go as far as Gant, and Gant took it further than he would have approved."

"Do you believe this?"

"Yes," Jon said, looking down at Shinsky. "I'd have to say I do. A lot of the facts in the case are swirling in my head right now, so

I need to think it all through. But initially this does seem to fit what I've seen. We've been assuming that if GS people are involved, Render would have to be behind it. . . . But I think this all actually could have been done without his knowledge."

"Well, I'm not inclined to believe it," Rielle King said. "But it's enough for me to work with. Just the scandal of the payoffs alone will disqualify that asshole, not to mention the cloud of all the murders by people from his company. . . ."

She thought for a few moments, and then started thinking out loud again.

"On the other hand," she continued, "this evidence isn't as incriminating as what I'd hoped for. I can definitely use it as a threat to make him give up on the referendum, and probably leave the city. But if he got ahold of the testimony you have, he might be able to pin it all on Gant and keep fighting. . . .

"Send me the video right now," she concluded after another few moments of silent thought. Jon did, and when she got it, she added, "Now erase the video. I don't want it getting around and somehow making Render look better than I want him to look."

"It's erased," Jon said, after fiddling with his phone for a moment.

"Is the suspect who gave the testimony in police custody?"

"No, he's here with me."

"Good. Are you alone?"

"Yes."

"Could you eliminate him and make it look clean?" she asked.

Jon looked down at Shinsky again.

"Yes," Jon said. "In fact, that's what he wants me to do, believe it or not."

"Good. Then do it."

Jon pulled out the gun he had put away after he secured Shinsky, and pointed it at the big man's head. He pulled the trigger twice, and the pounding sound of the shots reverberated through the air from floor to high ceiling of the old church building.

"It's done," Jon said.

"Good boy," Mayor King said on the other end of the line. "Keep playing your cards right and you'll be a very rich man."

"Thank you, Ma'am," Jon said.

"Just clean up that mess."

"Yes, Ma'am," Jon said, and hung up the phone.

He stood still for a few moments, then he looked at the video of Shinsky's testimony, which was still on his phone, and sent it to another cell phone he had before Mayor King had given him this one. Then he looked at Shinsky himself, who was alive and well on the floor, because Jon had fired just above his shoulder.

"You promised," said the big man, clearly disappointed that he wasn't dead.

"I did," Jon said, "but you know what they say about promises."

Looking around and noticing that no law enforcement or GS agents had arrived yet, Jon called Halladay to find out what had happened with their pursuit of Sturm.

"We lost him," Halladay said. "Now we just got back to the Below, and are checking it out."

"What's in there?" Jon asked.

"A lot of explosives," Halladay answered, but he must have had his phone on speaker, because Jon then heard Amira say, "But there's even more missing."

"You think Williams took them somewhere?" Jon said, remembering Sturm's comment about the bomber "partying" in another part of the city.

"Are you talking about the stuff in that room?" Shinsky spoke up from the floor, and Jon just looked at him without answering. "I know where he's taking it." Jon looked at him some more. "He's gonna put it below the Flatiron Building—the plan was to kill a few birds with one stone when the sun comes out. It'll cause more panic than ever when police headquarters goes up, and it'll thin out the force so that GS will have to secure the city. It might even get rid of the Mayor herself, if she's there at the time."

"Did you hear that?" Jon said into the phone.

"Yeah," said Halladay, then Amira chimed in again. "There are some underground maps here with some markings that support what he's saying."

"Are they in that room now?" Shinsky asked.

"Yeah, why?" Jon responded.

"They need to get out right now. Williams and Sturm rigged it to blow at Dayfall, and Sturm set the timer while I was in there. The sick bastard wanted me to sit there for a while knowing I was gonna buy it, and the blast would be the first chaos crime of the day, killing a bunch of people in the subway and the streets above."

"Halladay, Amira," Jon said. "You need to get out. . . . Shinsky says it's rigged to blow, on a timer."

"I found it." Jon heard Amira's voice in the background on Halladay's phone, and he could almost feel the pall that fell on both his partners.

"The count is down to a few minutes," Amira said. "The good news is I know how to diffuse the detonators; the bad news is I doubt we can get all of them in time. And it only takes one of them to set all this off—that's why they use so many."

"Stop talking and get out of there, for God's sake!" Jon said, but he didn't sense that either of them was moving.

"The thing is," Amira said, "there's a lot of people above us who will probably be killed or wounded if we don't stop this. And it would take both of us to even have a chance to do it in time."

Now Jon's two partners had to make a life-or-death decision. He could almost see them looking at each other. He thought of telling them to leave again, that they could still get far enough away, but then he held his tongue.

"How do we do it?" Halladay asked Amira.

"Just take the two green wires out of the back of each of the detonators," she said. "But they have to be unscrewed—that's what takes a while."

Jon listened to them moving around in the room, visualizing their panicked fingers trying to turn thin casings as fast as they could in the cramped little space, and feeling a sense of utterly helpless dread.

"Takes a while, for sure," Halladay grunted as he continued the frantic work. "You're not kidding. . . ."

"What's the timer say?" Jon finally blurted out, unable to hold it in anymore.

"Don't wanna take the time to look at it," Amira responded through heavy breathing. "I did the ones close to it first, and moved away. I'll check if I can."

Moments that seemed like minutes passed, until Amira finally spoke again.

"It's at thirty-nine seconds," she said.

"Can you get all of them in time?" Jon asked, and then pictured them looking around in desperation.

"Not even close," Halladay said.

"Get the hell out of there!" Jon screamed.

It sounded to Jon like they'd started running—he couldn't tell for sure—but right after that it sounded like a geyser had sprung up from hell itself, and the line went dead.

Even though the restaurant was far away from the blast, the walls and floor were jarred violently enough to throw glasses and dishes off some of the tables.

Jon covered himself briefly, afraid the roof might fall in. When it didn't, he let loose with a string of profanities and looked up again at the stained-glass ceiling, this time with anger. He vowed to put that God back on the shelf, or better yet, cast him into a pit.

27

Jon's vengeful thoughts soon transitioned from a God he had never seen to the real live people who were behind the various crimes he had now uncovered. Politics didn't concern him enough to be confused or distracted by their motives, but he did care about justice, and he knew that it was due for Gant and the two remaining mercenaries. He also knew that Render and Mayor King should face the consequences of their actions. And he was worried about what Williams was apparently doing under the Flatiron Building, mostly because of the innocent people in that area, and the fact that Mallory was one of them.

He wasn't sure what, but he needed to do something quickly.

He didn't have a car, because Amira had driven them and the keys were with her when the Below blew up. So he went with a gut feeling again, and called Ari Hegde as he got Shinsky up and ready to move outside. Jon knew that Hegde and Dixon were sympathetic to GS, but was counting on his guess that, like much of the MPD, they were more loyal to Render than to Gant. He also knew that whatever their politics might be, cops were usually devoted to other police, and the two Chaos Crimes officers wouldn't want their friends at the Flatiron endangered.

"We're on our way right now," Hegde said when Jon asked him if he was near the blast. "Almost there."

"I'll be outside John's Pizza on West Forty-Fourth," Jon said. "I have one of the killers in custody, and a lot of info you'll want to know."

When Hegde said they would come to him, Jon hung up and directed Shinsky toward the front entrance of the restaurant and out onto the street. He wanted to be outside when the two cops arrived, so at least there would be other people around if his gut feeling was wrong and things went south.

The first thing he noticed when he stepped outside was the emerging daylight. The storm was over, and it had obviously done what was predicted by clearing out most of the remaining "black smoke clouds," as they had been called. There was still a thin layer of gray clouds on the east side of the sky, but the sun was shining through them much like it would normally before the nuclear night had fallen. Since it had just risen and was near the horizon, however, the many tall buildings of Manhattan blocked it from hitting most of the streets directly. Seeing that, Jon remembered that the NYU professors had said it would likely be an hour or more after sunrise before the Dayfall would cause the apocalyptic effects they had predicted.

Even though Jon knew they had been paid to say all that, he wondered now if they had been right about the effects, but wrong about the timing, and whether something unusual *was* going on. One reason was Shinsky's reaction to the daylight, even though most of it was still blocked by the buildings. The big criminal was rolling his head and pressing his eyes tightly together, and his body jerked as he tried unsuccessfully to lift his manacled hands up from his back to shield himself from the light. At first Jon thought this might be the kind of effect the NYU professors had predicted, but he himself didn't feel it, and he realized that it could simply be a natural response for someone who had lived for so long without any sunlight. This interpretation was confirmed as Shinsky soon began to adjust to the partial daylight, and calmed down considerably.

Another reason for Jon's initial concerns about a possible "Dayfall Effect," however, was the flurry of activity he saw on the street around him. Crowds of people and cars were moving in nervous waves away from where the explosion had occurred, while cops and emergency workers were trying to get to it. But although the clamor of sirens and panicked voices was certainly chaotic, it wasn't necessarily apocalyptic. Jon realized that this was probably what would happen anytime there was a huge explosion on a street in Manhattan, and he remembered that the three killers had done this and much more to cause the mayhem at the earlier times when the sun had come out.

So Jon concluded that the daylight itself probably wasn't causing anything unusual, at least not yet, and he turned his thoughts to what he would do if it didn't go well when Hegde and Dixon arrived. He figured he could run back into John's Pizza and the underground, since they probably didn't know about the access point there, or how to navigate the tunnels. He looked at the map of the underground on his phone to see where he could go down there to elude any pursuers, and he reloaded his gun in case he had to slow them down or stop them.

The two cops from the Chaos Crimes division soon arrived, with several other police cars in tow. They all parked on the street outside the restaurant, but Hegde and Dixon parked closest to him, and were the only ones that approached him when they got out of the car. The other officers either stayed in theirs, or stepped out among the migrating crowds in order to be available to assist them, or direct them out of the way of emergency vehicles that were passing on their way to the scene of the explosion.

Jon and the handcuffed Shinsky met Hegde and Dixon about halfway to their car.

"Who's this?" Hegde asked, gesturing to the big hairy man.

"He's one of your Chaos Crimes perps," Jon said. "Congratulations for apprehending him." This was the bone he was throwing out in the hope that it would induce the two cops to help him out. "We need to take him to the Flatiron now, not just to book him but also to protect him from some very powerful people who want him dead."

"We don't want anything to do with that," Hegde responded, looking at his partner.

"Nothing," Dixon said, shaking her head.

"Okay, listen," Jon said quickly, going to Plan B. "There's another reason we have to go to the Flatiron right now. Another of your perps is still on the loose, the one responsible for the arson during the daylight hours, and I have it on good intel that he's laying a huge amount of explosives right under our headquarters." This was an appeal to whatever altruism and cop loyalty Jon hoped they still had in them. "If we don't stop it, this will be the worst chaos crime yet, by far."

This approach seemed to work better, as the two officers looked meaningfully at each other and pulled one another back closer to their car to confer. As they did, Jon could hear an APB being broadcast over their car radio and whatever portable ones they were wearing. He couldn't make out most of the words because of the noise on the street, but he could have sworn he heard his name spoken more than once. Maybe he was just inferring it, however, from the fact that Hegde and Dixon glanced back at him repeatedly as they listened, and the bad feeling he got from their facial expressions.

When the APB ended, they rested their hands on the guns at their waists and approached Jon and Shinsky cautiously, stopping at a safer distance this time.

"That was from the Mayor's office, by way of the Commissioner," Hegde said, looking hard at Jon. "Seems that *you* are the prime suspect in the Dayfall murders now, and what's worse you just blew up two fellow cops. Amira Naseem and Frank Halladay are both dead, and according to reports you were in the room with them just before they died, and were even talking to them on the phone when they bought it. What kind of sick—"

"Total bullshit," said Jon, in shock despite the fact that he should have seen this coming. He looked at Shinsky, who was the only witness to the truth of what happened.

"If you have something to say, you better say it." This was from the normally laconic Dixon, adding to Jon's surprise. "You're pegged as a cop killer, so as soon as someone in uniform recognizes you, you're a dead man."

She looked around at the various officers in the vicinity, none of whom were looking their way. Yet.

"I'm being framed by the Mayor," Jon said. "Shinsky can confirm it." He looked sideways and up at the big man, who nodded his head briskly. "Look, you guys can believe it about her, can't you? After all, you're GS sympathizers, right?"

This time Hegde spoke up.

"The APB also said that all GS agents have been directed to look for you and exercise extreme prejudice against you."

Jon's heart sank, but then the Indian man added, "Listen, man, I don't believe everything I hear, especially when it stacks up so nicely, but I'm gonna have to take your gun."

Hoping that the two cops might be objective enough to escort him and Shinsky to the Flatiron, or at least check into all of this more, he reluctantly handed his gun over to Hegde.

And then he caught the eye of a uniformed cop across the street who was looking right at him, and then down at his cell phone. The Blue Shirt gestured to a few of his friends spread across the street, and they all started trotting purposefully in his direction, hands on their guns.

"Oh, shit," Jon muttered, backing away slightly, and then one or two of the approaching cops drew their weapons. Hegde and Dixon turned away from Jon and Shinsky and spread their hands to slow the others down, but the guns kept coming up and out, so Jon backed up more and thought hard about whether he could make it back into the restaurant without getting shot in the back.

Salvation came from the unlikeliest of places, as Shinsky suddenly decided to fulfill his own death wish. The addict/assassin screamed primally at the top of his lungs and barreled ahead into the middle of Hegde, Dixon, and the other oncoming cops. His wild charge effectively distracted them all for a few long moments, in which they riddled him with a hail of bullets while being careful not to shoot one another. In the time it took for his large lifeless body to finally crash down onto the asphalt, Jon had already disappeared inside the restaurant and sent up a quick prayer of thanks to the suicidal criminal.

Jon dashed down the stairs before any pursuers had even entered the pizzeria, used the key to get through the door in the basement, and made sure it was locked when he was on the other side. He was assuming that none of the cops pursuing him would have access to the underground, but just to make sure, he headed along the tunnel in the opposite direction from the Below where the explosion had taken place and found a dark spot to wait. He turned off his flashlight and watched to see if anyone came from the direction of the door, or from the ruined tunnel beyond it.

No one did, so Jon leaned back against a wall and thought for a moment. Then he pulled out the phone the Mayor had given him, and tried to call Hegde again. But the phone wouldn't connect this time. He tried to call 911 and some numbers he knew outside of the city, but none of them worked. Finally, he saw the icon for Mayor King on the main screen and tapped that.

"Despite your best efforts," he said when she answered the call, "I'm alive and well, and I *will* come to get you."

"You shouldn't have called those two cops and told them the suspect was still alive," she said. "At least not on a device I control. But I was hoping you'd reach out to me. . . . I feel you deserve to know what's happened since you did do the job I brought you here to do. You solved the case and gave me what I needed to get Render out of the race. Thank you."

"So why does everyone want to kill me now?" Jon asked, though he could guess the answer.

"I confronted Render with the taped confession of the killer, and he agreed to back out of the referendum vote tomorrow, in exchange for secrecy about his involvement. Even though he wasn't actually behind the murders, he would still be implicated in the public opinion because of his participation in the fraud. Render also demanded that Gant be spared any exposure. . . . He's appalled at what his lieutenant did, but the man is a lifelong friend and Render wants him to be able to leave the city without prosecution."

"And I know about the crimes both of them have committed," Jon said, "not to mention yours in telling me to kill Shinsky. So you all need me out of the way, and it's extra convenient for you to pin all the murders on me."

"It's nothing personal, Jon. You're simply being sacrificed for the greater good. Isn't that what you came here for . . . to make this city a better place?"

"What happened to Render's commitment to protecting life in the city?"

"His love for his company and for Gant is greater than your one life, I'm afraid."

"Not to mention his love for himself," Jon said. "And what about *your* gratefulness to me, for what I've done?"

"I'm afraid my love for the city outweighs that consideration."

"And yourself," he responded angrily.

"Why don't you just turn yourself in, Jon?" the Mayor said

calmly. "If you don't, we'll have to find out who your girlfriend is, and make her an accomplice in your crimes. Which won't be hard."

Jon winced at the mention of Mallory, but was glad that King didn't know her name yet. And the plan he was leaning toward began solidifying further in his mind.

"Fuck you," he said.

"Okay, have it your way." The Mayor sighed. "With all of the MPD and GS wanting your blood, you'd better not show your face on the surface."

"That's why you left my phone on," Jon said, looking down at it and realizing this for the first time. "And were hoping I'd call you. So you can track me."

"Smart boy. Well, I have to write a speech to give in an hour, when Render and I will be making a joint announcement about his withdrawal, and about how all the scary theories about Dayfall were fabricated. Everyone will see that their fears were unfounded and the daylight presents no danger to the city, and they'll all know that I can keep them safe as their Mayor for a long time. Thank God there's no term limit anymore."

"There's always a limit," Jon said, and hung up the phone.

He frantically studied the map of the underground for a few more moments, memorizing selective parts of it as well as he possibly could in a short amount of time. Then he dropped the phone on the cement below him and stomped on it violently until it was in pieces.

28

The most self-preserving option Jon had at this point was to use the underground key to try and get out of the city somehow, find some federal agents and leverage them in an attempt to get protection while he worked with them to bring down the Mayor and Render.

The problem was that the pyro killer named Williams had taken enough explosives out of the Below to blow up the whole Flatiron District. That meant a lot of cops and other civil servants would die, and even though he didn't know most of them, he had taken vows to do everything in his power to protect them. He thought about what Halladay and Amira had done, how they had willingly sacrificed themselves for a lot of people they didn't know. And he thought about the likely danger to Mallory, who was working in that area, and how great it would be to have the chance to get to know her better.

With all that in mind, the decision was not really that hard, and then it was just a question of how to get to the Flatiron. He didn't want to head directly south in the tunnels under Broadway, because some of the lines were still in use, and there would be too many people and police and GS agents along that route. They all knew where he was right now, because of the call on the Mayor's phone, so they would expect him to travel that route and "come to get her" as he had promised. So he decided to travel east along the 7 line, which was unused because its tunnel to Queens under the East River had flooded in the River Rise. When he reached the maze of tubes below Grand Central Station, he could switch to other unused tracks like the 4 or 5 lines, which also led down to the Flatiron District. From what he had been able to tell from studying the underground map, this plan would take him fifteen or twenty minutes out of his way, but would avoid the more significant dangers of the direct route.

Thankfully he was able to find his way to the unused tunnel of the 7 line without going back up to the surface. He had seen the route on the map twice, once when he was waiting for the other cops in front of John's Pizza, and the other when he'd studied it before destroying the phone. And he was even more grateful that there was no one in the stairs and hallways leading to that tunnel, or inside of it when he got there. So he jogged alongside the tracks heading toward Grand Central, shining the flashlight periodically in front of him to make sure there were no major obstructions. He didn't want to use it too much, because if there happened to be someone ahead of him they might see it. Police and GS employees would be suspicious of any activity they noticed in the underground, because that was his last known location.

The jogging reduced his travel time to the Grand Central area by about half, and in less than ten minutes he started to see some light up ahead. He hugged the side of the tunnel as he approached it, and then peered through a small bright window in a door that was a part of the wall at the end of the tunnel, which had been erected to seal it now that it was in disuse. There was a train concourse on the other side, populated by commuters and a few Gotham Security uniforms standing guard at several places in it.

Jon knew the GS presence was typical; the company had taken over subway security from the Transit Authority after the flagger—that was one of the reasons they were able to remake the subterranean world for their own use. But he wondered if there might be a greater proliferation of such guards right now because of him. Or maybe it was because of Dayfall, since the commuter crowds were light and didn't seem to warrant that much security.

Regardless of the reason, that obviously wasn't the way for him to go, so he doubled back slightly into the dark tunnel and found a door on the right side with stairs leading downward. He knew the subways farther below the station were more likely to be empty, because of flooding and the fact that a lot of ongoing construction had to be abandoned when the River Rise occurred. Sure enough, there was a vacant platform two levels down the stairs, and he was soon able to find a tunnel that ran south, confirmed by an old sign he located with his flashlight.

Jon picked a pathway in the middle of the two sets of tracks that seemed smooth ahead of him, as far as the light could reveal, and started jogging along it. He ran in darkness as much as possible, but the fourth time that he turned the flashlight back on, he immediately sensed something wasn't quite right in the darkness ahead. He didn't sense it quickly enough to stop jogging in time, however, and soon found himself stepping into the air, flailing both his legs and arms, and free-falling for what seemed like an eternity.

In seeming slow motion, he waited for the inevitable collision with the rock floor below to break all the bones in his legs, snap his spine, and finally burst his head like a ripe fruit when his broken body jerked it forward to the ground.

Jon got lucky again. His legs hit the surface of a body of water instead, and his feet and knees were slowed enough by it to be uninjured when they touched the submerged floor about five feet below. The shock of striking anything when he expected certain death was enough to take the wind out of him, and he almost lost consciousness, but he was able to recover enough to push his head back up above the surface. He also managed to get his feet under him enough that he could stand, with his head and the top of his shoulders now out of the water.

What he couldn't do was see anything. The flashlight had flown from his hand during the drop, and it must not have fallen close to him because sweeping his arms around him in the water didn't help him find it. So he just stood still where he was for a few moments, as a feeling of fear caused by the total and unbreakable darkness started to come over him. He knew he was not really in danger at this point, however, so he forced the irrational terror out of his mind, and tried to think about what to do now.

His fall probably had been a good thirty feet, judging by the length of it and his impact on the water, so he must have dropped off the edge of an unfinished tunnel into a larger cavern—maybe one that had been dug for two levels of tunnels and tracks—and was now on the ground floor. That meant the way he wanted to go would be in the opposite direction of the mouth of the tunnel he had fallen from. But in the pitch black he couldn't tell which direction that was, so he moved slowly in the one he was facing, with his hand outstretched in front of him, and kept moving until it hit something.

What it hit, after about twenty feet, was an iron wall, with an uneven surface that had deep recesses every few feet, with metal objects half-protruding from them. Jon felt one of those objects, and it reminded him of a thick flying saucer with a ring around it that narrowed as it proceeded outward. He moved back and forth along the surface of the wall and soon discovered it was not a wall at all, because it ended on both sides and was only about as wide as a subway tunnel. That seemingly unconscious comparison, and the fact that his feet could feel the tracks running under it, led Jon to figure out that it was the front of a huge boring machine that had been used to dig the tunnels, and was left down here in these watery graveyards after the flooding.

A few minutes of further consideration gave Jon a sense of direction. If what he was facing was the front of the machine, then behind him would be either a rock wall meant for boring or a tunnel already bored. Behind and above him would be the tunnel he had fallen from, and ahead of him would be the way south. He could either make his way along the tracks and through the water in that direction, or hopefully find a ladder and ascend to the level above at the other end of the cavern, to continue moving that way. The second option would be better, he realized, because he couldn't be sure that the lower level tunnels would go through, even if this end of them had been dug already. Besides, he didn't want to be in this disgusting water for too long.

He couldn't do anything about that problem yet, so he simply pulled his way around the edge of the boring machine and pushed himself along its side. He wondered how long it would take him to feel his way to the other end of the cavern, and find a way up to the next level, and he began worrying that all this would be for nothing if he didn't reach the Flatiron in time to stop the detonation of the bombs.

While he was still moving along the side of the massive "earthworm," he heard a distant rumble ahead of him and caught some weak glimmers of light entering the cavern. As the sound grew louder, it seemed familiar to him, and he soon remembered it as the motor of one of the little boats that Shinsky had used to escape in the flooded tunnel the day before.

Jon felt the side of the big dead tool for a way to climb up to the top of it, and soon found a place that worked for him. By the time he was secure in a spot high up on the machinery, the headlight from the dinghy was shining brightly from a tunnel up ahead and illuminating much of the cavern. As Jon had imagined, it was very large and had four big open circles at both ends, two on top of the other two, where the trains would come into this bi-level station. Yellow tarp lined the sides of the whole upper level, and other abandoned machinery could be seen poking out of the water on the bottom floor.

When the light came through the tunnel mouth into the cavern, Jon could see that there was only one dinghy, with only one driver in a GS uniform. Which was a relief, because it meant that this was merely a random patrol rather than a posse sent here specifically for him. Feeling confident, Jon readied himself to jump onto the little boat and take it from the GS agent.

But the dinghy driver didn't come all the way to the far end of the cavern where Jon and the boring machine were. He slowed and stopped the motor next to a medium-sized crane that had been abandoned in the middle of the bottom level, and stepped up on the part of the cab that wasn't under the water. The GS man started urinating off the side of the roof into the water, and as he did he spoke into his radio, saying that he had reached the end of his loop and would be heading back.

Jon was now stuck in his hiding place, far from the dinghy and with no way to reach it before the man finished and drove it out the other way. Not knowing what else to do, he said, "Hey!" really loudly and ducked back down to where he couldn't be seen.

He heard the GS agent call for backup and start the dinghy's motor again, and then prepared himself as it started moving toward him.

29

Jon hoped the dinghy would pass on the other side of the boring machine from the one he was clinging to. He got his wish, and he was able to stay undetected until he heard it move beyond his position.

He pushed himself up and over the top of the big cylinder, hoping his foot wouldn't get caught in the array of machinery up there, and saw that the man was facing the other way, holding his flashlight in front of him and scanning the water and tunnel mouths in that direction. Apparently it hadn't even occurred to him that someone might be on top of the big machine, so Jon had the few seconds he needed to launch himself toward the man before he could figure out what was happening and pull his gun.

Jon wanted to hit him with his whole body, but missed slightly, so he had to grab him and pull him down. The momentum spilled both of them off the side of the dinghy, which kept purring slowly along its path as the two men thrashed about in the water. The GS agent must have gotten more of the rancid liquid in his mouth because of his surprise, so fortunately for Jon he had to surface quicker and gasp for air, and even more opportunely, he happened to surface right next to the side of the big machine. Jon simply stood up beside him, and while the man was coughing out water, grabbed his head and slammed it with full force into the iron casing. The man immediately stopped moving and slumped face-first into the water.

Jon wasn't sure whether the GS agent was dead or just unconscious, but didn't have time to find out. He wedged the man's arm in between some of the nearby tubing on the side of the boring machine, so he wouldn't drown if he was still alive. Then Jon made for the dinghy—he could tell by the sound that it had motored over to the side wall of the cavern and was stuck against it. As he did, he heard two more similar engine sounds deep in one of the two tunnels to his left, coming from the north, and could see their lights in the distance.

He climbed into the little boat and pointed it toward the other end of the cavern, turning the throttle up as high as he could while still being able to control it. By the time he reached the other end of the big chamber, he had pretty much figured out how to drive it at full speed, as the other two GS dinghies streaked out of the tunnel and into the cavern.

As Jon had hoped, one of them stopped so the driver could tend to his unconscious comrade, but the other dinghy continued in his direction. Jon fired his ride into one of the two big holes on the south end, driving it in the very center of the tunnel for a few moments until he was confident he could keep it going straight, and turned off all the lights, both front and rear, so his pursuer wouldn't have a target to shoot at.

The same bizarre, fearful feeling caused by total darkness hit him, but even worse now because he was moving at a high speed and could smash into a wall on either side if he wasn't careful. He also realized, too late now, that there could be some kind of abandoned equipment, like another boring machine, blocking the middle of the tunnel somewhere up ahead, which could abruptly end his trip. But he was banking on the fact that the first GS agent had come through this tunnel himself, and had been moving at a pretty high speed.

By the time the pursuing craft was in the tunnel behind him and shining its headlight in his direction, Jon could see that he had arrived in another cavern, about half the size of the one he'd just left, except this one had no tunnels at the south end—just a big wall covered in yellow tarp. It made sense to him now that these structures were dug for the East Side Access, which he had seen on the underground map. That system had been meant to stretch north to Queens, so this was the southernmost tip of it, and this cavern was probably the maintenance space where the trains would be laid up and worked on.

As Jon proceeded into the cavern, he moved the dinghy to the left so the pursuer's headlight wouldn't be hitting him anymore, and he soon discovered another tunnel veering off into the wall on that side, smaller than the other ones but big enough that he could navigate it with the dinghy. He turned his front light back on to make sure it wasn't sealed up ahead, which it wasn't, and he gunned the engine to put distance between him and the other boat, in the hope that its driver wouldn't realize right away where he'd gone.

Not too far into this smaller tunnel, he found a platform with stairs and a freight elevator leading up, and he was able to turn off the dinghy's motor and listen to see if the other one had entered it. Not hearing anything, Jon headed up the stairs, not wanting to test the elevator or possibly get trapped in it if someone was at the other end.

The long stairway ended at a concourse in the south end of Grand Central Station, and Jon looked at it through a small window in the door. There were fewer people here, and no Gotham Security guards to be seen, at least in this particular spot. The signs said that the entrance to the platform for the 6 line was just across the concourse, so that meant the unused 4 and 5 were somewhere on this side of it.

He checked through the window one more time to make sure he couldn't see any security personnel, and then stepped out of the door and moved along the wall to the right, scanning for any possible access to the old unused lines. Now that he was visible to the few commuters who were in the concourse, he became conscious of how wet, dirty, and smelly he was, and how much his body ached from jogging, climbing, and fighting—not to mention all the nervous tension. The dirt and smell actually came in handy once along the way, however, when he saw a GS uniform coming toward him and he joined a couple homeless men next to a shoeshine stand, quickly sitting down in the midst of their rags and bags. He lowered his head, not just to conceal his face but also to hide the blood that had dripped on his shirt earlier from the bottom of his chin.

The guard walked by without noticing him.

No one else noticed him, either, before he was able to find a roped-off, disabled escalator with the sign above it removed, and head down it. There were a few lights hanging at broad intervals in the tunnel at the bottom of it, enough for him to find the catwalk on the far right side of the tracks, but not enough for him to be seen as he started walking south on it. The catwalk was perfect, because there would likely be no obstruction to collide with on the darkest parts of it, and the far right side was perfect, too, because that's where the access to the Flatiron Building would be.

As his eyes adjusted and he found nothing to stumble on in his path, Jon started to jog again, reflecting bitterly on how royally he had been shafted by Render and the Mayor. Then he thought about Amira and Halladay and Mallory and started to jog faster. In less than ten minutes he passed the old platforms of the Thirty-Third Street Station, and in another ten, having slowed to a walk for a while to catch his breath, he went by the Twenty-Eighth.

If he remembered correctly, the Flatiron Building and Madison Square Park would be coming up on his right soon, before he got to the next station, so he started looking for the access point he had seen on the map. He had passed several others along the way, which probably led to the basements of other buildings on Broadway or Madison Avenue, and he was assuming that the one he wanted would look the same. There was usually a small tunnel, like a hallway, that had been dug by GS engineers and ran perpendicular from the main subway, with the access door requiring a key at the end of it. The length of those passageways depended on how far they needed to go to reach the various buildings to which they wanted access.

Before long Jon found the corridor he wanted, or at least he was pretty sure it was the one, and turned into it. The already limited light from the tunnel outside only lasted about a hundred feet into the smaller one, and soon he had to feel his way along the wall on one side with his right hand, the other held out in front of him. It was only about another hundred feet until his left hand hit the metal of one of the GS access doors, and after feeling his way to the lock, he used the key to open it.

On the other side of the door was more dim light and another abandoned subway tunnel, this one running almost parallel but slightly diagonal to the 4 line he had traveled along to get here. He guessed this was one of the lines that ran under Broadway from Times Square, which was the more direct route he had decided against earlier. If he was right, this one should pass right next to the basement of the Flatiron Building, which itself was on Broadway. But he wasn't sure which direction he should go. To the left, which was presumably south, he couldn't see anything but more tunnel and then darkness after that, but to the right he could tell it opened up into a larger space, probably a station platform. Since the Twenty-Third Street Station was the only one in this area, and it was right next to the Flatiron Building, he took a right and headed for the open space.

As he did, he heard a train traveling through another parallel tunnel to his left and stopping up ahead of him, so now he knew that some of the tracks on this line were still being used.

When he got to the platform, he saw tile mosaics reading 23 at the top borders of the walls on the platform, and a similar tablet lower down spelling out 23RD STREET STATION. He also noticed that there was a seemingly random collection of various kinds of hats painted on some of the tiles, and wondered what was up with that. But as he made his way deeper into the station, he was focusing on more important things, like the commuters who could be boarding and debarking from the trains on the two platforms that were in use on the other side. A makeshift wall had been erected between them and the unused platform he was on, but there were enough well-spaced doors in it that he felt a pang of fear that a security guard might come through one of them and shoot or arrest him before he could find Williams.

That feeling was only momentary, though, because what Jon now saw up ahead on the abandoned track made him realize that he wasn't very far from the explosives expert.

A small utility pickup truck with GS markings was parked next to the platform facing south, equipped with an extra set of flanged steel wheels that allowed it to travel on the tracks. Jon quickly figured out where it had come from, because in its rear bed was a collection of the cube-shaped explosive devices that had been taken from the Below near Times Square.

Jon peered over the back gate at the group of bombs in the bed, and saw that on top of them was a detonator timing apparatus with a green light shining on it, but no minutes or seconds activated yet. He noticed that Williams had stretched two sets of colored wires over the side and onto the platform, where another pair of bombs sat side by side, with green lights lit on them as well. Then the wires stretched farther to an open GS door on the right side of the platform, where there was another pair of bombs—and so on, through the doorway and into the dark hallway on the other side of it. Jon peered down it and could see the pairs of green lights stretching for about thirty feet until they turned a corner and disappeared out of sight.

He turned back to the truck bed and thought about messing with the timing apparatus, but realized that Williams clearly knew what he was doing, and wouldn't leave any way to disconnect the chain of bombs without setting them off, or at least alerting him. The former soldier had obviously laid them in such a way that they could not be tampered with, and planned to start the countdown when the other end of the chain was finished.

Jon was pretty sure where that would be, so he headed into the dark passageway, navigating through it by the little lights on top of the bombs, and trying not to step on any of them.

30

Around the corner at the end of the small tunnel was another one just as long, and that one ended in a set of about eight hastily carved steps that led down to a small hatchway only about half as tall as Jon. When the Gotham Builders had created this access to the basement of the Flatiron Building, they were clearly more interested in concealment than appearance or ease of use. Perhaps the mayoral and police offices had already been moved there when GS was securing the underground, or maybe they knew it would happen and had the foresight to construct this access. Either way, it worked for Williams to get in without being detected—the deadly chain of green-lit bombs and wires continued through the open hatch and into the basement of the building.

Jon crouched and craned around the edge of the hatchway to make sure he wouldn't be seen by the mercenary from the other side, then quietly squeezed through it and ended up in a tight strip of space between a high metal wall in front of him and an even higher rock wall behind him. He stepped sideways to the right, toward the end of the metal wall, which was about ten feet away, and had to be even more careful in the cramped floor space not to disturb the wires or explosives with his feet. He didn't have to worry about being heard, however, because of the hum of heavy machinery coming from around the corner of the iron wall.

When Jon reached it, he peered around and saw Williams at least twenty feet away, laying the last of his explosives at the foot of a big electrical generator that was about the size and shape of the concrete mixer on the back of a cement truck. The killer was crouched down and facing mostly away from Jon, but the young cop wasn't confident that he could reach the man and jump him before Williams saw him and pulled the gun that was resting on his hip. So Jon scanned the rock wall to his right and noticed a partially open doorway built into it, leading to some kind of recessed room.

When he could see that Williams's face was completely turned away from his current position and his hands were well occupied, Jon moved quickly across the floor and stepped through the half-closed doorway. He made sure the bomber hadn't noticed him, and then looked around quickly. It was a small room, really a large shaft, that was less than ten feet wide but stretched all the way up to a big grate on the street far above.

When he looked back out of the doorway, he could see that this subbasement of the Flatiron Building was a huge cavern, not quite as big as the one he had fallen into under Grand Central Station, but almost. He estimated that the ceiling of the chamber was about thirty feet high, and he knew there was a basement level above this, since that was where he and Halladay had practiced shooting at the gun range. He also was able to figure out quickly the original purpose of the shaft—ventilation—because across from him there were the decaying remains of two enormous old coal furnaces, which reached almost to the ceiling and looked like something from an old movie set. The far left side of the furnaces was the iron wall that concealed the secret access hatch through which he had entered.

The modern generator that now provided power for the building, next to which Williams was working, sat to the right of the old furnaces, in the middle of the cavern. To its right were several metal staircases, one winding up to an entrance on the other wall near the ceiling, and the other stretching to nothing that Jon could see, perhaps an old exit to the street that had been sealed off.

Jon turned his attention back to Williams as the mercenary stood up and dusted off his hands like he was done.

It was now or never, so Jon summoned every bit of remaining strength he could and exploded out of the ventilation shaft toward the ex–Army man, hoping to grab the gun if he could get to him before being seen, and he almost managed it. But Williams turned at the last second, so all Jon could do at that point was grab his arm to keep him from drawing his gun. Jon tried to make use of the element of surprise and twist him to the ground from that position, but the other man was much more agile and skilled than he looked. When Jon pulled his right arm across his body to keep it from the gun and spin him off his feet, Williams spun his left elbow around and connected hard with Jon's face. Then he kicked

Jon's legs out from under him while the young cop was still reeling from the blow, and sent him sprawling to the floor.

The mercenary stood over Jon, not even bothering to draw his weapon. He shook his bespectacled head in disgust, then turned around, crouched down again, and set the timer on a piece of equipment that was like the one in the truck out in the tunnel. Jon saw the numbers appear and start to count down on the timer in front of him, and imagined that the same was happening on the other one.

Williams turned back to Jon, and this time he did have the gun in his hand. He pointed it casually down at the helpless detective and moved his finger to the trigger. Jon tried to keep his eyes open, but they involuntarily closed when three or four shots thundered out and echoed throughout the huge room.

Williams's body jerked violently as he was hit in the back by at least two bullets, and he fell to the ground dead with a thud, right next to where Jon was lying.

Jon's eyes had reopened in time to catch Williams's body falling, and now he shook his head and focused beyond where the mercenary had stood above him. Ari Hegde and Brenda Dixon were halfway down the winding metal stairs that stretched down from the top of the chamber on the other side, still pointing their guns in his direction, and there was another figure behind them that Jon didn't immediately recognize. When they were sure Williams wasn't moving, they hurried down the rest of the steps and came running over to Jon.

"Are you all right?" Hegde said to Jon, helping him up as Dixon checked Williams's neck for a pulse that was no longer there.

252 • MICHAEL DAVID ARES

"Yeah, thanks," Jon said. "How'd you know who to shoot from that far away? There's not a lot of light in here."

"Your shirt," Hegde explained, gesturing below Jon's chin. "I remembered the blood."

"Why'd you come here?" Jon asked.

"You told us about it, remember?" Hegde said. "We didn't really believe you after the APB, but thought we should at least check it out since we were coming back down here anyway. Poppy here let us in."

Now Jon recognized their companion—it was the building superintendent that Halladay had introduced him to, the one whose father had passed the job on to him.

"Oh, no, listen," Jon said, his relief suddenly turning to panic. "We have to stop these. . . ."

He hurried over to the timer on the bombs and noticed it was down to about ten minutes, which was only twice as long as Amira and Halladay had to diffuse the bombs in the Below, when there weren't nearly as many.

"No time to get more help," Jon thought aloud. "But there are four of us," he added, and didn't hesitate any further when he thought of what his partners had done back at the Below. "Here's what we do. . . . You have to unscrew the green wires where they go into the detonators, and you have to do every one of them, because just one is enough to blow them all."

"How do you know this?" Dixon said. "I don't wanna mess with them if we don't know what we're doing."

"Amira knew," Jon said quickly. "Remember, I was on the phone with them. . . ." He looked at the three of them. "Come on, if we all work together we can do it."

Hegde and Dixon now looked at each other, and then back at Poppy.

"Awww, fuck it," the super said. "My dad and I didn't nurse this ole lady all these years just to see her get blown to shit."

The two Chaos Crimes cops looked at each other again, then nodded to one another and said, "Okay" to Jon. Hegde made a very brief call to someone above about evacuating the building, though they all knew that there probably wasn't enough time for anyone to get far enough away. Jon explained that they should start next to the generator with the bigger group of bombs and then work down the line toward the subway and the truck.

"But *make sure* you get every one," he added with emphasis. "There are always two together along the line. Don't just do one and move on, thinking you're done, or we're dead."

Jon showed the other three how to disconnect one of the detonators on the pile of explosives clustered near the generator, and then they all jumped in and went to work. It went quickly while they were working on that pile, but then they moved to the line of bombs stretching across the floor and had to figure out how to do those as quickly as possible without missing any. After a few anxious moments of discussion, they decided to form a line, and when one of them was finished detaching their green wire, he or she would move up to the next one that was undone. At first, this led to some awkward shuffling and bumping into one another, but soon it was going more smoothly.

"Shit, now we can't see the timer anymore," Dixon said as they moved away from the generator.

"Don't panic," Jon said, clearly the default leader here, because Dixon had looked at him. "Does anyone have a watch?" He knew

254 • MICHAEL DAVID ARES

that none of them could be taking the time to fumble with a cell phone.

"I do," Poppy said, so Jon told him to use the watch, in case they weren't going to make it and decided to run, like Amira and Halladay had tried to do. Poppy moved back toward the timer to read the numbers there, and pushed a few buttons on his watch.

When he read off the time left, they all felt a surge of adrenaline and doubled down on their efforts.

When they reached the thin strip of space between the iron wall of the old coal furnace and the rock wall of the basement cavern, they had to scrap the method they had been using, because there was no way they could step around one another any longer. After more hurried discussion, Jon made an executive decision for time's sake, and stepped carefully to the fourth detonator in the narrow corridor, telling the others to get the ones behind him, and then they would all move four ahead when they were done with that one.

Poppy didn't grasp the idea well at first, and the first effect of the stress they were under showed up when Hegde blurted out, "It's not rocket science, for God's sake," after trying to explain it to the super. Poppy responded immediately with a burst of profanity, but then they all immediately shut up and went to work in the way Jon had decided, with Poppy jumping in to disconnect the detonator behind Jon.

More profanity ensued, however, when Jon happened to notice, near the end of the tight corridor, that Poppy had missed one of the green wires going into a pair of bombs behind him.

"You've gotta concentrate," Jon said to the sweating super. "Do we have to go back and check all the ones you've done? I don't think we have time for that."

"No, that was the only one," Poppy said, wiping his brow.

"I don't wanna die because your feelings got hurt," Jon said. "No offense."

"None fuckin' taken. Let's go."

Jon climbed through the hatch in the wall after he finished his last detonator in the cramped space, and soon the other three did the same. Now they could resume their former method of "leap-frogging" one another, because they had more room to move around in the two long dark hallways stretching ahead of them toward the subway tunnel and the other pile of bombs in the truck.

But after Poppy read aloud the time that was left according to his stopwatch, and they started hurrying even more through the first passageway, they faced their biggest problem yet. The super wasn't the only one who was sweating by now—all four of them were having trouble gripping the small metal casings that had to be unscrewed in order to detach the green wires. No matter how much they wiped their fingers on their clothing, slippery sweat continued to trickle onto them.

"I can barely turn them anymore," Hegde said. "With either of my hands. It's gonna take twice as long at least, if we can even get them all off."

Jon straightened up from the detonator he was working on, having the same problem, and gave voice to something they were all thinking.

"You're right," he said. "I'd say we should take off, but I don't even know if we have time to get far enough away. What does the timer say, Poppy?"

The super pressed a sweaty finger to his watch for a moment, and then let out a loud grunt of frustration.

"Fuckin' thing," he said, shaking his head. "I tried to hit the fuckin' light so I could see it, and I musta cleared the fuckin' timer by mistake."

Great, Jon thought.

31

"Use your shirts," Poppy said, grabbing a small swath at the end of his, showing them how to use it on one of the casings, and redeeming himself for almost killing them twice in the last few minutes.

Jon stood in place for a few moments, his heart pounding, thinking about whether they should continue or not. But then he thought of Amira and Halladay again, and that was enough. He grabbed a bottom corner of his shirt and went back to work on the detonator below him. The others followed his lead, though Hegde and Dixon's shirts were too short and they had to take them off to use them.

A few minutes later—Jon couldn't tell how long—they rounded the corner into the last passage before the subway tunnel and kept on unscrewing the green wires, switching to different parts of their shirts when the ones they were using got too wet. The entire time Jon and his eerily silent companions felt like they might be blown to bits at any moment, but though they might all have been tempted to skip out on the others and attempt to save their own skin, none of them did. And before too long, they'd gotten close enough to the bed of the truck to see the timer there, and were relieved that they still had more than two minutes left.

They continued to diffuse the line leading to the truck, and then they all leaned into the bed and took care of all the bombs stacked in there. Soon they were done, with forty seconds to spare, but Jon couldn't help checking the whole pile in the trunk again, and peering once again down the nearby passage to make sure there were no little green lights still shining.

"Should we try to turn off the timer?" Hegde asked, staring at it nervously while it counted down to thirty and beyond.

"It's just a timer now, right?" Jon said. "It doesn't do anything. I guess I don't want to mess with it, in case it's rigged somehow." He looked at the others, unsure. "I don't know. . . ."

The timer hit twenty, then ten, and all they could do now was watch.

Hegde grabbed Dixon's arm and leaned into her.

Poppy looked at Jon and saluted him as if to say, *Nice fuckin' knowin' you*, and Jon nodded back.

The timer hit zero and nothing happened, and the four of them started shouting, jumping up and down, and hugging one another.

After the celebration subsided, Hegde pulled out his phone to call for the cleanup of the explosives, and noticed that he and Dixon had been asked repeatedly by text in the last few minutes to come to the park above. . . . Apparently "something weird" was going on up there. He looked up the platform toward the exit that would lead to the park, and said that was where they needed to go.

Poppy wanted to help with the cleanup, so after a few more hugs he headed back toward the basement of the "ole lady" he loved so much.

"What should we do with you?" Hegde said to Jon, while he and Dixon were putting their shirts back on.

Jon's head was spinning from the ordeal he had been through, but thoughts of Mallory still somehow managed to find their way into his mind. He thought about how glad he was that she wouldn't be endangered by the explosives anymore, but he remembered the Mayor's threat about implicating her in his alleged crimes, and started to consider how he could keep her safe from that.

"As far as I'm concerned," Hedge said before Jon could respond, "you can walk right now if you want, after what you did." He looked for a confirmation from Dixon, who nodded.

"Walk if you want," she said.

"But obviously this'll go a long way toward clearing you," Hegde continued. "So if you want to come with us, we'll help you work it out."

Jon thought about the reasons why he had first called these two cops, and realized that there was even more reason now to trust them. So he gestured for them to lead the way and followed them up the platform, continuing to mull what his options might be, especially in regard to Mallory, whom he couldn't stop thinking about.

When they reached the park exit and started up the steps, Hegde and Dixon both visibly reacted to the unfamiliar phenomenon of bright sunlight shining into the stairway from above. They stopped halfway to the top and took out the sunglasses they had been issued as part of the department's preparation for Dayfall. Then they nervously proceeded up the rest of the steps, with their arms out in front of their heads like they half-expected to be accosted by someone or something.

Hegde was the first one to top the stairs and see what was outside in the park, and he immediately stepped back down and restrained the others from going any farther. At first Jon thought that some kind of apocalypse *was* going on up there after all, but it turned out to be something else.

"I just realized," he said to Jon. "I'm sorry, but I'm gonna have to cuff you for now. Half the force looks like it's out in the park because of the evacuation, and they still think you're a cop-killer. But if we have you in custody, hopefully they'll leave us alone till we can get it straightened out."

This made sense to Jon, and he really didn't know what other options he had at this point, so he put his arms out in front of him and let Hegde put the handcuffs on him. At least they weren't cuffed in the back, so he would still have some ability to use them in a fight if he needed to for some reason, or to go for someone's gun.

With the two cops on each side of Jon, they stepped up and out into Madison Square. The Flatiron was ahead of them as they came out of the exit, and they could see people filing out of the left side of the historic building and crossing the large patio area there to make their way into the park, presumably because it was farther from the endangered building and had a lot of open space for standing and waiting. As Jon scanned the procession of evacuees, he noticed the tall thin tower of One Madison behind them, and the two MetLife Buildings farther to the left, across the park—the one with the clock tower and the shorter one that served as the Gotham Security headquarters.

Hegde and Dixon guided him in that direction, because the person on their staff who had contacted them had said he was in the middle of the park. As they moved that way, Jon started to become overly conscious of how many police were milling about in the park, along with the many civilians. Presumably most of them had come from inside their headquarters and were waiting for the all clear to go back in, and thankfully very few of them even looked at John, let alone noticed who he was. Almost all of them, as well as most of the civilians, were watching one of the two large TV screens, which stood at the north and south ends of the park.

When they got closer, Jon was able to take a good look at one of the screens, and could tell by the text at the bottom that the public announcement by the Mayor and Gareth Render was about to be broadcast. A room with glass walls that looked vaguely familiar to Jon was filled with reporters and cameras, as they waited for the two power brokers to step up to the currently empty podium.

"Isn't that—?" said a man who greeted Hegde and Dixon, and pointed at Jon.

"Yes," Hegde answered, "this is Detective Phillips, and he is voluntarily in our custody. Jon, this is one of our men, Malachi Croft. What's going on, Mal?"

"Well," the man said nervously, "we were all told just before the sun came out, by the Mayor's office, to relax because the Dayfall scare was all a hoax, the science was bogus, etc. But in the last hour we've been getting some reports from around the city about unrest and violence, and then we got the word to evacuate, so everyone out here was really tense for a while. It was really weird, and I have to admit I got a little scared. But then the tension seemed to ease a bit when the press conference came on. . . . Now everyone here's preoccupied with that."

He gestured in the direction of the screen at the south end of the park, toward which he was facing, and Jon and the others turned to look. The Mayor and Render hadn't started talking yet, but from some more of the words at the bottom of the screen Jon was able to tell why the room seemed familiar to him. It was the big living room in Render's condo at the top of One Madison, where Jon and Halladay had visited the Gotham Security boss. Jon guessed that the Mayor, who was completely in the driver's seat right now, had chosen that location for the announcement because of the threat to the Flatiron, but also probably to make a statement and stick it to Render by humbling him in his own residence.

Jon looked beyond the top left side of the big screen at the very tall and thin skyscraper itself, and noticed that the sun was just to its left, and a little more than halfway up its height. The skinny shadow of One Madison stretched across the street running in front of it and the southern tip of the park. But because there were no other very tall buildings immediately behind it, and because there weren't as many trees in the park as there had once been, most of the police and civilians in the center of it were standing in direct sunlight.

Jon was accustomed to seeing the sun, of course, because the total darkness of nuclear night had not reached as far as his home area in Pennsylvania. But he had to admit, as he looked around at the crowd, and down at his own slightly shaking hands, that there did seem to be something weird going on in the atmosphere. There could have been tension in the crowd merely from the evacuation threat, and in him because of the handcuffs and being around so many cops, but the feeling didn't seem to be that easily explained. And maybe there would have been more fear and panic happening if there weren't so many police there, making people feel safe.

Jon looked back at the screen and saw that Mayor King was now behind the small lecture stand that had been placed in front of the glass wall in the condo. Gareth Render took up a spot just behind her and to her left, looking more like a subservient minion than the proud man who had wanted to replace her. And behind both of them was the clock tower of the MetLife Building, shining with its first sunlight in more than ten years.

The Mayor wasted no time, but began speaking directly about how Render had agreed to back out of the referendum and why there was no reason to fear Dayfall. The apocalyptic theories about it had been proven to be false, she said, and there had already been several hours of daylight this morning without incident.

"Not what I'm hearing," Croft commented to all three of them, holding up his radio. Jon wondered if the Mayor didn't know about the reports yet, or was simply ignoring or minimizing them.

But no one would find out, at least not from her, because at that moment several loud cracks and the shattering of glass could be heard both from the TV screen and from the tops of the buildings behind it. On the screen Jon could see the Mayor going down in a spray of blood, the transparent wall behind her breached by several bullets. Then he looked up and could see that the shattered glass was on the side of the penthouse that faced the MetLife tower, so the shots had probably come from the archways just under the big clock.

A loud wave of shocked gasps surged through the crowd in the park, and the tension suddenly became much more palpable than before. But no one moved yet, because on the TV screen Gareth Render could now be seen standing upright in front of all the panicked members of the press, who were pressed against the floor or clinging to one another in an effort to protect themselves.

Jon immediately thought, as did many of the others watching, that the Gotham boss had brazenly ordered the Mayor's assassination, and was now about to declare himself the Dictator of Manhattan.

But then Jon noticed that the look on Render's face was not triumph or madness, but bewilderment. The graying older man turned around to face the tower from which the sniper's rounds had come, and spread his hands as if say, *Why?*

Then half his head disappeared as several more shots rang out, and his big body toppled to the floor next to the Mayor's.

And then all hell broke loose in the park, and in the rest of the city.

32

More shocked gasps from the civilians quickly turned into panic as it now seemed that *no one* could keep them safe. Some clutched at and huddled with their loved ones, others impulsively ran for the shelter of shade or a building, and still others started demanding explanations or help from the police in the Square.

Many of the cops instinctively pulled out their sidearms and started scanning the park, especially when civilians approached them. Jon noticed a few of them fixing their eyes on him and moving in his direction. He looked at Hegde and Dixon in a plea for his own protection, holding his cuffed hands out in front of him. But the normally laid back, even lackadaisical pair of detectives had their own guns lifted halfway and pointed in Jon's direction. And they both had a wild-eyed look that Jon had never seen on their faces before.

"What did you do?!" Dixon shouted at him.

"Me? What?!" Jon shouted back, waving his cuffed hands, which were shaking a lot more now. "It's Gant! He obviously he didn't want to be sidelined, or leave the city. Despite the best efforts of his old friend to protect him. He's the villain here. . . . We need to find him and take him in!"

As he blurted this out, Jon watched as the two or three cops who had recognized him and moved in his direction had trouble navigating the panicked crowd that surrounded them. One of them was confronted by an angry couple and had to deal with them, and another was knocked off his feet by a family of three, holding hands and frantically trying to find their other child. A third cop managed to make it to their little group, and now stood in a tense pose behind Jon with his gun pointed at Jon's back.

"Whoa, hold on," the officer named Malachi Croft said, stepping closer to Jon with his hands up and his gun still in its holster. He seemed to be a lot more rational than the others, and confirmed it when he said, "Put those away and let's talk."

A gunshot suddenly rang out not far from them, all the cops around Jon ducked, and the noise and chaos multiplied intensely in the park.

A screaming Goth girl ran over to Croft, randomly it seemed, and tried to liberate his gun from its holster. When he pushed her hand away from the leather clasp, she yelled, "Help me!" and clung to his arm. Two young men appeared from the direction she had come.

"Kitty, come on," one of them said as they approached, "We just want to keep you safe."

The Goth girl screamed again, and the uniformed cop who had joined their group swiveled and pointed his gun at the two other men. Jon could see that he was sweating profusely and the veins were standing out on his forehead.

"Come on, man," one of the young men said, also noticeably sweating. As he did, he very unwisely moved toward the overwrought policeman.

"Guys!" Croft yelled. "Settle down!"

A big dog, with a leash trailing behind it, ran straight through the uneasy gathering, and in the confusion, the young man accidentally veered even closer to the cop, and the cop shot him. The Goth girl screamed even louder than before, and Croft finally did unclasp his holster.

As a large group of freaked-out people migrated into the space where Hegde and Dixon were standing, and his captors became preoccupied with them, Jon took off running to the west, in the direction of Mallory's bar. He half-expected to be shot in the back for the first twenty seconds or so of his flight, and regretted that he couldn't swing his arms freely to run faster. He heard several gunshots from various directions, but didn't feel anything hit him and kept moving as rapidly as he could.

He slowed when he realized he was near the big bronze sculptures where Sturm had attacked him with a knife. He ran behind one of them and risked a look back. The Goth girl had managed to get Croft's sidearm, or someone else's, and was waving it wildly around her, fending off a small group of people that no longer included Hegde or Dixon, as far as he could tell. It was hard to see because people kept running by between him and that spot, but he wondered if the Chaos Crimes cops were fleeing the scene, too.

He took a moment to scan the park and its vicinity, and noticed other seemingly random scenes of bedlam and mayhem. He noticed how the largest groups of people were crowding into the buildings around the Square, or at least attempting to. Whether or not the sunlight was actually having a physical or psychological effect on them, they definitely wanted to get out of it.

One particular mob scene was taking place at the Gotham Security headquarters at Eleven Madison, on the east side of the park. Jon could see police and civilians, who were in the sun, shouting at the security guards who had formed a ragged line in the shade at the entrance to the building. Some of the civilians were throwing various objects in their direction. There hadn't been any gunfire yet, probably because the GS sentries were ready to engage in it if needed.

Knowing that no such security existed at The Office, and that no one was currently pursuing him, Jon pushed himself off the statue and headed toward Mallory's bar.

When he reached Fifth Avenue, on the west side of the park, he stopped to figure out the best way to get to her. The street was jammed both ways with cars and taxis, some of them occupied because people thought they would be safer inside of them, and some of them unoccupied because people thought they would be safer in a building. Horns were blaring, creating a cacophony of noise that almost drowned out the one created by screams of panic and shouts of rage. While studying the street, Jon could see some of the fearful citizens climbing into unoccupied cars, and even some trying to get into ones that were occupied, causing more chaos and violence.

To his left, the traffic jam at the intersection of Fifth and Broadway had spilled over into the large pedestrian patio called Flatiron Plaza. Motorists trying to bypass the jam had driven up onto the cement there, smashing into tables and chairs and umbrellas, and at least one pedestrian. Jon could see the victim's body lying on the left side of the Plaza, since the cars were giving it space and jostling for other paths through the intersection. As Jon instinctively moved forward to help, one of the cars in the jam decided it didn't want to wait any longer. It swerved out of the crowd of cars and ran right over the body, just to gain fifty feet or so on the others.

To Jon's right there were several different-sized mobs fighting to get into the stores and restaurants to the north on Fifth Avenue, so it seemed that going straight across the street from where he was, and passing through General Worth Square, was the easiest way to get up Broadway to the bar. He took a deep breath and waded into the river of cars, jumping back at the sudden movements some of them made when space opened up ahead, and trying to steer clear of the altercations happening at others.

Jon made it through to the other side without incident, but then looked back across the street to see a greater danger approaching. Coming from inside the park, and moving in his general direction, was a group of about seven or eight uniformed cops who had banded together to restore order, or whatever passed as order in their strained psyches. They had formed a phalanx of sorts in order to be able to protect themselves from all directions, but also to do more than just protect themselves. One of the cops shouted into a small megaphone that "anyone perpetrating acts of violence will be shot on sight," but they were shooting more than just violent people. As Jon watched, a woman in a Gotham Security uniform approached them peacefully from the left, as if she just wanted to talk to them, and two of the cops on that side fired about five rounds into her, without any hesitation.

Jon wasn't sure where the cops were heading, but it occurred to him that they might be making a wide circle around the Flatiron in an attempt to restore some degree of control to the area. Whatever their intent, which was probably capricious because of the effects Dayfall was having on them, Jon knew that he didn't want them to see his handcuffs or recognize him, because he doubted he would survive the encounter. So he looked around for a hiding place, and ducked behind a big umbrella that had provided cover for one of the tables in the little square and had fallen on its side.

As he crouched behind the umbrella, and tried over the din to hear signs of which direction the cops might be moving, he starting noticing for the first time that the wound beneath his chin was throbbing, and it seemed now to become more and more painful as he thought about it. He reached up and touched it gingerly, finding that it wasn't bleeding out, but was decidedly moist and sticky. It hurt even more when he touched it, and especially when his head jerked down involuntarily because a series of gunshots split the air not far from him. He peered out carefully from the side of the umbrella and saw that the vigilante cops were now in the middle of Fifth Avenue, and were shooting anybody who was jostling to get into a car, or trying to move theirs in an aggressive fashion.

Jon turned away from the carnage on the street and thought about making a run for it from behind the umbrella, toward Mallory's bar. He looked for other cover in that direction and saw the big monument to General Worth, from whom the little square had gotten its name. It was a fifty-foot high granite obelisk with a thick base that had two bronze reliefs, one of a man on a horse and one of something else that Jon couldn't identify. The monument was surrounded by a little patch of grass with a small cast-iron fence around the outside of it. And right in front of the fence sat a young woman who was sobbing and cradling the body of an older man.

Jon tensed his body and readied to leave his crouch and hiding place, planning to run to the other side of the monument as fast as he could. But then he looked back at the young woman on the ground at the foot of the monument.

It was Mallory.

33

Jon pressed his eyes closed and shook his head, in case he was hallucinating, but when he looked back at the woman, it was still Mallory. And the older man she was cradling was her father. . . . He was recognizable even from this angle.

Jon threw caution to the wind, ignoring the danger of the cops in the street, and ran over to her.

"Mallory," he said as he slowed his approach.

She squinted at him through tear-stained eyes, not recognizing him, and he realized that the sun was behind him. He moved sideways and closer until his shadow covered her head and she could see him better.

"It's me, it's Jon," he said, holding up his hands, but then realizing the handcuffs didn't look very good.

"Oh, fucking great," she said, shaking her head. "I didn't think this day could get worse."

"What happened to your dad?" Jon asked, ignoring both what she said and the continuing gunshots and screams to his right.

"Too many people from the street were crowding into the bar, and he tried to stop them. They beat him really bad. . . ." She choked up again. "I was taking him to CityMD on Twenty-Third, but I only got him halfway. He's dead." She looked up at Jon again, and her eyes went from grief to hatred in a moment. "This is what happens when your fucking Mayor is in charge!"

"She's not my—" Jon started. "Listen, you were right about Render. It was Gant behind the murders. I tried to stop him, and the Mayor. . . . I kept you from being blown up." He held up his cuffed hands again. "Look, the Mayor framed me. . . . I'm not on her side. I wasn't, I mean . . ."

As Jon searched for words to mollify her, he glanced back at the street to see that the group of murderous cops was almost to his side of Fifth Avenue, though a bit south from where he was. He hoped they would turn farther south as they continued their sweep of the area.

"Did you say CityMD on Twenty-Third?" Jon suddenly asked, a weird look on his face. "Is that across the street from a big home store?"

"Yeah," Mallory said, with her own odd look. "But . . . what the hell are you talking about?!" She started crying again.

Jon looked at the cops again to see which direction they were moving, and this time one of them looked back at him. Jon was sure the Blue Shirt recognized him when the cop started talking to his comrades and pointing toward him.

He felt a kind of panic he had never experienced before, and his chin started pulsating with the worst pain yet, which spread to the rest of his head. He had to force himself to think about whether he had implicated Mallory by talking to her, or whether the cops would ignore her if he ran away by himself. He was about the do the latter when the cop with the megaphone settled the issue with what seemed like a form of divine revelation.

"Hey, you," the cop's voice rang out. "Stay there, both of you!"

Since he said "both of you," Jon took this as a sign, and reached down with his cuffed hands to pull Mallory to her feet.

"Don't touch me," she said, shrugging him off.

"Look, Mallory," he blurted out, "see those cops coming our way? They will kill both of us. You have to trust me, and come with me *now*."

"I'm not leaving my dad," she said, but seemed conflicted because she could now see the cops, the look in their eyes, and the guns they were raising as the first of them cleared the last row of cars on the street. Though they were still at least a hundred feet away, the only thing that kept them from a clear shot at Jon and Mallory were the obstacle of the tables and downed umbrellas in the little square.

"Your dad would want you to stay alive," Jon said, holding out his hands again. "Come on!"

She didn't take his hand, but after a few moments of consideration, she laid her dad's body gently down and stood up, staring in fear at the oncoming cops when she saw the one in the front raise his gun higher and point it directly at them, after nonchalantly blowing away a pedestrian who had gotten too close to him.

"This way," Jon said, giving up trying to take her hand and diving into the jam of cars to his left on Broadway. As he navigated quickly through them to the other side of the street, he glanced back to make sure Mallory was behind him, and was glad to see that she was. He glanced back farther at the squad of cops, and was even more happy to see that a suicidal motorist had turned out of the left side of the jam and barreled into several of the tables and umbrellas, directly in the path of the cops. Jon didn't know if the driver was angry at them after witnessing their street-shooting spree, or trying to save him or Mallory, or what. But whatever the reason, it was definitely suicidal, because the cops paused their pursuit to riddle the car and driver with bullets.

Jon and Mallory streaked through the last of the cars on Broadway and around the bank building on the corner of Twenty-Fourth Street. Jon pulled her against the wall on the other side and looked around the corner to see what was happening with the cops. Other motorists nearby had become enraged at their deranged brand of justice, or were trying to protect themselves, and they were pulling out of the jam and trying to run over them with their cars, or smash other cars into them. At least one of the cops was hit, and they all seemed occupied, at least for now, with firing into all the cars around them.

"Was this the way you were gonna go?" Jon hurriedly asked Mallory, panting for breath. "To the urgent care?"

"Yeah," Mallory answered, still puzzled, "there's an alley in the middle of the block that goes over to Twenty-Third." She watched as John nodded, then added, "But my dad's dead. . . . Where are we going?"

Jon peered back around the corner and saw that while three of the remaining Blue Shirts were still occupied in some way with the cars on the street, four of them had now broken away and were coming after him and Mallory.

He grabbed her arm and started pulling her down the sidewalk. She shrugged it off almost immediately, but did run after him. The sidewalk was almost empty, except for a few dead or injured bodies that they had to swerve around—most people by now had sought shelter inside buildings or vehicles. The street itself, however, was packed pretty tightly. . . . It was a one-way going west toward Broadway, with only one lane for cars trying to move between the ones parked on each side.

Jon left the sidewalk and ran into the middle of the cars after the murderous cops had rounded the corner behind them and could see where they were. Before he and Mallory could reach the left turn into the alley, some of them fired, their rounds sailing past them in the air or hitting the cars near them.

Jon and Mallory turned into the alley and ran into a small crowd of noticeably frightened people who were hanging there because it was in the shade of the buildings on each side. When the group saw his handcuffs, they gave him a wide berth, but he stopped abruptly after passing through and turned around to face them. He snarled maniacally and stepped forcefully toward them, which caused many of them to retreat back toward the north end of the alley, where the cops would soon be entering. Then he turned back around and ran toward the other end of the alley.

Due to her own feelings of disorientation, Mallory couldn't see the method to Jon's madness, and she was even more confused when he passed the urgent-care facility at the corner of the alley and Twenty-Third Street, and began crossing it toward the big home store on the other side.

"What're you doing?" she called out.

She breathed heavily as she said the words, but noticed that she wasn't nearly as tired as she thought she would be, after half-carrying her father for a block and running at full speed for another two. It occurred to her that this extra physical energy and adrenaline might be an effect of the sunlight.

Rather than continuing toward the doors of the big store, Jon suddenly veered to the right and headed down the sidewalk.

When they weren't much farther down the block, the four relentless policemen emerged from the alley onto Twenty-Third, and only had to scan the street for a few moments before they saw Jon and Mallory headed west along it. Even though there was even more distance between them and their targets than on the last street, they again fired their guns numerous times as they pursued, this time hitting some of the windows near where the couple was running. At one point, Jon felt some small pieces of glass hit him as a pane shattered in front of him and he ran through the resulting shower.

But they weren't hit by any of the bullets before Jon was able to disappear down a subway entrance built into the sidewalk, near the end of the block close to the intersection of Sixth Avenue. Mallory followed him down, still not sure that he was completely sane, but having no other good option for safety from the obviously insane cops.

They had to slow and stop when they realized the subway platform below was filled with refugees from the street. There was someone sitting or standing on almost every patch of floor, some of them wounded and only some of the wounded being cared for by others. There was very little talking going on, but there were some soft cries and gasps, especially when the handcuffed Jon led Mallory to their right along the platform, and they had to push their way through the crowd to move in that direction. These people were much more docile than the ones on the surface above, probably because they had been out of the sun for a while. But they were definitely scared.

No one else besides Jon and Mallory seemed to be moving—perhaps they were waiting for a train to arrive so they could try to leave the city, or get home. The feeling in the air, however, was that no train had arrived for a while, and none would likely be coming.

Mallory had no idea where Jon was going, and wondered if he did. She could also see him becoming more and more agitated, as moving through the throng was slow going, and they were losing ground on the cops, who would be arriving at the subway steps at any moment. She herself was becoming more afraid, and started pondering the idea of leaving Jon by hiding in the crowd of people or taking off across the tracks.

They reached a section of the platform that widened away from the tracks and was beyond where a train would stop. There was much less of a crowd there, only a few people sitting out near the edge of the platform and none in the open space behind that. Jon stood in that open space, and was looking around frantically.

Mallory just stared at him for a moment, ready to put her Plan B into effect, when he stepped toward her rather violently, grabbed her by the arm, and whispered something into her ear.

"What? Why?" she said, pulling away from him.

"Just do it!" he half-whispered and half-shouted, with a look of desperation on his face.

34

"Get away from him, he's crazy!" Mallory shouted at the people sitting and standing near the edge of the tracks, shooing them in the direction of the crowd she and Jon had just passed through. Then she added, "He's losing it!"

Jon waved his handcuffed hands in front of him and let out a wide-eyed snarl, like he had in the alley a few minutes before, and sure enough, it worked here, too. As every one of the frightened people near him and Mallory withdrew quickly away from him, that sudden movement and the screams some of them let out caused the larger crowd on the other side to also retreat up the tunnel in a brief but chaotic frenzy.

As this was happening, Jon grabbed Mallory again by the arm and pulled her toward the back of the platform, where he produced a key from his pocket and opened a big metal door that was built into the wall there. Before she had time think about what was going on, Jon pushed her through the door and closed it quickly behind them.

"I needed to get those people away so no one would see where we went," he explained, and she just nodded slightly, still not fully understanding.

This Below had a light switch inside the door, which Jon turned on, and about ten steps leading down to several rooms below. Jon started down the stairs, gesturing back at Mallory.

"Come on," he said, "We'll be safe here. . . . I don't think the cops know about this place, and by the time they get through that crowd they'll think we took off down the subway tunnel."

At the bottom of the steps there was a central room about twenty feet in diameter, which was empty except for a wooden cabinet on the left side. It was obviously not currently in use, unlike the other two Belows Jon had seen earlier. There were four doors near the corners of the main space, three of which led to smaller rooms with bunk beds in them, and one that led to a bathroom. Jon darted in and out of all of them briefly, disappointed that he didn't find any weapons but happy to discover that the cabinet held some dry goods and food stores.

"There's coffee," Jon said, with his head down inside the door of the cabinet, then straightened up and turned around to see Mallory standing in the middle of the room with an angry look on her face.

"I don't know what I'm doing here," she said. "How did you know about this place? How'd you have a key for it?"

"I saw it on a GS map yesterday, and noticed the big store and the urgent care near it on the map. Wasn't totally sure, but it worked out."

His wide eyes and skewed smile seemed odd to Mallory, and made her feel more suspicious of him.

"If those cops are really gone," she said, "I need to get back to my dad. . . ."

She started to turn toward the steps, and Jon moved close to her, saying, "Whoa, whoa, hold on." When she shrugged off his hand from her arm and turned further, he moved even closer and put both handcuffed hands over her head and arms, locking her into an involuntary embrace with the chain and the cuffs pressing against her arm.

"You can't go up there yet," he said.

"Let me go," she hissed, and started to struggle against him.

"We were just in the sun," Jon grunted as he held her. "We need to settle down."

"*You* were," she said, and thrashed about more.

As she did, her shoulder slammed into the wound under Jon's chin, which caused him to scream and swear, but it also distracted him enough that she was able to wriggle downward and out of his grip. When she was free, she hauled off with her right hand and punched him in the face as hard as she could.

"Don't *ever* . . . ," she spat out, as he reeled back a step and grabbed his cheek.

Then he stepped up close to her again, and they stood facing each other silently. The expression on both their faces was inscrutable to the other—the meaning and the interpretation of them seemed to be complicated by the lingering effects of the Dayfall. It could have been love or hate or pity or resentment or anything else in between that he felt, or she felt, and it could probably end up changing in the blink of an eye. But they continued to stand still and stare at each other, until Jon's cuffed hands moved slowly away from his cheek in the direction of Mallory's neck.

Her eyes glanced down once very briefly, but then her gaze returned to his eyes, and she didn't move another muscle as Jon's hands continued toward her throat. It looked like he was going to choke her, and it looked like she wanted him to do it. But when his fingers were almost touching the skin below her chin, he moved them up slowly and began to softly cradle and caress her cheeks with them.

Jon tilted his head slightly to the side and down, and kissed her tenderly on the lips, then more deeply.

Then they suddenly heard the door of the Below being unlocked at the top of the stairs.

Not knowing who was coming or what else to do, Jon led Mallory quickly and quietly into the room at the back right of the Below. They situated themselves behind the partially open door, and Jon peered out through the crack at the hinges. He was thankful for the loudness of the footsteps on the stairway, and hoped whoever it was hadn't heard them moving across the floor.

The Dayfall Killer named Sturm emerged from the steps into the central room, holding a sniper rifle in one hand and a case for it in the other.

The ex–Navy SEAL didn't check the adjoining rooms, obviously assuming no one else would be in the Below, but stepped right over to the cabinet on the other side of the room from where Jon and Mallory were hiding. She placed the gun case on the top of the cabinet and started to disassemble it with her back to them. Jon wondered if the rifle was her only weapon, and thought of trying to jump her while she was taking it apart. But before he could even consider whether he could get to her across about ten feet of space, or whether he should wait for her to move to a different position, she stopped what she was doing abruptly and looked up at the lights in the ceiling.

Evidently she was wondering why the lights were on. She methodically rotated her neck to the left and then to the right, scanning the doorways to the other rooms, which were all dark inside. At one point her eyes seemed to be pointed directly at Jon's, and he had to battle a wave of fear rising inside him by reminding himself of the fact that there was no way she could possibly see him with the lighting in the big room and the lack of it in the little one. But he also remembered Halladay's comment about how good Navy SEALs were at what they did, and how Sturm seemed to have a sixth sense about her in the two previous altercations.

He tensed and got ready to do something—though he wasn't sure what—if she moved toward them. But all she did was turn back to the rifle, lay it down temporarily, and take off her coat before continuing to work on it. When she did, Jon noticed both her powerful body and the handgun resting on her back right hip. Mallory saw it, too, as she spied through a lower part of the door crack, and then she and Jon looked at each other with raised eyebrows.

Mallory whispered something quietly into Jon's ear, he nodded at her, and they both silently slipped off their shoes. A few moments later they both stepped softly out from behind the door and started toward Sturm, hoping she would not hear them or turn around before they got to her.

Jon was slightly in front of Mallory, and when he was about four or five feet from Sturm, the killer suddenly started turning around and reaching for her gun. So Jon lunged toward her with his arms out in front of him, stretching the handcuffs over her head to her neck, and pulling them tight in a choke hold. Sturm arched in pain and began to thrash about wildly, propelling Jon's legs up in the air and sideways, which made it hard for Mallory to get to the rifle parts as she had planned. But Jon held on for dear life, Sturm wasn't able to liberate the handgun at her waist, and Mallory eventually reached the biggest part of the rifle and picked it up.

She swung it toward Sturm's head as hard as she could, but just then the mercenary's body jerked violently to the side, and the heavy piece of wood and metal slammed into Jon's shoulder instead. Both Jon and Sturm grunted loudly as their connected bodies staggered a few feet across the floor, but somehow they didn't actually fall over. The murderer's head swung around in the right direction, however, and Mallory's next blow landed squarely on it.

Sturm's body jerked violently once more and then slumped to the ground lifelessly, with Jon going down on top of it. He checked to make sure there was no pulse before he extricated his hands from her throat, and then stood up face-to-face with Mallory, as they had been before the killer arrived.

"Good plan," Jon said. "But I need you to stop hitting me."

"Sorry," she said, looking at the rifle butt and then laying it down on the floor. Then she stared at Sturm's body, and at her hands, as if there was blood on them. "I can't believe I killed someone. . . . I feel bad for her."

"Don't," Jon said. "She deserved it, believe me. In fact, she might have been the one who murdered your fiancé."

"She worked for Gant, right? He was behind it all. So what's gonna happen to him?"

"He'll get his," Jon said with satisfaction. "I saved a video that will put him behind bars for the rest of his life."

Remembering how he had sent Shinsky's testimony to his personal cell phone, Jon crouched down at Sturm's body and found hers, thinking he might call Hegde or someone else and see if they could leave the Below. But there was no service.

"Must be pretty bad out there still," he said, pocketing the phone and putting his arms around Mallory again.

"What do you think caused all that?" she asked.

"Don't know. I guess one of the theories was actually right, or more than one, maybe. I'm just glad we're in here and not out there."

He kissed her again, and then hugged her tight.

"Never thought I'd be happy to be handcuffed," he said, as he looked at the cuffs over her shoulder while they were embracing. "But I don't think we could have won that fight without them."

Then Jon noticed something else—the tattoo on the back of Mallory's shoulder.

"I see the whole clover," he whispered in her ear, "all four leaves."

He didn't know if this was a lingering effect of the Dayfall, or what, but he didn't care. And Mallory didn't either; she just gasped and squeezed him tighter when she heard it.

Before he could look back at the tattoo again, to see if it was still complete, the lights went out in the room.

"Must be *really* bad out there," Mallory said.

"At least we have each other," Jon said.

"And two guns now, in case anyone else comes."

"Yeah, we'll wait it out for a while," Jon concluded, realizing that even the wound under his chin was feeling a lot better. "We'll be all right."

And they clung to each other in the darkness of the Below.

ACKNOWLEDGMENTS

Thanks to Isaac Asimov and Brendan Deneen for inspiration and ideas, and also to Brendan for his terrific editing work. Thanks to Paul Patterson, who served as a cop for thirty years and made sure the depictions of police work were realistic. And thanks to Jill, for clinging to me in the darkness of the Below.